I0769242

ISBN-13: 979-8-9905379-2-7

Her Blood Runs Cold

In Xypha's Shadow: Book Two

Samantha Tano

About the Author

Samantha Tano is a science fiction author based in Rhode Island. She has worked as an award-winning journalist and development editor. She is a proud and vocal transgender woman. Her first novel published in 2024, her micro-fiction has appeared online in *Deep South Magazine*, and she has appeared in *The Boston Globe*. You can find her reading in coffee shops around New England.

Acknowledgments

I am eternally grateful to my friends who have supported me, pushed me to keep going, and reminded me that writing is integral to my existence. The people who helped me bring this book into the world are incredible at what they do: Sam Willow, my editor; and cover artist, Caitlin b. Alexander. Again, I have to specifically thank Kelly, M, and Jess for their close, earnest readings, love, and support. Finally, I said when I finished this book I was going to thank my psych meds for making any of this possible—so shoutout Bupropion and Paroxetine.

To every trans person whose parents made it all about themselves.

1

The Wind

A biting wind blew south across the Isidis Valley. Pale clouds hung low in the sky; snow and frost fell silently over the chis, signaling the end of the blood-soaked autumn. The people of the valley spoke of that autumn only in whispers, as if their words could thaw the hard ground; and with spring, the Lipine River would swell beyond its banks, flooding the fertile valley in yet more bloodshed.

As winter settled in, the chis shortened and shed the sacrificial panicles; the upper quarter of the sheaths bent and formed a layer on the ground. Wild stirrols moved with greater caution and predators lay low on the bed of browning detritus.

Jo did not speak.

Her boots crunched over frozen chis.

She stopped.

The wind whispered in her ear, despite the thick ibi wool headband covering down to her earlobes. The girl moved again, step after deliberate step, plasrifle pressed to her shoulder—stalking.

The minbing expanded their territory in the winter. Herds moved south, away from even colder lands in a great sweeping arc that touched the valley. The ungulates sported thick coats, black, twisting antlers, and a mouthwatering smoked meat that Jo could not stop thinking about.

She moved quietly up a slope, keeping a westerly track north of the river.

The hill looked over a tight hairpin curve in the Lipine. The ice fragmented and the river moved along, quickening around the bend. Eight minbing idled there, sipping from the cold water, crunching the ice at the bank with their black hoofs.

Jo lay on her stomach, a thick coat keeping her warm and dry.

The minbing stood almost 200 meters away. She dug her elbow into the ground and steadied her rifle. The wind blew across her shot in short gusts. Jo closed her eyes and slowed her breathing, taking in the sharp winter air through her nose, releasing warm fog from tight lips. She closed one eye, steadied the rifle, and waited for the right moment.

At the river's edge, a minbing buck searched the ground with its tongue and flat teeth, ripping the last remnants of grass from the mud and slush. She aimed right for its heart.

Wind swept by, shifting, passing over Jo's right shoulder.

The minbing lifted its slender head, ears pricked.

Jo squeezed the trigger.

Scrack.

The minbing leapt in shock and terror; the other seven scattered, bounding away in panic as the shot echoed. When the front hoofs of Jo's prey hit the ground, they gave out; the minbing fell to its side. For a moment, it scrambled, hooves tearing into the dirt. Then, it settled, dropped its head, and died.

Jo lowered the rifle and let out a long breath.

At the water's edge, Jo knelt beside the minbing. She lifted the head by its black antlers, which reached toward its back. Jo leaned her rifle against the animal and removed the glove from her right hand before running her fingers through the animal's thick coat. The prospect of dragging the minbing up the hill on her own made her legs burn and her heart ache.

She missed Sora.

Jo stood, groaned and growled, mouthing off in full voice against the wind and the cold. Trudging up the hill, she retraced her steps all the way back to where she'd left Allie, her favorite stirrol. Tied to a burrey tree branch, the stirrol turned its long face to watch Jo approach.

Allie shook the snow from her mane. Jo slung herself up in the saddle, patted Allie on the neck, and gently urged her forward. They returned to the downed minbing much faster than on Jo's two feet, but the animal still had to be lifted onto the stirrol's back. Jo definitely took pride in her strength, but, at almost seventeen, even she had her limits. She dismounted into the snow and led Allie by the reins toward the riverbank. Retrieving a twilight fruit from a saddlebag, Jo coaxed Allie into kneeling on her front knees, then lying on the cold, wet ground.

"Sorry," she murmured, "but this is the only way I can get this thing up."

Jo tied the minbing's front hoofs together, then the back two; she could lay it over Allie's back, behind the saddle, then cinch it tight with the tiedown straps. The minbing weighed probably twice as much as Jo. With a loud scream or two, which echoed through the valley almost as much as the rifle shot had, Jo hauled the animal up and over Allie's back as the stirrol munched on the twilight fruit without a care.

That was, until a body floated down the river.

Jo and her stirrol startled at the sight. A young boy floated facedown, spinning in the current after emerging from under a thin layer of ice. Jo gripped the reins to keep Allie near, but her eyes remained locked on the boy. He couldn't have been more than seven years old, dark hair, handmade clothes. Jo felt relieved that she could not see his face. Despite the layers she wore, she shook as the body drifted away around the bend. Tossing the reins over Allie's neck, Jo looked back toward the east. She climbed into the saddle and clucked her tongue and rode along the bank.

It wasn't long before she came upon the small homestead. Three families had settled together near the riverbank. Their homes sat across from each other, a stone well in the middle of a dirt lane worn down by foot and wagon traffic. Only the hissing wind and the crunch of the stirrol's hoofs made any sound. Jo took in her surroundings before she dismounted and approached one of the homes cautiously, her heart racing.

The sight of the first body stole her breath. A woman lay in the lane, her hair, clothes, and face frozen. Blood mixed with snow and frost around the body. Jo bit her lip to keep it steady. She scanned the rest of the village, spotting the other bodies: two women, three men, and two more children.

Her eyes watered and she could not prevent her lip from quivering and her hands from shaking. Her heart pounded in her chest; tears froze to her cheeks. Any other time, she would have turned to her sister for guidance. But Sora was gone, and Jo stood there, alone as the wind whistled between the homes. She sniffled and wiped her nose with the back of her glove.

A curiosity drew her toward the dead woman. Jo knelt beside her, looked into the wide, frozen eyes. The woman's frostbitten skin had begun to blacken in spots, while others remained white as snow. The bodies must have been here a few days, but she honestly did not know for sure. She returned to her stirrol's side, drew her knife, and cut the minbing loose, pushing it as Allie stepped forward. The body fell hard to the ground. Leaving the food behind was not ideal, but Jo needed to ride fast. She could lead someone back here and get the minbing, later.

She climbed back into the saddle, spun Allie around and pressed her heels into the stirrol's sides. Allie leapt and galloped away to the northeast. As she pounded up and over the hills, Jo's eyes burned in the wind, unable to fight back the fear in her heart.

Then she remembered the words: *A vengeful fire.*

The Thin Man.

She had stood across from him that night, rifle in-hand. He'd warned her. Of course *he* had already started one fire; but now she feared another. Jo could have ended everything those months ago. But she remembered the Thin Man's other words: *You're not a killer. Not yet.*

The Thin Man was right—something else had been unleashed in Silas's absence. Jo cursed herself—her fear and weakness. Even more innocents had paid the price for her failure.

The sun dipped below the eastern horizon, casting a beautiful orange glow over Verisport. Windows, bright in the dark, looked out at Sora from the small shanties on the southwest side of town. Smoke rose from chimneys made of stone. The great flight tower loomed over the spaceport on her left, the last vestiges of the sun's light glinting off its wind-blasted edges. A pristine, white Xypha drop ship descended into a docking bay, bright lights on the bottom of its hull searching the ground.

Sora shivered—she told herself it came from the cold wind behind her—but there was more to it, something she didn't want to admit.

The market lay dark and quiet. A final group of vendors boarded up their stalls by faint lamplight. Sora missed the sweet smell of fruits and baked treats. Supper came with the night, and the air smelled of ale, liquor, salted meats, fire, and smoke. A short, cylindrical automated brush rolled by to sweep the snow in the street.

She went out of her way to ride past the area where Silas Purvida's place had once stood just a couple months ago. Only the building's dark, glistening omniite skeleton remained aboveground. She stared through the open space between the two buildings on either side, the dark night ahead, snow covering the ground.

A storm had passed through here—a deliberate instrument of destruction, tearing this place from its foundation. Sora thought of that autumn; the tumultuous season that had blown through her life like a cyclone. She thought of Alix—her smile, bravado, her arms like steel cables beneath soft, smooth skin.

Sora smiled and closed her eyes, recalling Alix's warmth beside her in the simple cot on board the *Shadow*.

But Sora also recalled the fear she'd felt upon witnessing the rage within Alix. When Felix and Wick had left the village to go after Alix, Sora hadn't been able to go with them—the fear of seeing Alix dead, or the trail of bloody debris in her wake—had kept Sora away. Like a storm over the valley, Alix had inspired awe and terror at what she could unleash. The storm's beauty and strength had won in the end, and Sora smiled at the memory of Alix returning to her shop, beat to hell, but alive. Then, winter had settled like a blanket, quiet and calm. For two months, Sora had stayed with Alix and Felix in the *Shadow*, working to repair the ship.

Now, Sora returned to Verisport alone.

Jesse's shop radiated heat no matter the temperature outside. A large fire, and plasma generators emanated a permanent warmth within, which could be oppressive in the summer, but now felt welcoming against the cold. Sora shook the snow off her shoulders, calling out to Jesse as she walked through the heavy curtain at the front of the store.

"Jess! It's me, Sora."

From behind a door, Jesse's head popped out, hair wet with sweat, their face dirty, as usual. They cocked an eyebrow, "What are you doing here?"

"Just had to get out for a while," Sora leaned on the workbench near the large fireplace.

Jesse emerged, wearing a thick apron over a thin shirt with no sleeves. "You want me to put you to work?"

"Please, no. I feel like that's all I've been doing for months."

"Oh, you sure that is *all* you've been doing?" Jesse smirked and put a smelly arm over Sora's shoulders.

"Shut up," Sora elbowed her friend in the ribs, knocking them away. They both laughed and Sora sank into Jesse's embrace, feeling small in their muscular arms.

"Come on, you want something to eat?" Jesse must have seen the weariness on Sora's face. "My treat." Jesse tossed the apron on some kind of half-exploded engine before pulling a heavy coat off a rack in the corner and slipping their arms into the fuzzy sleeves.

Sora regretted going back out into the cold, but she huddled close to Jesse as they walked, hanging on their arm. They entered a noisy saloon down the street, a frequent haunt for Jesse and other folk with scarred, calloused hands. After pushing through the door, Jesse waved to the bartender.

"Jess!" Li cried out, "Who is your hot date?" He winked at them as he spun a bottle in his hand.

"This is my friend Sora," Jesse said.

"Emphasis on *friend*," Sora said playfully, peeking around Jesse's shoulder.

"Go have a seat there in the corner, and I'll send Sara over your way."

Jesse put up their hand in acknowledgment. They found the table he mentioned, sat and hung their coats on the backs of their chairs. The room hummed with excitement, full of people who had been driven in by the cold to seek the bottle and a bit of warmth. Men to their left drunkenly wagered on arm wrestling; a table to the right played Solar with stained and frayed cards, betting the day's pay. In the back of the small room, someone played a stubo.

They drank a bottle of chisik together. Then, began working on another. Li and Sara served excellent flin, ibi steaks, and roasted woboes. Jesse didn't say a word as they devoured every morsel. Sora ate a little slower, but no less eagerly.

"So, why did you *actually* come into town? I know where the ship is. You traveled days to get here, Sora," Jesse said, mouth half full.

Sora stopped poking at her plate with her fork, "I wanted to go see Jo."

"But you didn't?"

Sora shook her head. "I didn't know what I would say. I feel terrible."

"How about, 'Hey sis, I love ya'? Or something like that?"

"Very funny," Sora groaned. "We didn't exactly leave on the best of terms."

"I know, I'm sorry."

"It's alright. Anyway, I got in late, so I wanted to come stay with you for tonight, and I'll ride out in the morning."

"You're always welcome, of course," Jesse downed the last mouthful from their bottle.

Stories and songs passed around the room. Jesse laughed with food in their mouth. Li came around the bar to break up a fight. Everyone yelled and threw their bread at two men who spilled drinks and disrupted a perfectly good song. A cheer went up as the combatants were tossed outside into the cold. Sora raised her glass, any serious thoughts and regrets fading out of mind.

Until the marshal walked in.

Marshal Rayburn Skye stood opposite the noisy saloon. The soft glow of fire and lamplight from the windows lay across the street. But the marshal stood in shadow, hat pulled low as he watched and waited as people gradually filled the saloon. Hours wore on, and he shifted his weight off his prosthetic leg, the gears and joints even more stiff in the cold.

"Alright, positive ID, marshal," Cole's voice said over their comms channel. "He's at the bar."

"Keep your cool," the marshal said, as if his chief deputy stood right next to him.

Two months. He'd been at this for two months since Alix had burned down Silas's compound. She'd killed twelve men in the street, and the bodies inside had been too burned to bother counting. But many of Silas's men had cut and run when the storm had hit. The marshal had spent the past two months rounding them up, trying to put an end to any last, minor fragments of Silas Purvida.

"Heading inside," the marshal said.

Looking both ways, he walked across the street. He didn't check for stirrols or skimmers, but eyes watching him. This saloon wasn't a usual place for men carrying plasbolts; so, before entering, he made sure no one else stood outside, waiting for him to make a move.

The marshal pushed his way in, and a cool breeze came with him as the door opened. The jovial company within fell silent. Even the musician in a far corner stopped playing. The marshal's boots thudded on the floorboards, one landing more heavily than the other.

Some conversations returned, but in hushed tones. The marshal kept his focus solely on the bar. It was enough for some in the room to shrug and continue their games and arguments. Others, like the man to the marshal's right, stayed silent as death.

"What can I get for you?" Li asked the marshal.

"Chisik," the marshal pushed his hat back, giving a friendly smile to the bartender.

Li brought out a bottle and poured the marshal a glass. It wasn't the best chisik the marshal had ever drank, but it wasn't the worst, either. He remembered the aged Black Barrel that Silas had served him, back when Silas had still had an office—still had breath in his lungs. *Black Barrel*, the marshal thought, *yet another business of Silas's that now has no owner, like a leaf in the wind.*

"Want me to make a move?" Cole said.

The marshal glanced at Cole, who was already fidgeting. The young man had a problem with his nerves, a little too jumpy for this line of work. *But, who else is as eager to do it? Certainly no one with Cole's moral compass*, the marshal said to himself, taking a drink.

Cole stopped asking after the marshal continued to ignore him. The marshal waited, and waited, feeling out the mood in the room. Conversation began rising again, the deep thrum of the stubo, the clink of utensils against plates, the shuffling of cards. Only two people still snuck glances at him. He'd recognized them both: the scrapper Jesse, and the mechanic, Sora.

The saloon was only a short walk from Jesse's shop, so the marshal wasn't surprised at all to see them inside. This was likely a regular place for them to eat and relax. But he still felt their eyes on him, waiting for something to happen—wondering, fearing if he had come here for them. He'd meant what he'd said those months ago, when visiting Jesse the first time. He hadn't intended to detain them for helping Alix and Felix sneak into the spaceport. Jesse posed no threat to anyone, just a scrapper looking to make some crits.

"Can I get you another?" Li said, noticing the marshal's empty glass.

"Actually," the marshal cleared his throat, "I'm looking for a man named Berrin. You know anybody by that name?"

Li cocked his head and narrowed his eyes, genuinely thinking on the question. "No, I don't believe so."

"He's a heavy man, about your height. Got dark eyes and wearing an old red coat. Missing a finger on his left hand."

The man beside the marshal shifted on his stool.

Li's eyes widened, and his eyes darted toward the man.

To the marshal's right, the hand with four digits that had been holding a cup, tried to drop below the bar without notice.

"Why don't you keep that hand where I can see it, friend," the marshal said, still looking at Li.

The hand stopped. It rested on the bar again; the man turned his head. "You're playing a dangerous game, marshal," Berrin said in a harsh, raspy voice.

"Let's not make a disturbance," the marshal replied, finally looking Berrin in the eyes.

"How about I spray your brains all over this bar?"

A plasbolt charged up, the signature whining, the chambers spinning. Berrin slowly put his hands in the air, his eyes darting back and forth, sensing someone behind him. Cole held his plasbolt to the base of Berrin's skull.

"You'd do well not to move," Cole said in his most intimidating tone.

It's not bad, the marshal thought. Then, he got off his stool and swept his gaze around the saloon. Everyone's eyes now locked on him, Cole, and Berrin. He put his hands out. "Nothing to worry about, folks. We'll be on our way."

Berrin sneered, but he had no real chance to save his neck. It was over for him. Cole pressed the barrel firmly into Berrin's neck, and the three of them headed outside. Berrin walked with his hands up, Cole behind him, and the marshal last. The marshal tipped his cap to no one in particular, to everyone in the bar, and slowly conversation rose behind them once more.

Out on the boardwalk, the marshal stood by as Cole locked Berrin's hands behind his back with a set of fetters. The marshal smiled at the man. "You'll be staying with me for a while."

"You ain't got no cause to hold me."

"Your friends sold you out, Berrin. You're the last piece of Silas's puzzle, back in the box."

Berrin spat on the marshal's coat. The marshal looked down, then back up—and swung a heavy fist into the man's gut. Berrin crumpled over, coughing, gagging. The marshal wiped the spit off his coat with a handkerchief.

"Cole, pick that son of a bitch up."

The pale moons drifted across the Celestinian sky, Ava moving over the face of Tasca. Thin, grey and purple clouds moved south, slowly dissipating. A swirling wind blew through white peaks. Shadows fell on the north side of the mountains; glaciers glittered blue in the moonlight. Near the tree line, where dark-needled slape and still-green ghissh trees offered concealment, the *Shadow* lay upon rocks.

Carefully stacked and joined rocks replaced the ship's shattered landing gear. The explosion two months ago had rendered the legs beyond repair on the port side. The starboard legs still worked, but the rock pilings kept the port side up, out of the snow. The ship lay parallel to the rising foothills to the south and the tree line only a few meters away on the other side. The personnel ramp opened toward the dark forest, grey mist hanging among the black trunks.

Alix sat at the top of the ramp, knees up at her chest, gazing into the cold night. Despite the chill, she wore a grease-stained tank top. She tilted her head back and blew a short breath to watch it rise, swirl, and vanish. The cough and burning in her lungs returned. She wrapped her right hand around her mouth until the coughing subsided, but she could still feel the molten heat of the fire back in Silas's compound.

When she pulled her hand away, she looked down at the burn scar on her palm. She traced the scar with her left pointer finger: the metal backstrap from her old Plasveld-7s. The marshal had given her the pair as a gift when she'd come of age; she remembered the searing pain of gripping the Plasveld in Silas's burning saloon, and then killing the Thin Man with a final shot. She'd left the Plasvelds behind, but the reminder would never leave her.

Alix smiled at the familiar thump of Felix's boots on the ramp. He sat beside her, the stained, drab shirt contrasting his sleek, semi-translucent artificial skin. In her peripheral, Alix caught the faint lights beneath his bare arm. She leaned her head against his forearm—even sitting, he was too tall for her to rest her head on his shoulder.

"Still trouble sleeping?" Felix's voice carried a deep, distant reverb like a raspy voice echoing in a dark cave.

"Mm-hmm."

"I finished the repair on the lateral temp regulators. We're making good progress."

Alix closed her eyes and nodded. She knew the more accurate statement: *Felix is making good progress*. He worked almost nonstop, effortlessly, to repair the *Shadow*. Alix contributed as much as she could, but her body, and brain, seemed to rebel every day.

"Thanks," she whispered.

"Are you sure you don't want anything to help?"

"It didn't work, remember?"

"Well, we could try other substances."

"Honestly, I'm tired of trying." Alix snuggled closer and Felix settled his arm around her.

"Aren't you cold? Let's go in."

Alix shrugged. The cold actually felt comforting, a sign that the nano hyperfluid inside of her was not just taking over—that she was still human, after all. At the time, when Alix had plunged the needle into her body, hoping against hope the same nano-fluid that coursed through Felix could save her life, she couldn't even have comprehended the consequences. The only thought racing through her mind that night had been death, the gathering dark on the edges of her sight. Afterward, the fires and the trail of death at Silas's place had prevented her from processing anything. The nightmares had begun, the horrific memories of blood, tears, and black lines beneath her skin.

She tried a deep breath, but couldn't draw her lungs full. They still burned, weak from the smoke and chemicals inhaled amidst the fire. Felix held her tight as she coughed. Then, the dull headache returned, the back of her skull throbbing, the neck pain, muscles tightening. *The goddamn headache.*

Months ago, she would've fallen asleep in Felix's arms in no time. But now, when she closed her eyes, she saw faint purple and red swirling remnants of light that passed through her lids, creating residual patterns of the world around her. But the usual patterns began to give way to an utter dark, and light then grew around the edges, pulsing with the rhythm of the pain in her head. Patterns returned, moving, swirling, becoming vague shapes of a world that wasn't physically around her, like a lucid dream, the metal structures and machinery so familiar: the interior of a Xypha superstructure—the Rings over the Cradle.

Alix sat in that dim, cold space: young, barefoot, starving. But the scene shifted and faded. Another emerged from under her feet, but her child self remained in place. Instead of the darkness of her hiding spot within the Rings, a bright, hot light surrounded her. Burning flames twisted into the night sky. Screams pierced her heart. The world burned all around her. She tried to will herself to look into the fire-coated trees, through smoke and mist—the orchard.

Alix opened her eyes.

"Are you okay?" Felix's voice was full of concern.

"Just remembering Sora's orchard."

"That was not your fault."

"Wasn't it?"

Felix gripped her tight. "Have you heard from her?"

Alix coughed. "Not since she left."

"I'm sure she made it home okay."

Alix coughed again, then growled to clear her throat. "Come on, let's go to bed."

She stood and offered her hand to Felix. He definitely didn't need the help getting up, but he took her small hand in his and then, towering over her, pulled her close by the waist. His eyes sparkled, catching moonlight like raindrops on a twifruit leaf. He smiled and lifted her chin. She stood on her tip toes to kiss him, wrapping her arms around his neck before Felix lifted her off her feet and carried her back into the ship.

Alix stretched, arms out and over her head, legs wide, one hanging out of the blanket; she quickly pulled it back under. With a long yawn she relaxed, then cuddled closer to Felix. A smile spread across her face, and she shook her butt closer to him, rubbed her head on his chest, felt the flow of energy moving from him and through her, like subtle vibrations. As she opened her eyes, she took in their cabin on the *Shadow*. The sight of the dark metal surfaces, the clothes on the floor, the sliding door of the locker half open—it was enough to bring a tear to her eye. She missed home so much, and now, she savored every day of the past two months as much as she could.

She couldn't believe that she had fallen asleep—and remained asleep—for the entire night.

Her body began protesting. A growl rolled in her stomach; a sharp pain pierced her bladder. She moaned and pushed her face down into the pillow. Then, she threw the cover back and put her bare feet on the cold floor. Felix lay quietly behind her. She tugged the blanket back over him, a comforting gesture more than necessary for his warmth. She blushed thinking about the night before: his touch from her toes to her breasts, her lips, the snapping electricity in wet kisses. A shiver ran through her again.

Alix opened the squeaky hatch from their cabin into the head. She brushed her tangled hair with her hands, tying it up on her head like a whippix nest. Behind the mirror she retrieved vials and the metal plunger. She put her foot up on the toilet seat, inserted a vial into the plunger, and injected the hormones into her hip.

She yawned again and braced herself for the headache to follow, but there was nothing.

After relieving herself, she had to address her growling stomach.

Alix's bare feet pattered on the cold metal deck as she snuck through empty hallways to the cockpit wearing only a tank top and underwear. She sat in the pilot's chair, *her chair*, and checked the power core and generator status. She dialed up the output just a little to improve the heating system. Green lights flickered and shifted all around her. The canopy remained dark beneath the shield flaps. But she imagined the white winter outside, and made out the wind whistling around the angles of the *Shadow*'s hull.

She flicked on the coffee brewer in the galley before moving back and forth between the sink, the cooktop, and the icebox. As she cracked eggs into a pan, she felt grateful to Wick for having stocked the galley with a clutch supply run before the winter had settled. She welcomed the heat of the cooktop. The smell of coffee spread, already perking her senses from the anticipation of its warmth—and caffeine.

Humming to herself, Alix dumped the scrambled eggs onto a small metal plate. She flopped into the circular bench seat against the hull, and put her legs up on the table. As she ate, she pulled up a diagram of the *Shadow* projected above the table. She and Felix had gone through and noted every repair that still needed to be made. With Sora's help, they'd initially focused on the damaged engine, and it had proven to be worse than any of them had thought. The engine repairs had taken so long, they'd barely had time to get to anything else before the first snowfalls.

In the meantime, they'd fixed the hole torn in the hull by the explosions, a black and blue patch of Alloyn steel, bent and shaped, welded in with the rest of the hull. That had at least made it warmer inside the ship. There were countless damaged wires, tubes, and hoses. Every day some other wiring problem emerged that meant she had to crawl through cramped spaces under the deck, reach deep into open panels, searching for the right connectors and circuits.

Felix walked into the galley bare chested, stretching his arms and neck. The soft blue lights running along the upper edges of the galley made his head and shoulders shimmer. Pulses of light flowed like delicate streams under the surface of his skin. His stark blue eyes spun in their sockets. A warm smile spread across his face when he saw Alix at the table, cramming eggs into her mouth.

"How'd you sleep?" he said.

"Pretty good," Alix replied with a wink, the satisfaction in her voice muffled by the mouthful of eggs.

Felix slid into the bench next to her and Alix moved her legs off the table to lay them in his lap. He let her finish slamming down her breakfast, studying the same diagram of the ship she had been reviewing.

"What're we working on today? The CO_2 scrubbers? The intake oxidizer?" Felix flipped through systems that still needed repairs.

Alix finished the last of her coffee. "Dealer's choice."

"CO_2 scrubbers it is." Felix swiped away the diagram above the table.

Just then, a shrill beeping echoed from the cockpit.

Alix and Felix looked at one another: they'd received a transmission from either Wick or Sora. Felix started to slide out of the bench seat, but Alix stepped on the table, jumping over it to hurry into the cockpit. When she reached her chair, the seat spun around to face the windshield. Her hands worked instinctually to connect with whoever had sent the call.

"Good morning!" Wick's voice passed through static into the *Shadow*'s cockpit.

A moment of disappointment hit Alix, as she'd hoped to hear Sora instead. "You're back?"

"You bet. I picked up everything we needed, and then some," Wick responded.

"What does that mean?" Alix rubbed her eyes. She waited for the bad news that Wick had concocted some stupid plan that would inevitably lead to trouble.

"Hey Alix," Sora's voice sent Alix's heart aflutter.

Alix sat up as if she'd been caught in an unflattering position. She quickly changed her tone, "Sora? What are you doing there? I thought you were going back home?"

"Well, I was, but I stayed with Jess for a night. We ran into the marshal."

"Shit."

"What happened?" Felix now stood behind Alix, hand on her chair, the other up on the instrument panels overhead. Although, they weren't over *his* head unless he leaned over the dash.

"No trouble directly, but we are pretty sure he saw us. He picked up some guy, probably one of Silas's men who was in the wind."

"Well, Felix and I will meet you in town."

"Copy that."

Alix stared at the dash as the transmission ended. She dwelt on Sora's tone and wondered if it meant anything significant. Sora had left the *Shadow* to go see Jo, or so Alix had thought. *Surely she didn't just leave to get away, right?* Alix sighed and wondered if Sora's tone had been distant, as if maybe things had run their course.

Felix leaned his face in front of Alix's stare and she snapped back to the present. She smiled, leaned forward, and pecked him on the lips before hopping out of her chair and heading back toward their cabin. He followed behind.

"Don't forget, the hike into Alloyn is strenuous," he said.

"I know," she yelled from within their cabin.

Felix stood in the hatchway watching Alix pull on a pair of trousers, smell a shirt that had been in the floor, and toss it over her head anyway. "We've got to take it slow," he said.

Alix popped her head out of the shirt, though she hadn't put her arms through, yet. "Okay, okay. I'll take it easy!"

2

The Town

Alix's cough turned into a hard wheezing as the oxygen escaped her lungs. She fell to one knee, and Felix rushed to her side. An outstretched palm kept him from helping her up as she shook her head. The cough subsided, and Alix drew in breaths as deeply as possible, but they remained shallow. The high altitude strained Alix's weakened lungs even more, and when she stood, she swooned as the blood rushed to her head. This time, Felix gently put his hand on her back.

"I'm okay," she said, more annoyed at her weakness than Felix helping her. Before Felix could speak, she continued, "Don't say I told you so."

"I wasn't!" Felix smiled. "But we still have a kilometer to go."

"Great, I was just getting warmed up," Alix quipped. She side-eyed Felix as he waited for her to continue.

The game trail ran up through the foothills, and when they reached the top of one hill and lost sight of the *Shadow* and the forest behind, they finally came to a dirt road. Alix sighed, relieved to at last have some decent footing. Now that the road provided enough space, Felix walked beside her and they strolled toward Alloyn at a leisurely pace.

Ahead, the town emerged from rocks and slape trees: stone buildings, stone walls, and stone pathways between them. Alloyn lay in a small valley, collared by mountains rising high to the south, lower peaks to the east, and hills to the north. The road into town approached from the west and the townspeople expanded up the short slopes with houses of stone and wood. Sweepers moved along the cobbled streets, pushing and brushing snow into large piles to allow people and wagons easy passage. Binox pulled wooden wagons and carts, loaded with ore from the mine.

In the winter, the town depended entirely on itself, but Wick's coming and going in the *Procella* had become a welcome change—it also meant the townsfolk had taken a liking to him, and anyone associated with him. Alix saw the *Procella* sitting on the only landing pad in town, jutting out from the northern hillside high above the rooftops. The mine lay below it, reaching into the mountains, the shafts and caverns spreading into the rock above and below the town. Alloyn was a primary source for local metals used in the Isidis Valley, but Alix had never run supplies in or out of this place. She had only been to Alloyn once, and the memory brought a smile to her face, but she tried to hide it, and the twinge of fear that followed.

The *Procella* sat with its cargo ramp open. Wick savored the chance to boss around the workers who unloaded containers from his ship. Alix heard his valley farmer accent over the gusts of wind that swirled between the mountains. She and Felix approached the ship and Wick held his hat down with one hand while waving to them with the other. Then he broke into a frustrated drawl at a worker who started to remove the wrong container from the ship's hold.

"Power goes to his head," Alix said to Felix.

Before Felix could reply, Alix caught sight of Sora walking out of the dark interior of the cargo hold. Alix quickened her pace, almost into a sprint, but then checked herself to play it cool. Still, she grinned ear-to-ear as she met Sora at the bottom of the ramp.

Sora, brown skin rich in the morning light, wearing a loose blue shirt, her dark, curly hair tied up on her head, cocked an eyebrow. She ignored the cold and while still on the slope of the cargo ramp, looked down at Alix. Sora's eyes were drawn to the long, pale fingers on Alix's hips; she had a habit of standing that way, her hands near the plasbolts that currently weren't at her sides. Sora remembered the last time they were together, that those fingers could do more than squeeze a trigger—so much more.

"Do I have to say it first?" Alix said, finally, crossing her arms.

"Say what?" Sora stepped a little closer.

"I missed you."

"Oh, you did?" Sora started to walk past Alix.

Alix grabbed Sora's arm and pulled her back and in close before kissing her; Sora dropped her bag, and held Alix's face in her hands. Their mouths opened and the cold air threatened to dry their lips. Alix bit her bottom lip, tasting the twifruit Sora had eaten on the ship, or maybe that was just the way Sora tasted on any given day.

"I missed you too," Sora said at last.

They laughed together, but Wick brushed past them to make a point. "Alright you two, break it up."

"Aye, aye, captain," Alix said in a deep, sarcastic tone.

Before Sora could pick up her bag, Alix swiped it off the ground and slung it over her shoulder. She carried it proudly as Sora clung to her other arm, and together they made their way toward the hangar and warehouse built into the mountain. Felix was inspecting containers removed from the *Procella*, but he smiled and waved at Sora.

"Welcome back!"

"Nice to see you again, Felix," Sora said.

"How is Jo?" he said.

Sora looked down at her boots. Her shoulders dropped. "I didn't go home."

"Why not?" Alix said.

"Well, once we saw the marshal, I got worried that maybe it wasn't safe."

It wasn't a lie, but Sora still felt guilty: about not seeing Jo; about using the marshal as an excuse to change her plans. She and Jo had been through rough patches before, but the forced proximity of their living arrangements made it pretty hard to leave things unsaid. Now, with Sora hundreds of kilometers away, she felt unable to bridge the gap—afraid to admit what she wanted to say.

"Did he say anything to you?" Felix said.

"No, he was too focused on whoever he was apprehending. There was another guy with him," Sora recalled.

"Cole," Alix said.

Felix nodded.

"What are we discussing?" Wick strolled up, pushing his hat back on his pale, balding head.

"About whether we should ditch you once you deliver the last parts we need," Alix said.

Wick gave her a side-eyed glance, likely recalling the time she'd almost killed him in Keizur's End. But things had gone haywire, and she'd promised to get his ship back. She'd kept her promise, and he'd stuck with her and Felix, even though sometimes he remained the punching bag.

"Oh, almost forgot," he said at last.

Wick pulled a soft, black pouch from the bag at his feet before tossing it to Alix. Glass clinked as she caught it, and she quickly opened the pouch to reveal many vials of hormones. Her sarcasm faded away, and she smiled at him, genuinely. He tipped his hat.

"Now, let's eat," Wick said.

He picked up his bag and disappeared into the giant hangar inside the mountain. Alix stuffed the hormone vials into Sora's bag and hefted it over her shoulder. Sora clung to Alix's arm, then let her hand slide down until their fingers interlocked, causing Felix to smile at them, his bright eyes glowing, the morning light glinting on his face.

A wide cobblestone lane split Alloyn in two, running west-to-east from the wagon road straight to the mine entrance at the base of the mountains, roomy enough to accommodate teams of binox, skimmers, and foot traffic all at once.

Alix and the others strolled down the lane, observing the snow piled at the edges and how the undaunted townspeople trudged past, thick coats and furry boots protecting them from the biting cold. Felix caught a few staring eyes, but none full of hostility. Alix paid no attention; she and Sora whispered to one another until Alix saw a shop off the central lane and remembered the parts list Felix had assembled.

"We've got to get a few things," she said. "Do you want to wait?"

"Just find me later," Wick said. "I'm starving. I'll leave my beacon on."

"No problem," Felix said.

Wick strode ahead as the others entered the shop where a short man with red, wind-burned cheeks and a knit hat sold an array of reclaimed spare parts. Alix pulled up her to-do list on the syncpad on her left arm.

She followed the short man around, reading off the list as he picked things from shelves and dug through crates and trunks, as Felix followed with a wood box the man had let them use, which slowly filled to the top until it weighed so much only Felix could carry it. Alix made sure to keep firing off the parts list as they went, not giving the man a chance to interrupt. Finally, Alix swiped the list from her syncpad and leaned on a large U-shaped counter in the center of the shop.

Sora crouched by a shelf in Alix's peripheral vision, her curiosity drawing her to tinkering with the small parts and gadgets around the shop. Sora was always eager to work with her hands, to find something to disassemble, reassemble, and repair. Alix stared at Sora's back, the tight trousers hugging her rear.

"What do we owe you?" Felix said to the proprietor as he lugged the box onto the counter, everything inside shaking and rattling.

Alix shook herself from her trance and turned to give the man her best polite smile.

The proprietor stammered, trying to do the math in his head, as he hadn't kept notes while retrieving everything. "Well, uh, two thousand."

Alix pulled out a pouch of crits from her coat and weighed it in her hand. She laughed anxiously as she counted. "What can I get for... seven hundred?"

The proprietor eyed Alix, then the crate, and began removing parts from the box. He laid the entire box's contents on the counter and rubbed his chin. He pushed some things to the side, and with each item, Alix started to speak or reach out her hand to stop him. But she bit her tongue and quietly seethed. In the end, they had barely a quarter of the things on her list.

At least the smaller amount meant Felix didn't have to carry the huge box back to the *Shadow*. Instead, he put everything in a rucksack he had rolled up in his coat.

"It was a pleasure, miss!" The proprietor beamed with satisfaction.

"Yeah, yeah," Alix groaned. She could've carried their remaining crits in one hand.

Alloyn grew busy toward midday. Men and women in blue, dirty coveralls emerged from the massive opening in the mountain and headed down the center lane as their shifts ended, while lines of men and women in not-yet-stained outfits moved toward the mine to take their place. Bells clanged around the necks of heavy binox, their hoofs clomping on the stone as they pulled carts laden with iron ore, wood, barrels of water, ale, bales of animal pelts, and much more.

Alix, Sora, and Felix found Wick inside a pleasant restaurant just off the broad lane. The restaurant was laid out in a wide rectangle, with a stone floor, and the entire front face open to the outside air. A huge fire burned against the back wall, and the heat warred with the cold, allowing in just enough of a chill for Alix to keep her coat on. Wick waved at them from a table in the back corner, still chewing his food.

Alix settled beside him, and as soon as her very rich, very dark coffee arrived, she drank it to supplement the fire in trying to keep herself warm. Sora brought her chair close to Alix, their shoulders near to touching as Sora's left hand rested on Alix's thigh beneath the table, warming her even more.

Groups eventually filled the restaurant for their noon meals, mostly miners who'd had the chance to clean up after a shift. Some of the diners stared openly at Felix from their tables. Alix shot them dirty looks, which caused the prying eyes to look away. The bag of gear, and goods, sat on the floor while Alix kept her back to the wall so she could watch the entrance and anyone who might approach them—an old habit. Felix didn't need a view of the entrance, or even need to visibly *see* anyone to keep tabs on everyone and everything in the room.

The early afternoon passed pleasantly, and Alix appreciated the never-ending cups of coffee. They sat in near silence, enjoying each other's presence, the calm between them a far cry from the circumstances in which the crew had assembled back in autumn. Wick sat back in his chair, smoking a cigar, extremely satisfied.

Felix gazed into Alix's eyes, a silent communication between them; he knew the peace and pleasure on her face, which he hadn't seen in quite some time—at least not since Xypha had arrived on Celestine.

The crowd in the restaurant died down after a couple hours, but Alix remained hesitant to leave. Ideas passed through her mind while at the table, perhaps because she didn't feel so cooped up. She had spent months in the *Shadow* recuperating and repairing things. Now, she almost felt back to full strength, but the *Shadow* remained out of commission. Xypha remained overhead, and in the valley. She had almost no information about what they were up to back in the valley— *back home.*

Alix sat back and lifted her cup for a drink but noticed the lack of coffee inside. She craned her neck and searched the restaurant for a server. Instead, she found a blonde woman, stunningly beautiful—and familiar. Alix couldn't help but stare as the woman walked across the room toward the bar and the doorway into the back of the restaurant.

"Oh no," Alix whispered.

"What?" Felix said.

"I think I saw someone I know."

"Is that bad?" Sora's voice was low, on edge.

"Well..." Alix grimaced, thinking hard about the answer to *that* question.

Years ago…

The heavy front door opening and closing shook Mia from the very edge of euphoria. She opened her eyes wide, her chest heaving, sweat running down her face. Heavy footsteps on the floorboards echoed as her husband put his things away. Alix popped her head up from under the blanket, her face and lips red and wet.

"What the fuck," Alix breathed.

"He wasn't supposed to be—" Mia started.

"Mia, where are you?" her husband called out, gruff and impatient.

Alix rolled out of the bed, hitting her knees on the floor, scrambling to get dressed. She had her pants on and one arm through her shirt when a large hairy man threw back the blanket curtain over the bedroom doorway. Mia sat wrapped in the bed's sheets, her blonde hair disheveled, her face and chest flush.

"What the fuck?" the man roared.

Mia tried to stammer excuses. "Rolfe, please just—"

The man eyed Alix's belt and Plasvelds hanging on the chair. Alix had rolled the other way and stood on the wrong side of the bed from them. He went for the belt—so did Alix and Mia. Rolfe gripped the belt with large hands, but Mia managed to pull on one end enough for him to fumble with drawing a Plasveld.

Alix threw a punch into his jaw.

Rolfe swung the back of his hand at her.

The blow sent Alix staggering, and warm blood dripped from her nose to her lips. Rolfe grabbed Mia by the throat, lifted her and threw her against the wall. Her hands grabbed the back of her head. Rolfe turned back to the belt, but Alix was already there. The training from Spiros kicked in, and she began pummeling the larger man in the ribs, the kidneys—ducking under and leaning away from his wild, haphazard swings. She cracked his nose, a couple ribs, and sent him staggering out of the bedroom, clutching his face.

Alix's eyes blazed with fury as she followed. She wiped the blood from her nose with the back of her hand, then wiped the hand on her pants. Rolfe crawled back toward the front door; Alix stalked her prey.

Rolfe spilled out of the house, coughing, and bloody, as Alix strode calmly out behind him, buckling the belt around her waist. The large man put his hands up, sitting in the dirt street.

Alix sneered and drew the Plasveld on her right hip.

In her mind, the grey coveralls Rolfe wore resembled the Xypha slipsuit worn by the security officers who had discovered her within the walls of that station—she'd clawed and scratched, bitten, kicked, and screamed. Then, she'd only had a knife to kill them, her young hands dripping with blood.

Now, she leveled a Plasveld at Rolfe's chest.

Mia staggered to the front door, wrapped in the sheets, panic in her eyes as she saw Rolfe on the ground, hands up toward Alix.

"Please, I'm sorry. Just listen—" Rolfe begged.

Mia shouted, "Alix, wait!"

Zmmph.

Rolfe lay dead.

Alix's hand trembled. She held the Plasveld on the dead man, as if making sure he wouldn't move again. Mia's gentle touch shocked Alix back to reality. She turned her head to look at Mia, her eyes watering, searching, tears beginning to roll down her cheeks. Alix returned the Plasveld to her holster.

"I'm—I'm sorry, Mia," Alix stammered.

"You have to go," Mia replied, knowing the trouble that would come.

There were a million things racing through Alix's mind. She tried to move her lips, but Mia's eyes pleaded with her to leave, to escape. Alix touched Mia's face; Mia brought her hand up and held Alix's hand to her cheek for just a moment longer.

"Now, go. Run!" Mia implored.

Alix ran.

Now...

Alix finished recounting the story, her eyes down, staring into the coffee mug. She looked up, afraid to see Sora's reaction.

Sora studied Alix through narrowed eyes, a subtle smirk on her lips. Alix wondered if Sora disapproved of the murder, the affair, or both.

"That was her?" Wick said. "You're sure?"

"Trust me, I would never forget her," Alix said, then she paused and looked at Sora again, whose eyebrows now raised, waiting for Alix to keep talking. Alix felt like she was digging herself an even deeper hole.

"Is there a place you've been where you *haven't* killed someone?" Sora crossed her arms.

Alix scrunched her face as if she'd just been punched in the ribs. "We should get out of here."

"What about paying?" Wick whispered.

"It's nothing, let's go," Alix whispered back.

"You don't even know if she's mad at you!"

"I killed her husband, then skipped town."

"You said he was abusive?" Sora asked.

"He was!" Alix tried not to raise her voice. "It's not about *her* being mad at me."

Alix, Sora, and Wick leaned forward over the table as they argued in hushed voices. They didn't notice a server walk up to the table, a pot of coffee in her hand, until she spoke.

"Coffee?" the server said in a sweet tone.

Alix, still bent low to the table, tilted her eyes up, and froze. The server's eyes widened like the ceramic saucers on the table, her lips quivered, and slowly, her brow wrinkled as realization settled in, "Alix?"

Nervous laughter overtook Alix. She leaned back in the chair and scratched her head just under her pony tail. "Yeah, it's me, Mia."

"I can't believe it," Mia stammered. She nearly dropped the coffee pot on the table. "I didn't think I'd ever see you again!"

Alix held her arms out, "Well, surprise!"

Mia stared in disbelief, eyes darting to the others at the table, none of whom she knew. Mia opened and closed her mouth a few times, and Alix tried not to squirm in her seat as she waited for a response. Mia remained as beautiful as the last day Alix had seen her.

With a sarcastic smile for Alix's benefit, Sora reached out her hand, "I'm Sora."

Mia finally stuttered as she shook Sora's hand. "I'm so sorry, I'm Mia, um…Alix and I were…"

"Don't worry, darling, we heard the story," Wick added.

Alix kicked Wick in the shin, jostling the cups, plates, and forks as Wick jerked his knee up and hit the table. "This is Felix," Alix gestured with one hand. "And this is Wick."

"Hi. Nice to meet you," Mia blushed.

"Y-you look great!" Alix took matters into her own hands and picked up the coffee pot to pour herself another cup.

"So do you," Mia said, but she narrowed her eyes and looked a little closer, as if assessing her properly.

"Thanks," Alix stared down at her cup. "The past several months haven't been that kind to me."

"Are you okay?"

"Oh, we're fine," Alix waved her hand to dismiss any concerns. She took a sip and held the warm cup in both hands. "Listen, Mia, I'm sorry."

Mia shook her head. "He was a terrible person, I know that."

"No, I'm sorry that I ran out, and didn't get in touch again. I'm *definitely* not sorry I killed him."

Felix put his hand to his head.

Mia let out a gentle laugh and covered her mouth with her hand as if to hide some kind of shame for laughing at her husband's demise—even if he did deserve it. Alix stared into Mia's green eyes; her hands trembled. Mia's smile stirred Alix's heart. That smile told of years spent safe and thriving. But the passion between them had faded, and Alix had rediscovered that feeling—a nascent passion—just with someone new.

"Rolfe's still got family here. Brothers, they uh…" Mia started.

"Want to kill me?" Alix said.

"Yes."

"Well, what else is new?" Wick chimed in.

Alix broke her gaze away from Mia to scowl at Wick. He put up his hands in defense and shut his mouth. The idea of people hunting her down came rushing back. *Had she softened, or relaxed too much in the past two months?* Alix had never felt as naked as she did right now without her Plasvelds. Replacing them leapt to her top priority, but that wouldn't be easy. Alloyn wasn't exactly a town where one could buy an array of weaponry; not to mention, she was low on funds.

"I guess we'll have to steer clear. We were just talking about leaving, anyway," she said.

"Where are you staying?" Mia asked.

"My ship is outside of town."

"This is my place, so if you need anything, you can always come check with me here."

"You own this place?"

"Don't sound so surprised."

"I guess we better pay the bill, then."

Mia laughed. "It's on the house."

* * *

Shadows fell over Alloyn as the sun set behind the high peak to the east. Beams of pink and gold light reached the rooftops, and the snow on the mountainsides took on an orange, pink, and purple shimmer. In the street outside Mia's place, Alix pleaded her case to the others.

"Why don't y'all go back to the *Shadow*. I'll hang back and find some…"

"Some what?" Sora put her hands on her hips, eyes narrowed as she tried to anticipate Alix's argument.

"Come on, I've got no bolts. It's killing me. If there are men in town who want me dead, I would like to not be caught with my hands empty."

"Or you could come back with us, and just continue to lie low?"

Alix bobbed her head as if she was actually weighing that option. "Yeah, but, if I did that, then the next time we came into town, would there be a bunch of guys with bolts waiting for us?"

Sora and Alix stared at one another, their faces continuing the argument: Sora scowled and shook her head; Alix smiled, eyebrows raised, her head cocked to the side. Sora rolled her eyes and threw her hands up. *It's like fighting with Jo*, she thought.

"Fine. We've got work to do, though. So hurry," she said.

"I know! I will be right behind you," Alix said.

Alix reached behind Sora and brought her in for a kiss. Sora smiled, unable to resist the playful charm. At first the kiss was brief, but Sora kept Alix close, their lips softly locked, Alix giving Sora's bottom lip a playful bite before pulling away. Alix took a deep breath, then started to cough.

"Sorry," she said in between gasps of air.

"Ah, another reason it's a great idea for you to stay behind," Felix said.

"Shut it," Alix said once she finished coughing.

Felix smiled, the light in his eyes catching the sunset, almost changing their color. Alix had to stand on her tiptoes to reach up and kiss him, an electricity passing from his mouth to hers. When she turned to leave, Wick stood in her way.

"Don't I get a kiss?" he said.

Alix cocked her fist, ready to throw a punch—Wick flinched, his hands up to his face, taking a step back. Everyone but Wick laughed; Alix started coughing again, shaking her head as she covered her mouth. She softly put her fist onto Wick's shoulder as she passed him, and finally the cough subsided. She walked down the lane, cool and confident, as if she was merely headed out for a peaceful stroll.

"This is a bad idea isn't it?" Sora said to Felix as they watched Alix leave.

Felix shrugged. "Maybe. But I've been with Alix long enough to know when she's going to do what she wants to do, no matter what you say."

Sora blew a puff of air through her lips. "I guess I'm still adjusting."

"It's okay. You care about her; of course you want to protect her."

"Thanks." Sora kept her eyes down the lane, but Alix had long disappeared into the crowd, or onto a side street.

"Come on, you and I have work to do," Felix said.

"I'm staying with the *Procella*," Wick added. "Give me a ping if you need me, or when you come back to town." He started to walk away, then paused and turned back, "Or if Alix gets into trouble, whichever comes first."

An old man shuffled along a street, lighting oil lamps set on wooden posts every few meters. A soft yellow glow spread from the lamps and windows, contrasted with the dark stone of Alloyn, but the light gave off a false sense of warmth. The temperature plummeted as darkness overtook the town. The first bright moon wouldn't lift over the peaks for another few hours.

Alix sat on a bench across the street from a shop. She cinched her coat tight and kept her head warm beneath the hood. Earlier, she'd walked by the store a couple times, noticing the case with plasbolts laid on soft cloth. Traffic on the street died down as the light faded, and no one had gone in or out of the shop for the past hour. Alix looked up and down the street, then hopped off the bench before opening the shop door and slipping inside.

A short man popped out from behind shelves when he heard the bell. "Hi there," he said. "We're just about closed for the day."

"Oh, I will only be a minute," Alix assured him.

"Well, what do you need?" He wore a dirty apron and busied himself wiping down the shelves with an old rag.

Alix nodded toward the case. "Let me see those bolts."

"Ah, sure."

Alix thought the man sounded nervous, so she tried to remain pleasant and nonthreatening, acting as if the plasbolts were just a curiosity to her. But once he opened the case, her skill belied her innocent tone. She picked up the weapon and spun the chamber, turned it over in her hand, and inspected the long barrel. The grip was made of a red stained wood. She shrugged and set it down. Another was more to her liking, although it was no Plasveld. She gave it a once over, and spun it on her finger, back and forth, as the shopkeeper stared at her with raised brows, parted lips, and maybe a hint of fear. She winked at him.

"You got two of these, I see," she said. "How much?"

"For the pair? Twelve-hundred."

"For *these*?" She whistled. "You got charges?"

"Certainly."

"Let's see em."

He studied her, chewing on his lip, then reached below the case and brought out a box. He gave her a single cell charge, which she clapped into the chamber before giving it a spin. The plasbolt whined and glowed blue in the shop's dim light. The sound was like music to her ears and she finally felt whole again. Alix held out the plasbolt, spun it and caught the grip firmly in her palm. She closed one eye and panned the room, looking down the barrel. When she brought the bolt over to the shopkeeper, he laughed nervously, sweat gleaming on his brow.

"I think I'll take these two," she said. "And some charges. At least eight if you got that many."

"Sure, sure." He eyed the plasbolt. She didn't move. He licked his lips and swallowed. "Um that'll be fifteen hundred crits."

Alix knit her brows. "Nah, I said I'll *take* them."

The shopkeeper's mouth hung open. His hands began to shake. He spilled the charge box and the metallic casings clinked against the glass. Alix picked them up one by one with her left hand, stacked them, and then picked up the stack. She didn't have a replacement for her old belt, so she stuffed the stack into a pocket on the inside of her coat before picking up the second plasbolt, which she spun in her left hand and then dropped in the left pocket of her jacket. A smile crept across her face. She lowered the plasbolt in her right hand, and flicked the safety; the spinning chamber slowed and the blue glow died away.

"Pleasure," she said.

Alix threw her hood back over her head and walked outside, leaving the shopkeeper gawking after her, still shaking from head to toe. Outside, Alix stuffed her hands and the other plasbolt in her pockets, strolled down the street, and whistled a pleasant, carefree tune.

3

The Law

Alix wrapped her arms around herself to hold in what little warmth she had left after walking through Alloyn in the night. The streets lay quiet, and it let her mind wander away from the high-alertness she'd felt before obtaining new plasbolts. Although at the time she'd argued with Sora about staying behind, now, Alix wished she was in the *Shadow* with Sora and Felix.

She stayed off the center lane, and the side street sloped down gently to the west. Felix's voice chimed in her head, reminding her to take it slow, especially now that the temperature had dropped and the cold in her lungs brought on worse coughing fits. In between coughs, she cursed at herself. Even if her muscles felt strong, the lingering weakness in her lungs meant she couldn't do anything at full tilt.

Standing in the narrow street, Alix looked up at the moons now overhead. She pulled in a deep breath. Maybe she could will herself into healing. Of course she coughed and the ensuing hacks came so violently that she stumbled and caught herself with her right hand on a crate of refuse behind a stone building. She coughed into her left hand, pulled it back from her mouth and stared at the speckles of blood on her palm.

Goddammit, she thought.

When she climbed to her feet, Alix swooned and her vision blurred. A sharp pain throbbed in her head. She put her hands up as the pain persisted. Every muscle in her body tensed and she winced, forcing her to shut her eyes tight, waiting for the pain to subside.

Alix tumbled over into the crates and barrels of refuse, sending them crashing to the ground, the noise echoing along the street. Lying on her back, Alix tried to open her eyes, to get rid of the darkness, only to realize her eyes were already wide open. Her heart raced as panic spread through her body.

Then, her vision returned, but not of Alloyn, and not the moons on a clear Celestinian night.

Before Alix lay a dense jungle.

Smoke rose above the canopy.

The stars were strange.

The vision moved as if controlled by someone else; as if she'd been transported to another time and place. She could not control where she looked, and she felt and heard nothing around her.

An explosion swelled above the jungle in a brilliant flash of light against the night sky. A ball of fire rose and curled in a vortex of air—then the flames died out and left behind a column of thick, black smoke.

Alix could hear again. The vision of the jungle blurred and went black. Her sight returned like a curtain drawn back.

Two men stood over her. At any other time, Alix would have reached into her coat faster than the men could have reached for her. She would have shot both of them dead.

At any other time.

"That's her," one of the men said in a voice that sounded familiar, and a little anxious.

A strong arm grabbed her and lifted her off the pile of refuse. Alix looked at her surroundings through cloudy eyes, but she could still make out the man's face: pale, rough, and with a few days' worth of a beard. A lantern bobbed over his shoulder. Alix put her hand up to block the light but another arm pulled her hand down behind her back, and she felt cold steel encircle her wrists.

"Wh—what's going on?" Alix stammered.

"My name's Schelon and I am the law in Alloyn. Public intoxication, as well as robbery, don't fly here."

He thinks I'm drunk. "I'm not drunk," Alix protested, her voice weak and unconvincing.

"Yeah, sure," Schelon said. "I suppose you own these, too?" He held up one of the plasbolts.

Alix realized why the other voice sounded so familiar.

"Come on, we'll get you a nice bed for the night," Schelon said, leading her by the arm.

The following morning, Felix stood outside Mia's restaurant, listening. He glanced once over his shoulder to find Sora chewing on her cuticles, waiting for him to give her a sign. She had no idea how this worked, how *he* worked, but she trusted him because Alix trusted him.

At last, he turned and looked down at her. "This way."

They crossed the center lane and headed south. The town gently sloped upward, each street a little higher than the last, creating small terraces up the hillside. Felix tracked Alix's heartbeat. He knew that sound, that feeling, so intimately. They were close now. Once they reached town, within his sensor range, he blocked out all other input and focused solely on Alix.

He stopped at a small stone building with a heavy wooden door and a single window. Felix would have ripped the door down and barged in if he hadn't seen through the door and stone already and knew Alix leaned on the bars of a cell door inside. He smiled, partly because she wasn't hurt—and partly because he knew that Sora had an "I told you so" ready like a charged plasbolt.

Alix leaned her elbows on the crossbars of her cell door. The local lawman, Schelon, stood with arms folded across his chest, dismissing every word she said. Alix's own arms were bare: no syncpad to notify Felix or Sora. Her coat lay on a horribly uncomfortable cot behind her. She barely remembered arriving here, and she definitely hadn't taken the time to process just what exactly had happened to her last night.

"Where you from?" Schelon said.

"Nowhere," Alix replied.

"Well, Alix from *Nowhere*, this will be your home for quite some time until you tell me why you stole those bolts?"

"I told you. For my protection."

"Ah, so you're in danger?"

"You have no idea," Alix said under her breath.

"Usually you would just pay for a plasbolt if you weren't going to *cause* trouble."

Alix rolled her eyes. "Well, I seemed to be out of crits."

"Well, robbery carries a penalty of one cycle of work in the mine. No crits involved in that sentence, but maybe you could get some honest work after."

"Over my dead body." She glared at Schelon, who stood tough, but the kind of tough someone displayed when their adversary was behind bars and couldn't get a hold of them.

Just then, a heavy knock came at the door. Schelon startled, and his right hand went to his plasbolt. He gave Alix one last look, then approached the door, hand resting gently on the plasbolt's grip.

"How are we supposed to get her out?" Sora whispered to Felix as they stood by the door.

"We'll figure something out, don't worry."

The door creaked as it opened and a middle-aged man with pale skin and green eyes appeared, still holding the door with one hand. He looked at Sora first, since she was at his eye line, but he had to look up at Felix, and his eyes bulged as he gauged the sentient's height.

"What can I do for you?" Schelon said.

"Looking for a friend of ours. A dark-haired woman, about this tall." Felix held his hand up to represent Alix's height.

"She missing?"

"Well, she's in your cell," Felix said.

"Now, how do you know that?" Schelon let go of the door and stood fully in the opening, hands on his hips.

"We aren't looking for trouble. I *know* she's in there."

Schelon narrowed his eyes, looking back and forth between Felix and Sora. He pursed his lips as he thought.

"Alright, you can see her, but no weapons."

"We don't have any," Sora said.

Schelon stood by and let them walk past into his bare office. Only a simple wood desk and a couple of chairs sat inside, and a hall stretched straight back from the door toward the cells.

Alix beamed when Sora and Felix entered the hall. She let out a deep sigh and picked up her coat off the cot, draping it over her arm. But Sora did not share her relief.

"What the hell did you do?" Sora raised an eyebrow, arms crossed.

"It's good to see you, Alix! I'm glad you're okay, Alix!" Alix replied with an eye roll.

Sora's facade melted when Alix threw on her usual sarcastic charm. The corners of her lips twitched, but Sora regained control, increasing her glare.

"So, what did you do?" Sora asked again.

Alix shrugged. "I picked up some plasbolts."

"You *stole* some plasbolts," Schelon raised his voice from behind Felix.

"Details," Alix groaned.

Felix leaned on the bars, blocking Schelon's view. "You were supposed to stay out of trouble."

"Yeah, well, I'm not very good at that, now am I?"

Felix smiled.

Sora turned to Schelon, "What can we do to get her out, pay a fine or something?"

Schelon adjusted his belt and trousers and stepped around Felix so he was in the middle of the group. Alix glared at him, waiting for him to act high-and-mighty.

"Well, it doesn't work that way around here. No fine to pay, she's got a robbery charge, and being intoxicated in public."

"You were drunk, too?" Sora said to Alix.

"No I was not!"

"Then why did I pick you up passed out in a heap of junk?" Schelon said.

Everyone looked at Alix, waiting for an answer that she didn't want to give—not here, not in front of this man, and truthfully, not in front of Sora. She looked up at Felix, her eyes pleading. He would understand.

Felix shifted, but said nothing, probably just as unwilling to talk in front of the others.

"So what's the plan? She's just in here indefinitely?" Sora said.

"No, no." Schelon waved his hands. "One cycle of labor in the mine. That's always our penalty for most things, except of course murder or something."

Alix's eyebrows went up, one of the few times she couldn't keep her Solar face. Sora's eyes widened and she glared at Alix, who subtly shook her head. Felix took charge, speaking with the kind of reverence that Schelon couldn't resist.

"Well, that is the law, and we'll honor it. And Alix won't give you any further trouble." He made eye contact with Alix on the last sentence, stressing each word. She gave him a sarcastic smile in response.

Schelon frowned, but just shrugged his shoulders. "Alright, that sounds like an agreement."

"I guess I better get used to this shitty cot," Alix said, tossing her coat back onto the creaky frame.

The marshal pushed his hat back on his head and squatted on the balls of his feet, looking down at the dead man. Away to his right, a woman also lay dead, and many others. The wind blew at the marshal's back and whistled between the small homes around him. An obnoxious beeping wore on his senses. He tried to focus in on the man lying in front of him. The beeping just would not stop.

"Cole! Cut that thing off!" the marshal shouted.

"Sorry, marshal." Cole turned off the scanling in his hand and walked back toward the marshal.

"Nothing stolen, just a bunch of dead people," the marshal said when Cole stood beside him. The marshal stood with a groan, the prosthetic below his left knee creaking in the cold. *The damn thing always got worse in the winter.* "The wounds aren't precise."

"They weren't killed by trained men, you mean?"

"Or it was made to look that way."

The marshal followed the bloody trail that ran straight from Alix to this homestead. He stood on land once owned by Silas Purvida. Now, the ownership of the land was in dispute. A couple of men had ridden into Verisport to report the massacre. The marshal remembered the village those men had come from; he'd been there before, when looking for Alix and Felix. He remembered the mechanic in that village, too, Sora; he'd seen her in a saloon in Verisport not too long ago. He heaved a weary sigh.

He walked through the homestead, from one body to the next. Alix had murdered Silas and damn near every person who'd worked for him. Whoever she hadn't murdered, the marshal had apprehended and stuck in his cells in the port. It was true that he'd let Alix go, watched her walk away in the crowd from his favorite restaurant. The *Shadow* had left port thereafter, thanks to a scrapper who had helped Alix and Felix get into the port to try and take the ship in the first place.

Now, these farmers here lay dead—men, women, and children.

Someone wanted this land, and Alix had made it ripe for the taking.

"What's on your mind?" Cole said.

"What's ever on my mind, Cole—dead men. Dead men."

The marshal returned to the skimmer they had used to get out to the homestead. Alix could be anywhere, and there were many homesteads in the valley on Silas's former lands. They were all in danger. He did not possess the strength to protect them any longer.

"Let's head back to that village," the marshal said.

"Yes sir." Cole hopped into the pilot's seat.

The marshal fell into the other seat and the glass canopy closed over them, keeping the cold at bay. Along with Cole, there were only three other men the marshal could trust: Dunn, Rhodes, and Underwood. The three deputies had actually listened to Cole when the marshal had warned them about Alix coming for her ship. They, along with Cole, were the only four men serving him that had lived through that night.

"Who do you have watching the scrapper's place?" the marshal said.

"Underwood is over there," Cole replied.

"Spread too thin," the marshal mouthed under his breath.

"Sir?"

"We're going to have to keep an eye on the homesteads. But we're going to need help doing it."

Shouting drew Jo out from under a skimmer. She slid the creeper back and exited the shop. A crowd had gathered near the cistern. Sim and the other elders stood by Marshal Rayburn Skye and a much younger man. Jo climbed onto the stone cistern to see over the adults.

"Now folks, I know you're scared." The marshal raised his voice and his hands to try to calm the villagers. "But my men and I are spread pretty thin. We need some help."

"How exactly are we supposed to help you? We're just farmers, don't you have trained people?" one of the village men said.

"We're going to take three or four of your men, and one of mine to lead you. We're going to set up multiple groups across the valley from other villages."

"Then what's the plan?" Sim said, calm as always.

"We'll go to another village, until we have enough teams who can patrol the valley. At least until I can figure out who is responsible."

The villagers looked at one another, eyes troubled, trying to figure out if someone among them would make the first move. Families talked together quietly as the marshal watched and waited.

One of the men stepped forward—tall, umber skin, still well within his strong years. Another stepped up beside him, this man older, his face gaunt and dirty. The marshal nodded at each of them. He looked at the crowd, from one man to another. A little boy clung to his father's leg. It seemed the marshal would have no other takers. Until a third man walked through the crowd.

"I'll stand with you, marshal," he said. "The name is Dorn."

He was about the same stature as the marshal, but younger, although his hair had already turned grey. They shook hands.

"I appreciate you," the marshal said. "And you men, as well. Do we have one more?"

A long silence. No one else stepped up.

"Well, I know you all have been through a lot since the autumn. I don't blame any man who would want to stay and protect his hearth."

The crowd began to disperse. Cole and the volunteers exchanged pleasantries and shook hands. They began discussing future plans, and which of the marshal's men would lead them. Jo walked against the crowd and faced down the marshal.

The marshal studied her. "I remember you."

"Is that so?" Jo replied.

"That mechanic's little sister. I believe you two helped a woman and an artificial evade me."

"I did no such thing."

The marshal laughed. "So what's your angle? Why are you looking for a fight?"

"Because…" Jo had to catch a lump in her throat. She lifted her chin, defiant. "I had the chance to do something before, and I didn't."

The marshal nodded, and the orchard away to his left, burned black to stumps, told the rest of the story. He looked down at his boots. "You saw him that night?"

"I should've shot him myself."

"Well, why didn't you?"

Tears gathered in Jo's eyes. The Thin Man's words ran through her head: *You're not a killer—not yet.* She clenched her teeth and fought against the flood of tears. "I couldn't do it."

"Well, then I suppose you wouldn't do it, now," the marshal said.

He looked at the girl, studying her intently, then slowly shook his head.

"You remind me of someone," he said with a smile. "Sorry, darling. I put bolts in the hands of a young man once. And I am afraid that choice has led us where we are today. I ain't making the same mistake twice."

The marshal tipped his hat and turned away from Jo.

She yelled back, "Do I look like a young man to you?"

"All the more reason," the marshal replied.

* * *

Felix and Sora strode out onto the landing pad. Wick came down the *Procella*'s cargo ramp, arms up, his brow wrinkled.

"What the hell did she do?" he said.

"Stole some plasbolts," Felix replied, deciding to get right to the point. "We can get her out easily, but doing it means leaving Alloyn for good."

"Just when I got some work," Wick groaned.

Sora shoved him, hard. He nearly stumbled and tripped on the cargo ramp. "Which do you care about more?" she yelled.

"Hey, relax, I was just making a joke."

"We could use less of that."

"Okay, let's just think, and preferably, inside your ship," Felix said. He passed Wick and headed up the ramp.

Sora stormed in after him, leaving Wick to himself, licking his wounds. He finally came stomping up the ramp behind them, his voice echoing inside the hold as he yelled for the other two to wait up.

Inside the ship, they gathered around a table just outside the cockpit door. Sora paced along the hull and hugged herself, as if holding herself together. Felix could sense her heart pounding. Wick leaned over the table, interrupting the three-dimensional projection of the town on the tabletop.

"Will you sit still?" he finally blurted.

"No! I will not!" Sora shouted.

"Wick, leave her alone," Felix said, his voice like deep static.

"Well big fella, I see a way you can get her out of there," Wick said.

"How is that?"

"You know." Wick stared at him. He looked at Sora, who waited for him to elaborate, then turned back to Felix. "You know, the ghost thing."

"The *ghost thing*?" Felix raised his brow.

"Or whatever it is you do," Wick waved his hand. "You appeared out of thin air in the docking bay. I know what I saw—or I guess, what I *couldn't* see."

Felix stared down into the blue projection on the table. His mind recalled a far away memory.

Packed inside a dark ship, shoulder to shoulder with his brothers. Red light bathing the cabin. The expressionless faces around him, their eyes matching the red cabin lights. Felix could feel the weight of the plasrifle in his hands, the large pack over his shoulders. He remembered lights flashing outside—he could see them through the open hatch of the cockpit and through the windshield. Lightning and explosions.

An alarm blared. The bodies around Felix straightened. He gripped the plasrifle tight. The floor beneath his feet opened and he fell. The rush of wind hit him like an explosion, but Felix dropped like a sleek missile, whistling through the air.

The black jungle below rose up to meet him.

"Things are not yet that dire," Felix said, his mind returning to the here and now.

"Just saying," Wick shrugged. Then, he lowered his voice, "Would make it pretty easy."

Sora shook her head. "Well, what about that woman in the restaurant?"

"Mia?" Felix said.

"Yeah, could she help us?"

"Possibly." Felix rubbed his smooth face. "She could certainly give us information about the mine shifts, and the lay of the land."

"The mine shifts?" Wick said.

"The lawman said Alix would have to work in the mine as her sentence," Sora explained.

Wick let out a huge laugh. "Now, *that* I would pay to see."

A chill wind blew through small farmhouses, playing with the steep, wood shingled-roofs. Several families had clustered their homes together in the north valley where the soil grew tubers, leeks, herbs, and much more. They also tended small herds of ibi and brizcoe. But, now in the winter, the fields lay bare and the village quiet.

The *clop clop* of stirrol hoofs on the hard ground brought people to their windows.

Three men rode into the village, their faces covered against the cold, hats pulled low. They showed no urgency or interest in the people who peeked out from their homes. Mothers kept children inside as fathers threw on coats and stood in doorways, watching with caution. The riders dismounted and spread out. Two men wrapped in coats met them in the street.

"Can we help you? Need some water, or food?" one of the village men asked.

The only reply came from a plasbolt, burning a hole in the man's stomach. The second village man shared a similar fate—a plasbolt round through the chest as he tried to scream out to his wife and kids.

Men in the village attempted to burst out through their doors, plasbolts and rifles drawn, but their erratic and panicked shots found no targets. Men and women fell upon the street, verandas, and over barrels. The three riders moved methodically from house-to-house. The muffled sounds of plasfire could be heard from inside each home, and blue flashes seen in the windows.

A woman frantically ran, holding her son by the wrist as tightly as she could. The child wanted to yell and fight, but his mother's orders to keep quiet overruled his urges. She dragged him into a barn across from the houses. Stirrols inside stamped their hoofs and shook their manes, frantically pacing in their stalls at the shots and screams outside.

"Will, get a saddle, hurry," the mother pleaded.

He did as she said while she used a calm voice to bring a stirrol out, leading it by a simple rope halter. The boy threw the saddle onto its back. The mother used one hand to remove the rope halter and another to put a riding bridle over the stirrol's nose and ears. Once they finished, the mother pushed the boy up onto the stirrol.

"Now, get going, ride into Verisport. The marshal will help you," she said.

"I'm not leaving you here!" the boy attempted to remain strong, but could no longer hold back his tears.

"I love you, William," she reached a hand up to wipe his cheek. He pawed at her arms, trying to hold on to her. "You have to go!"

She slapped the stirrol's hindquarters and it startled, galloping out of the barn. The boy cried out, but had to keep his focus forward, holding the reins and securing his feet in the stirrups. He felt the cold air freeze the tears to his face and the mucus on his upper lip.

The boy's mother turned and before she could leave the barn, one of the riders stepped inside, plasbolt in hand. She stared at the light glowing from the chamber. The rider took one look at her, then shot her dead. Her body fell and bled into a pile of straw.

The rider moved around the barn; he searched nooks and crannies, tack rooms, and the loft for anyone else, but found no one. He holstered his plasbolt. The rider noticed a rope bridle on the ground, an empty stall, and a missing saddle.

"Casey! Find anybody?" a gruff voice yelled out over the cold silence.

Casey emerged from the barn to join his other two companions. They mounted their stirrols again. "Just some woman. I think someone may have ridden out of here."

"You *think*?" one of his partners said.

"Saw a halter on the ground, and an empty stall," Casey said.

"Well, I guess you better get moving and find whoever it was."

"Verisport is only a few kilometers southways, that's where they would go."

"I'll catch up to em, or follow the trail into town," Casey turned his stirrol southeast.

The other two men watched Casey ride off, then spurred their stirrols out of the village, heading west.

4

The Confined

Otto buttoned his shirt collar and straightened the gold and silver Xypha logo pin before smoothing down his dark hair on the left side of his head. The silver neural implant shined over his left ear. Silver buttons ran diagonally from one shoulder to the center of the Xypha suit jacket—pressed to perfection. Otto slipped a silver ring on the forefinger of each hand, and then one on each ring finger. Instead of being decorative statements, the rings contained microscopic sensors and circuits inside the bands, which allowed him to interact with the ship's projector interface.

The polished white stone surfaces in the washroom sparkled as Otto checked himself one final time in the mirror. His black boots clicked on the stone floor as he left the washroom and entered his luxurious cabin. A wide window stretched the length of the room on his right, the dark void of space beyond.

A call came in, tickling his neural implant. He used two quick hand and finger motions to accept the transmission and open a projected image of his security chief, Fenn Loucks, on the ground.

"I'm on my way out," Otto said.

"Just letting you know that Wray Egar is on our side," Loucks said, his thick face and broad shoulders visible in the video projection. A sneer crossed Loucks's face, as close as he got to a smile.

"Good. I trust you logged your expense?"

"No expense." Loucks shook his head. "He only needed some… convincing."

"Well, with Silas gone, I guess these people are free of the heavy hand. Good to return it to them, I suppose, it's what they're familiar with."

"Another thing," Loucks said. "I've completed the trace of that ship taken from port."

"I know the one."

"Seems it was taken up into the mountains. The scrapper who lifted it out is a person named Jesse, and they have a shop on the southeast side of town."

"Good work, Loucks."

"Should I pursue?"

"Give it time."

Loucks nodded. "What about that blood sample? DNA markers matched the Cradle database. My suspicion is it belongs to that ship's pilot."

"The one that Silas hired?"

"Yes sir. We were able to save enough of the servers under Silas's compound. He kept extensive dossiers, but this one was quite incomplete. Her name is Alix, but chromosomal evidence from the blood sample suggests she is actually a *male*. The change likely intended to obscure identification from our seekers."

"Is that so?" Otto rubbed his chin. "If I remember correctly, the marshal knows this person."

"More than that." Loucks looked away as if to check records in front of him. "He was one of the marshal's deputies, once."

"That could be a considerable point in our favor."

"Of course, he could be dead. The scene at Silas's was pretty bloody."

"Retrieving that ship suggests the pilot survived, or at least his friends survived." Otto cleared his throat and looked at himself one more time in a mirror on the wall.

"Do you want me to pursue in the mountains?" Loucks pressed the issue again.

"Let's see what we can do with the marshal on this point, first."

"Yes sir."

Otto waved away the projection, ending the call. The sleek white door to his cabin slid open and he entered a long, bright passageway. Men and women dressed in light grey slip suits stood by as he passed them. Some wore small hats that matched their suits, or sported tight, neat hairstyles. The silver implant remained a constant.

Three turns down other passageways brought Otto to the main lift that carried him down to the hangar at the station's center. A rush of cold air struck Otto when the lift doors opened on the hangar bay. Workers went about their duties preparing supply drops for the surface, refueling drop ships, moving cargo, fixing things, shouting at one another. The hangar walls were brushed grey omniite, the floor polished so much that Otto could see his reflection as he walked. The planet Celestine filled the view outside the hangar—swirling white and purplish clouds over green, red, and grey lands. At the edges of the hangar entrance, the atmospheric shield glowed a faint blue.

Two men moved about a boxy drop ship, white with a dark heat shield on its keel. A set of metal stairs angled down from the midpoint. When they saw Otto approaching, they stopped their pre-flight checks and stood erect. Otto's face showed no pleasantries, or any care about formalities. He simply walked by them and up the steps into the ship.

The dim cabin smelled of recycled air, constantly blowing from vents at the ceiling. Otto fastened his belt in the semi-cushioned seat as the two pilots ascended the steps and went by him toward the cockpit. The steps folded inward on themselves and drew back within the hull, a door sliding shut, hissing as the airlock sealed. Otto stared across the cabin, running through the playbook in his head, rehearsing his lines, contemplating any rebuttal, anticipating resistance.

He had planned to seize the opportunity ever since Silas had been killed months ago. Silas had served adequately as a proxy on the surface, allowing Xypha and Otto to gain influence over several council members—pathetic men who crawled on their bellies to Silas if it meant they could pass as a wealthier person living on the frontier planet. But Silas's hubris had gotten him killed, and Otto had always planned for the eventuality. He sat in his position *because* he thought of these outcomes, planned for them, anticipated them, ensured that a strategy would not fall apart due to some vainglorious frontier businessman.

Convincing several council members posed no true challenge to Otto. All he had to do was dangle the local currency in their faces, a metal of no value whatsoever, easily produced by Xypha actualizers. New positions of power, new homes, new businesses—all of these trivialities appealed to men who saw a valley as a galaxy. For now, Otto needed to make promises that he wouldn't keep. The day would come when he positioned Xypha in every corner and level of life so that these people would be powerless to extricate them.

The jarring vibrations of the drop ship's entry into the atmosphere rattled Otto's brain. He gripped the armrests, closed his eyes, and dreaded the environment into which he descended.

The marshal didn't often meet with council members outside official business, but he needed allies, and it seemed as if the number of people who could be trusted dwindled each day. Rounding up the last of Silas's men was one thing, but now the Verisport council had sold off all of Silas's lands and businesses. The marshal had assumed four of the seven council members stood with him, two of whom sat in his office right now. But he had underestimated Otto again, or overestimated the courage of Wray Egar.

Madeline Welf and Elme Grier sat in front of the marshal's desk, anxious and confused. Like the marshal, they could each trace their families back to the original settlers of Verisport—and like the marshal, they didn't wish to see it handed over to Xypha. Madeline pressed her red lips into a tight line, her long red hair with streaks of grey framed her tawny-beige face. She wore a flowing tunic, colored bluish green like the sea past White Sands.

"Wray assured us he would vote our way," she said, trying to make sense of the council meeting that had adjourned only an hour ago.

"Well, now we see what his word is worth," the marshal stood at his window, gazing over Verisport, feeling as though the city slipped further away from him every day.

"Giving Xypha space here to further expand and improve the port, I can understand," Madeline said. "But, now…"

"Now they own a lot of real estate in Verisport," Elme chimed in. "Lumber mill, stoneworks, scrappers."

The marshal shook his head and turned away from the window. The old prosthetic below his left knee sunk as he walked, weakened by years. He rubbed his forehead, thinking.

"At least they didn't get ahold of the lands west," he said. "Those farmers will be free of Silas's extortion."

"Yes, other than their train corridor," Madeline remarked. "It seemed a useful, and practical compromise. You should be proud."

"Otto sure seemed a little too happy to accept the deal," the marshal said as he sat.

"Those farmsteads and villages could have traded one landlord for another," Madeline pointed out.

"The fact that Cob Nell left his lands to his tenants helped our cause, there," Elme added.

The marshal rested his elbows on the desk, interlaced fingers by his face. He felt strange speaking of the valley's farmers in such a positive manner given the circumstances. *They are being slaughtered out there*, he thought. Regardless, Madeline and Elme were right, the compromise to have tenants keep their lands *was* a victory. Things could have been so much worse, especially with Wray siding against them on properties in Verisport.

He did not feel victorious, however. He had presented his plan to the council, to organize teams of men to protect the farmsteads. Some were quite interested and sympathetic; other members waved away the concerns too casually. He worried the violence had come as a response to the council's decision to let Silas's former tenants own their own land. If that were true, then he had many enemies in his midst.

"Relax, marshal. We did a good thing today," Madeline stood and smiled politely, bowing formally to an equal.

"Maybe," the marshal said as he stared into the middle distance.

"You worry too much, Ray." Elme waved his hand.

Worrying too much is what's held this place together for the past sixty years, the marshal thought. He tapped his fingers on the desk. The council members took their leave and the door slid closed behind them.

The marshal turned to the vizscreen above the right side of his desk. It had been months since he'd seen or heard about Alix. But now he began to worry as the violence in the valley inevitably drew her to mind. Having spied two of her acquaintances in Li's saloon made him nervous. He suddenly regretted not apprehending the scrapper, Jesse, a couple months back. He had not expected to see Sora again, either. The two together felt suspicious, but of course, it could be coincidental.

He'd plotted the attacks on farmsteads on the vizscreen, searching for a pattern. Each stood on Silas's former lands, but they did not appear to have any kind of direction. Attacks occurred near the Lipine River, up north, and in between.

Cole entered the office. The marshal's chief deputy wore a light blue shirt beneath a black vest, his young face shadowed by the brim of a white hat.

"What'd they have to say?" Cole said, referring to the council members he'd passed in the hall.

"Oh you know, how great of a job this all was, patted themselves on the back," the marshal responded.

"Well, I guess it could have been worse."

"Yeah, that's what people keep telling me."

The marshal didn't believe it, no matter how many people tried to convince him otherwise. The things he could control were dwindling. It left him feeling empty, weak—angry. He thought back to Wray Egar's face in the meeting. Wray wasn't as old as the marshal, or Madeline, but still, he was an elder member of the council, and up until today, seemed to possess a shred of decency. Wray and the marshal went way back, they had known one another as kids. Everybody loved to put them together, on account of a hominem, no matter how much they protested.

I thought I knew this man, the marshal reflected. A common refrain: the people he thought he knew kept surprising him. Alix, Wray, the valley itself—clouds that suddenly turned dark and angry, a turbulent storm sitting directly overhead. The marshal became aware of his clenched fists and furrowed brow, tight and painful. He sprang up from his chair, as best he could at this age, grabbed his hat and headed out the door.

Cole scrambled to follow.

The marshal and Cole burst into Wray Egar's furniture store. The storefront sat off the market square, with a painted sign above the door, and a bell rang when it opened. Inside, the dark, stained burrey wood floor held several pieces of handmade wood furniture. They had been carefully positioned with plenty of space between, to accentuate the boutique nature of the store.

Delicate lamps bobbed up and down in the air near the ceiling. A counter ran along the left wall. Wray didn't make the furniture himself, of course; he bought pieces from craftsmen in the valley, sold them to clients in Verisport, and pocketed a large fee. Wray emerged from a door in the back, looking nonplussed. He wore a crisp white shirt, a black tie and vest, and black pants.

"What can I do for you, Rayburn?" he said.

"Let's have a talk in private," the marshal replied.

Wray glanced over at the young man, who stopped his work behind the counter and looked from the marshal to his boss. "Can you come back another time?"

Wray wrung his hands. The young man behind the counter looked nervous as well, as if he knew what plagued Wray, and what had made him ask if the marshal could come back later.

"No, let's talk now," the marshal insisted.

"Right this way," Wray waved a hand back toward the door, though his shoulders sagged and his eyes were a little too wide.

When the marshal stepped through the door, he halted. Otto stood beside a dark wood desk in the cramped office, a disgruntled look on his face. Boxes and books and papers surrounded a black leather chair in the middle of the room. Bookshelves lined the walls, full of even more books, papers, and boxes.

"What the hell are you doing here?" the marshal said.

"Am I not permitted to do business in this city?" Otto said.

"You know damn well what I mean."

"Gentlemen, please," Wray tried to smooth things over.

The marshal turned back to Wray. "And here I thought you still had a spine."

"I don't like what you're implying—"

"Cut the shit," the marshal interrupted him. "I expected this kind of thing from Harold Volster. But, you, Wray?"

"I am operating in the best interests of Verisport," Wray said, though the words did not aim to convince the marshal.

"Is that what you tell yourself?"

"I have committed no crime," Wray insisted. "So, I would appreciate if you would leave my store, unless you desire to speak in a calm manner."

The marshal scoffed. "Pardon my anger." His stare pierced Wray's anxious heart.

"It is possible Rayburn, that folk in Verisport no longer agree with you about keeping Xypha out of town?"

The marshal raged, and no matter how afraid and guilty Wray looked, the man was right. He'd committed no crime that the marshal could prove. Before today, even the marshal had held no suspicions that Wray had taken bribes or made any backdoor deals with Otto. The seed had already been planted months ago, but now it germinated.

Perhaps Wray was right, the marshal thought.

"I ain't losing this town, this valley, to people like *him*," the marshal jabbed a finger at Otto.

"Who, now, seems to have selfish motives?" Otto said.

"You son of a bitch!" the marshal started toward Otto.

"Rayburn, please." Wray put a friendly hand on the marshal's arm. "I wish we could all work together."

"I think the marshal has other business to which he should attend,"

Otto said to Wray. Otto turned to the marshal, one eyebrow raised. "After all, who has been held responsible for the murder of Xypha engineers? Who has been held responsible for the attack on this city's spaceport? Has *anyone* been brought to justice for burning down Silas Purvida's primary business and residence? It seems you are reluctant to admit the truth: that one of your own deputies committed these crimes."

Wray looked from Otto to the marshal in shock.

The marshal glared at Otto. *He knows about Alix.* The marshal didn't let the accusation trip him up. "Who was brought to justice? *Silas*," he snapped.

"So, is that the kind of law in this town? Revenge? Your grudges seem to drive *your* brand of justice."

The marshal seethed, his fists still clenched; the Plasvelds on his waist called his name. His heart pounded in his chest. Otto was too good a player to smile as he spoke, delivering each verbal blow until the knockout. The marshal's mouth twitched, and he took a deep breath. There was nothing else to say—he stormed out of the office and out of Wray's furniture store.

The marshal bristled. *What* am *I doing here,* he asked himself after Cole had posed the question. Finding Alix meant death. He remembered that day in the valley, when Alix very well could have shot him clean. Felix's words echoed in his memory: *That's the only peace offering you're going to get.* The marshal traveled even further back. He remembered finding Alix, teaching her to shoot, giving her the instrument of death that she now wielded so well.

Otto was right. *I created this problem.*

He puzzled over what he could have done differently with Alix. If only she had listened to him, stuck closer to him, maybe this wouldn't have happened. Maybe if he hadn't allowed her to leave for Corto all those years ago. But now, it was too late. He had lost her. *No, she made this choice. She rejected the path I set out for her.*

He locked eyes with Cole. "It's time to stop giving ground." Without waiting for a response, he strode down the alley and out onto the street, searching for his target.

The marshal entered Jesse's shop hot with rage. Jesse stood beside their coffee brewer, a metal cup in hand, also steaming. Cole stayed back, hands on his hips, face a little pale. He looked like a man trying to eye a safe distance to be from an impending explosion.

Jesse set their cup on the metal surface behind them. "Howdy marshal. What can I do for you?"

"Cut the pleasantries," the marshal said, looking around the shop, which was filled to the brim with dark, twisted metals, oil, grease, and dirt. "I'm here to arrest you for aiding a known fugitive."

Jesse scowled. "I feel like we've discussed this before."

"Yes, and my lenience was clearly a mistake."

"You got no proof that I did anything."

The marshal stepped closer, toe to toe, looking up at the scrapper. "Why don't you take me downstairs? The records of Verisport's underground are even older than I am."

Jesse sucked their teeth and let their arms down, dangling at their sides, their blackened fingers and hands slowly forming into fists. "So what? You think having a hole in my floor is some kind of evidence?"

"I'm ordering you, in the name of Verisport law—"

Jesse smirked. "You know, I didn't even know that woman. But I know the kind of people she's at odds with. Silas, Xypha, *you*—what wouldn't you do in the *name of the law*?"

"I'm not the one who tore a dockyard to pieces," the marshal boiled over. "I'm not the one who killed men just doing their jobs!"

"You also ain't the one who put Silas Purvida in the ground where he belonged."

The marshal lunged forward, pressing his forearm into Jesse's throat, knocking them back. Tools and scrap clattered to the floor as their weight struck the shelves behind them. Cole started forward with his hand on the grip of his plasbolt, but he stopped. The marshal had his left arm into Jesse's neck, and the right already held a plasbolt. The room glowed blue, the whine from the charged cylinder the only sound until the marshal spoke through gritted teeth.

"I'm sick of being told what's right and wrong by people beneath me," he sneered. The blue glow from the plasbolt lit their faces as the marshal brought his hand up and put the barrel beneath Jesse's chin. "You're coming with us, and if you don't tell me where *she* is…"

"What? You going to kill me? Is that the law you're upholding, now?"

"It seems to be the only thing you people answer to."

The marshal stepped back, pushing Jesse's chest with his left hand, rattling the shelves again. He held his plasbolt out, directly at their heart. Instead of cowering, Jesse stood, head high, daring the marshal to pull the trigger. His upper lip curled and his chest heaved with intensifying anger—anger at his own helplessness.

"I've looked in her eyes," Jesse said. "And now, I've looked in yours. You ain't got what it takes."

"On the contrary. I've put more men in the ground than I can count."

The marshal held the plasbolt only centimeters from Jesse's chest. He felt so sure he could pull the trigger. What did this scrapper mean to him? And yet, he stood frozen. He studied Jesse's face and wondered how they could be so unafraid. Had he really come this far; had his age and authority worn to a brittle end?

"Tell me where she is," the marshal ordered. "Otherwise, I'm going to take you in, and raze this place to the ground."

Jesse held out their hands with palms up. "Go ahead."

"Cole!" the marshal shouted. "Lock them up."

"Sir?"

"You heard me." The marshal lowered his plasbolt and the glow and whine died down as the chambers slowed their spin. He holstered the weapon.

Cole secured a set of fetters on Jesse's wrists. They paid no attention to Cole as he did so, their eyes cutting straight through the marshal. Cole grabbed the back of their arm to direct Jesse forward, but Jesse jerked it away. They walked defiantly past the marshal and out of the shop.

"You think I'm the one being locked up," they said as they passed him. "You're already in a prison of your own making."

A bell rang clear through the mountain. Alix braced herself against the ear-piercing scream as she exited the lift and stepped into the large cavern at the top of the mineshaft. She shook her head after the bell finally stopped. Inside the cavern, men and women milled about, waiting to head down to work, or fixing machines and loading tools, all wearing the same blue ragged jumpsuits. Alix wore a red jumpsuit, to indicate her status as a prisoner.

Outside the office built into the left wall of the cavern, Schelon waited for her. He smiled, as if enjoying the idea of seeing Alix in service to the community. After three days, she hated that stupid grin.

"You got a little something there." Schelon pointed to his left cheek.

Alix rolled her eyes and kept on walking, not caring at all about the black dust and dirt covering her face, creating a stark contrast with the area around her eyes that the protective eyewear kept clean. Schelon followed and Alix just knew he still wore that shit-eating grin. The central lane filled with people and carts and animals in the late morning. Alix watched her hot breath against the cold. Light flakes of snow played in the air.

After a short walk, she reached Mia's restaurant, and while she couldn't turn left into the place, she saw Felix, Sora, and Wick sitting at a table. They'd waited there every day since her first shift, keeping an eye on her, and she winked when she saw them. Schelon couldn't forget Felix, and tipped his beige hat in Felix's direction. He put a firm hand on Alix's shoulder and directed her right, up the terrace steps.

The door clanged and Schelon punched in the code to lock Alix inside her cell. He began whistling as he walked back up the hall toward the front door and his desk. Once he was around the corner, Alix turned to the wash basin in the corner. The water was already a little cloudy, and as she washed her face, the basin filled with even blacker water, swirling around down the drain. Her face looked back from the dirty, old mirror, wavy and blurry. For a moment, she thought she saw a black dust speck in her left eye. She leaned in close, pulling her lower lid down to get a better view.

It wasn't dirt at all, and the blurry vision wasn't due to the old mirror. She watched as the black lines crept across the white of her eye, filling swollen blood vessels with the black hyperfluid. She panicked, stepped back and clamped her eyes shut, her hands over them for good measure.

Instead of seeing the fading light and patterns, a wide desert spread before her.

Sand dunes towered like mountains. The wind swept across the dunes; faint wisps of sand reached out from the crests of the dunes with each gust. She had never seen a desert on Celestine like this, and the sky did not show the purple hue of Celestine's atmosphere. Beyond the dunes, through the grey haze of a searing sun, she could barely make out a ruined structure: spires and beams, shards of metal reaching up. The great bones of the structure lay strewn across the land, as if she stood atop a dune herself.

Alix tried to open her eyes, but though she felt her lids open, she continued to see the desert. She lost her balance, reaching out for the cell bars, the basin, the cot, anything. She stumbled backwards, the backs of her legs hitting the cot and she fell backwards.

Her head struck the stone wall.

* * *

"Hey, wake up."

A splash of cold water hit Alix in the face.

Opening her eyes felt like a terrifying risk. She blinked and the light overhead felt like the sun at high noon. She could only open her eyes a little, and she held up her hand to block the overhead light, squinting at Schelon. He stood over her with a metal bucket.

"What the hell, man?" Alix groaned.

"You knocked yourself out, what was I supposed to do?" Schelon protested.

"I don't know, let me sleep?"

"Permanently?"

"Fine, point taken."

"You okay?"

"I don't know." Alix sighed and stared at her hands, rubbing her fingers together. "Do me a favor. Remember that sentient that came in here, Felix?"

"Yes," Schelon drew out the word to reflect his suspicion.

"Bring him here so he can examine me."

Schelon shook his head. "We've got a doctor in town."

"I don't need a doctor. I need *him*."

"You think I haven't heard this one before? *Oh please Mr. Lawman, I'm sick, get me out of here.*"

"Trust me, I wouldn't have to create some pathetic ruse to get myself out of here."

Alix tried to stand but lost her balance and Schelon grabbed on to her to keep her upright. In that moment, she gripped his shirt sleeve, pulled hard, and went for his plasbolt.

Schelon lost his balance, and with his left arm trapped by Alix's grip on his sleeve, and his right occupied by trying to fight Alix for the bolt, he couldn't steady himself. She swiped the plasbolt out of its holster, climbed to her feet and staggered back, shoulder against the wall. The whine and blue glow of the plasbolt chamber echoed in the small space. Schelon went down to one knee, and after the surprise wore off, he slowly stood with his hands raised. His expression turned to fury, but Alix could not be intimidated.

While she hid the fear beneath the surface, Alix glared at Schelon. A plan began forming in her mind, and for that plan to work, she needed to stay in Schelon's custody.

"Look, I could easily walk out of here. But that is not my intention. All I want, is for Felix to come take a look at me. This is twice I've passed out in the last few days and I would like to know why."

"You think I'm going to trust you?" Schelon nodded toward the bolt in Alix's hand.

She spun the plasbolt on her finger, then flipped it around so the grip pointed toward him. The charged whine began to fade as she motioned for Schelon to take it.

"I could've put you down. But I didn't," she said.

Schelon approached with caution, then, took the plasbolt. He returned it to its holster and searched Alix's eyes.

"Fine. Where do I find him?"

"Mia's place."

When Schelon returned with Felix, Alix sat on the cot, elbows on her knees, head down. She ran to Felix as soon as Schelon opened the cell door and flung herself into his arms. Felix held her tightly, her face pressed against his chest.

"How are you feeling?" he said in a soft tone.

"I *feel* okay." Alix pulled away from him and stood on her own strength. "But something is going on. I need you to check me for—" She glanced at Schelon. "Anything that might make me sick." With those words, she looked into Felix's eyes, stressing each syllable, unwilling to mention the hyperfluid around a stranger.

Felix nodded. All he had to do was take a step back and look Alix up and down. She let out a long, shaky breath. Whatever was happening to her had to be something related to that fluid, which had saved her life months ago. Since then, she and Felix had gone from fear of the fluid turning on her body and *killing* her, to accepting that maybe the stuff would just remain inside of her, an unprecedented symbiosis of organic material and intelligent nano-robotics. But the blackouts were something new, and the visions, the *memories*, were not her own.

"You look okay," Felix reported.

He made a show of stepping close, lifting her arms and putting his face close to her body, speaking so only she could hear. "What's been going on?"

"I'm seeing things," she whispered back. "And the fluid has been getting in my eyes."

"What do you see?"

"Places—places that I haven't been before. But they seem so *real*."

Felix paused and then rubbed his thumb down her face, cradling her cheek in his hand. His eyes spun as they often did when he focused on a thought. "The hyperfluid is not causing any damage, but it moves with a purpose. The nanoids have entered your brain. There is a concentration in the hippocampus."

"What's that do?" Alix said.

"Memory, learning, that sort of thing. It's unclear *what* the hyperfluid particles are doing, but they may be triggering *something*."

"But they aren't going to kill me, right?"

"I cannot say. You've blacked out?"

"Twice."

"I wish I knew what to do," Felix said, a desperate sadness in his voice.

"It's okay," Alix put her hand to his face.

She leaned up, hands on Felix's chest, and kissed him. The security of his embrace and the current that ran from his lips to hers, comforted her. She put her arms around his neck, and their lips parted, but stayed close.

"I love you," she said. Then she whispered, "I've got to get out of here."

5

The Gamble

Alix and Schelon followed the morning crowd down the lane. When they passed Mia's, Alix smiled at Wick and Sora, sitting in their usual spot. Schelon tipped his hat to them; but, as they passed the restaurant, he looked back, likely wondering why Felix wasn't with Alix's other companions. He shrugged and kept pace with Alix.

The cavernous opening to the mine filled with workers coming in as the previous shift headed out. Schelon stopped Alix at the mine office and let those leaving their shifts pass by. Everything in the dim cavern remained the same as the past three days. The same crews, the same sounds, the same tools and carts and ore. But Alix closed her eyes and took a deep breath.

"Alright, go on," Schelon said. "I'll be here to pick you up in a few hours."

"Thanks, dad," Alix joked.

She walked across the cavern to the wide lift, which wasn't full of other workers, but carts and tools. Schelon didn't like to send her down with a crowd of people.

Two men in grey jumpsuits stood on either side of the lift. With broad shoulders and stiff backs, they looked the part of security for the mine. They always met her here, and watched her as she worked, although she was easy to pick out in the red jumpsuit, compared to every other workers' blue suit.

"Morning fellas," she said with a wave.

The three of them took their places on the lift. One of the men operated the controls. The other stood close to Alix. As the security detail prepared to take them down, Alix felt the slight jostle of the metal floor beneath her feet, as if more weight had been added to the lift. She smiled wide, staring at Schelon, and waved at him. She felt a brush on the back of her suit and knew that Felix was with her.

The lift buzzed and metal clattered and gears groaned as the lift descended into the dark. Small yellow lights lined the shaft, creating deep shadows and brief moments where dull light fell across the faces of Alix and the other two men. Alix stuck her hands in the back pockets of her jumpsuit and felt the small earpiece in her left hand that Felix had dropped.

She used the stretch of darkness in between the faint glowing lights to put the piece in her ear, but she remained absolutely silent until the lift reached the bottom. It passed out of the shaft and into another open cavern with a ceiling just high enough for Felix to walk comfortably. Tunnels branched out all around them; some reached back to the west, passing under the town.

Alix followed the usual path, along a tunnel with an almost imperceptible downward slope to the east. She carried a metal toolbox in one hand. The tunnels echoed with whistling, hammering, drilling, yelling, and the unique buzz and pop of sonic explosives. When she heard one go off, she smiled and spoke to Felix.

"That's what we're looking for," she said as if he stood beside her. "Sonic charges, will fit in your hand easily."

"How many?" Felix replied in her ear.

"As many as you can carry and remain cloaked."

"When did you think up this plan?"

"You mean you don't think I had this in mind the whole time?"

"I know you didn't get sent to jail on purpose." Felix sounded amused. "When is the next lift up?"

"Every hour."

"Alright, I'll let you know when I'm on my way out. Be safe."

"You know me," Alix laughed.

A shimmering vein of blue-black metal ran along the tunnel wall. Alix set her toolbox down as men brushed passed her, leaving the deeper ends of the tunnel. When she turned to watch the crew leave, she noticed the lack of security detail behind her. Every day she'd been down in this dark, damp, loud hell, those two watchers had *never* left her side.

"Felix," she said.

Before he could reply, and before Alix could go on, six men emerged from the darkness on either side of her, three ahead and three crowding in behind. Their faces were cloaked in shadow, but the whites of their eyes remained clear, and their postures hinted at violence. They grasped wrenches and iron bars in their hands.

"Hello boys." She stood with her back to the vein, slightly nudging the toolbox with her boot.

"Alright, Red," one of the men said, referring to Alix by her red jumpsuit. "What're you down here for?"

"What does it matter to you?"

"Call it carrying out your sentence," the man said.

Alix nodded and rolled her eyes, realizing their plan. The man who had spoken stood taller than most of the others, but she could barely make out any of his face, likely by design. *I really need to craft a new pair of goggles*, she thought.

"Oh, so is this why they just send you down here if you commit a crime?" Alix looked at the other group, "You guys are the executioners?"

"Executioners? Did you kill somebody?" The man began tapping the heavy wrench against his palm.

"Once upon a time." Alix squared up.

"Is that a fact?"

"So why don't you get the hell out of my face, or you'll end up just like him."

The heavy man stepped closer to Alix; he stood a good bit taller than her, but she didn't back down. She felt the others behind her occupy space, moving in closer, too. She really had no other options if she wanted to walk out of the tunnel alive.

The incoming fight brought a smile to her lips.

Alix ducked and side-stepped, using their momentum against them —and the narrow tunnel to her advantage. She tripped a man, pushed one into another, and stepped back just in time to avoid a pipe to the head. She kicked over the toolbox into the feet of the man rushing toward her.

Alix kept backing up as each man pushed and stumbled by one another, tangled in the small space. These miners certainly weren't any good beyond a drunken brawl. Alix threw precise jabs and elbows, and brought her knees up into the men's noses as they tried to get to their feet. She would have broken bones if the security guards hadn't come around the corner in time. She held one of the men by the collar, a fist cocked back. She saw the light from globes bobbing over the guards' shoulders before they rounded the corner. Alix dropped the man she held and raised her hands, her chest heaving, her open mouth breaking into a laugh.

Schelon ran his hands down his face. Alix sat in a chair, hands restrained, the security detail standing close by. The mining officer in charge explained what had happened, at least *his* version of events. Alix shook her head and laughed every time he accused her of starting the fight.

"How would I have started a fight when these two guards were on my hips?" she pointed out. "Unless of course, they just happened to lag behind at a convenient point in time."

"Shut it," Schelon barked at her. "Mr. Wallace, thank you for your cooperation. I'll take it from here." He turned back to Alix. "Let's go."

Alix rolled her eyes as Schelon kept a firm grip on her right arm as they left the office and the cavern, emerging into clear daylight. In her ear, she heard the whisper of Felix's voice that he had made it out of the mine, thanks to her, although, it hadn't been part of the plan to create such a useful distraction.

Schelon jerked her when they neared Mia's, not giving her the chance to linger near where Felix, Wick, and Sora always sat to watch for her. Normally they wouldn't be there, since this wasn't exactly Alix's usual time to leave her shift. But the three sat at their regular table, and Schelon's eyes narrowed. He glanced back over his shoulder as he and Alix headed up the terrace steps to his office, and to Alix's cell.

"What the hell were you thinking?" he said.

"Hey, I told you in there, I was just trying not to get my head caved in!"

"You're lucky they didn't kill you."

Alix let out a loud, defiant laugh. "Please."

Back in her cell, Alix sat down on the cot like a scolded child. Schelon mumbled to himself. His grumbling continued around the corner and Alix craned her neck to make sure he was out of sight before she spoke to Felix.

"How much did you get?" she said in a whisper.

"Six charges," Felix replied. "What the hell happened down there?" His tone changed to disapproval.

"You heard what happened!" Alix tried not to raise her voice. "Those men jumped me. My security guys conveniently weren't around. Must be some kind of extra hazing for anyone serving a labor sentence."

"Did you get a look at who they were? Because, you know, it could have been—"

"It wasn't," Alix cut him off. "But it was too dark to really see their faces."

"Well, what's your plan?"

"Haven't quite figured that out yet." She massaged her temples and began to think.

"We don't need these explosives to get you out," Felix reminded her.

"No, of course not. Plus I'd like to avoid making a mess of things here."

"You're doing a great job so far."

"Shut up." Alix would've punched Felix if he'd been beside her.

"Well, do you want me to come get you tonight?"

She knew Felix was serious, and perfectly capable. Schelon and these bars stood no chance of keeping Felix out if he came to get her. She ran through how it might go in her mind. Felix would simply walk in, knock Schelon unconscious, or restrain him; and then Felix would rip the cell door off its hinges like twigs from a burrey tree.

"I think it's time to go," Alix said at last.

Sora watched Felix with anticipation and worry. He stared into the middle distance, speaking to Alix while sitting at a table in Mia's restaurant. Sora and Wick could only hear one side of the conversation. When Felix asked if Alix wanted him to break her out of the cell, they leaned forward. Mia lingered by the table after refilling their cups of coffee.

"Is everything alright?" she said.

Felix's eyes spun and he refocused on his friends' faces. "Well..." Felix hesitated. "Alix is fine. Whoever jumped her at the mine seemed to be participating in some kind of hazing ritual."

"Yeah," Mia groaned. "That's not atypical."

"So, what did she say about getting her out?" Sora said.

"I'll go get her tonight," Felix replied.

"You're going to break her out of there?" Mia's eyes flew wide.

"She can't stay locked up. Nobody will get hurt."

"You promise?"

"Trust me." Felix smiled.

Sora felt a burning in her chest as she watched Mia—a twinge of jealousy. She tightened her lips and looked across the table at Felix, chastising herself for letting that feeling take over, even for the briefest moment. *Mia is gorgeous, though*, Sora thought. She couldn't help but compare herself.

Did Mia still have feelings for Alix? Did Alix?

Sora tried to shake the thoughts.

Then she remembered Alix killing Mia's husband, an act of love and anger, intertwined like some kind of weed trying to choke out the flowers on a cirros bush. Alix had killed for Sora, too—far more than just one man.

Instead of judging Alix for her actions, Sora judged herself: *Am I wrong to hold so much affection for someone capable of such violence?*

"So what do we do?" Sora blurted out.

"Get back to the *Shadow*. We might as well keep working. Wick, you keep an eye on things here." Felix took over as the group's leader.

"Can I help?" Mia said, her voice quiet and unsteady.

"We don't want to put you in any danger."

"I can handle myself."

"Well, here," Felix produced an earpiece much like the one he'd slipped Alix in the mine. "This is coded to our private frequency. You can talk as if we're right beside you. This is your home, so if you notice anything out of the ordinary, let us know."

Mia smiled softly as she took it, and Felix patted her shoulder to reassure her. *He is so good at that*, Sora thought, *reassuring others that Alix would be fine*. Sora knew Felix also plotted how to get Alix out. It would be easy for him, but she knew anything they did would lead to danger—and ever more violence.

Just then, a voice shouted nearby, "Wick!"

Wick leaned around Felix, who turned with him to see several men approaching. Wick smiled in welcome, but then his gaze fell on Mia— her eyes wide. Wick furrowed his brow for a moment, but quickly threw the smile back on when the men stopped at the table.

"It's been a while, Brom," Wick said.

"I thought that was you." Brom stood tall, broad, with grey eyes and dark hair. Two other men flanked him on either side, younger, but just as stout. "What are you doing back in town?"

Wick leaned back in his chair and shrugged. "Been making a few runs the past month or so."

Brom looked sideways at Mia, and she wilted under his gaze. He turned back to Wick, "Well, maybe we'll have a drink or two later."

"If you're buying." Wick and Brom both laughed.

Their friendly nature did not extend to anyone else, especially not Mia. She had shrunk in on herself, cowering as if predators circled. Wick kept talking, but Sora and Felix's attention had shifted, and they watched as Mia's frame trembled.

"Sounds like a deal," Brom grinned. He glanced at Sora and Felix, but said nothing to them. Then, he refocused on Wick. "I'll let you get back to it."

"See ya around," Wick waved two fingers as the three men turned and left.

Mia seemed to let out a breath she'd been holding the entire time. Her knees almost buckled, and she put both hands down on the table. Sora reached out for her in case she fell.

"Who was that?" Sora said. "And how do *you* know them?" she added to Wick, voice low.

Wick shrugged. "Just some guys I did business with when I, uh, had a different employer."

"You mean Silas," Sora sneered.

"Yes, I do," Wick replied sarcastically.

"They're Rolfe's brothers," Mia explained.

"Ah, well that complicates things." Felix looked over toward the brothers' table.

"You mean those are the brothers of that guy Alix murdered?" Wick said.

"Yes," Mia sniped.

"They don't know who Alix is, right?" Sora said.

"No, they never saw her."

"Well, let's keep it that way," Wick added.

"I have a better idea," Alix proposed, having listened to the conversation through her earpiece.

"Oh no," Felix said.

"Hey, don't be like that."

"Alix…" Felix let her name drag. He covered his face with his hand. Everyone stared at him, bracing themselves for some kind of bad news.

"The brothers can offer a useful distraction," she said. "We need someone to break down the door. What better than a blunt instrument?"

"Do you have an idea that *doesn't* involve a shootout?"

Silence hung around the table.

"Okay, well, send the brothers to Schelon's door," Alix said. "I'll bargain with him to let me go, and we'll promise to never come back to Alloyn again."

Felix recalled the construction of Schelon's office and the jail. Like most buildings in Alloyn, it was made of solid stone, and there was only one entrance. Schelon wouldn't be able to hold his own if a bunch of bolts knocked down his door. But he could prevent any bloodshed if he showed up at Schelon's side. *Maybe Alix has a point*, he thought.

They needed to kick the kyper's nest, and Wick was especially good at that kind of trouble. "Wick, you've got a job," Felix said.

"I'm listening." Wick leaned in and rested his arms on the table.

"Alix wants you to go chat with your friends over there. You know who killed their brother."

"And then what?"

"Then, they'll look for revenge. Schelon can't withstand them just turning up and shooting down his door."

"What happened to 'nobody will get hurt'?" Sora frowned.

"She'll be fine," Felix said. "With pressure from the brothers, I'll give Schelon a chance to let Alix go, in exchange for a promise that we never come back here again."

"What makes you think he won't just hand Alix over to em?" Wick wondered.

"He's a more honorable man than that."

The group split in different directions from Mia's restaurant. Felix and Sora walked together back to the *Shadow*, while Wick remained in town to fulfill his role. Along the trail, the forest lay silent. No wind moved through the slape trees, their branches still laden with snow. The crunch and thump of Sora's and Felix's boots in the snow and frozen mud became the only sound.

"You think this is a bad idea," Felix said, as if picking up on her thoughts.

"What gave you that impression?" Sora replied sarcastically.

"Just a hunch." Felix smiled and looked down at her.

Sora understood what Alix saw in Felix. His presence and his smile were calming. "I'd be lying if I said the time in the ship, just working on repairs, wasn't a huge relief. The better she feels, the more reckless she becomes."

"That's just how she is." Felix shrugged.

"She's always happy to risk her own skin."

"It's what she's used to. Every day of her life was a risk. She's been fighting for survival for so long, comfort and quiet have become unsettling."

"How do you not worry about her all the time?"

"Who says I don't?" Felix chuckled. "I know she can take care of herself. We just have to be there when she needs us."

"Like the port? And Silas's place?"

Felix's voice buzzed, something that would have been akin to a sigh if his body had required him to breathe. "Yes."

A small sense of relief washed over Sora when she entered the *Shadow*. She could work on something, keep her mind focused. In the cargo hold, beneath the pale lights, she stared at the floor where Alix had once crawled. She remembered the story, the panic and desperation she'd felt in Jesse's shop when Felix had returned carrying Alix's body. When they had gone storming into the port to take this ship back, Sora had been able to do nothing but wait—wait with the feeling of Alix's kiss lingering on her lips.

Sora would feel helpless if it came to a fight. She wasn't like the others; she couldn't draw a plasbolt at a moment's notice and take someone's life. Sora didn't *break* things—she *fixed* them. Staring down at the cold metal floor, she imagined the pool of blood where Alix would have lain—where she would have *died*, if it hadn't been for an act of desperation.

Sora's hands trembled.

The workbench remained strewn with tools, parts, and hardware from the last time someone had sat there and worked. Sora settled on the stool and took a deep breath. She picked up small pieces of metal, wire clippings, and tiny fasteners and gathered them into a little pile before grabbing the goggles that protected her eyes from the bright burn of the plaspen. She began to slip them over her head, but paused, removed the goggles, and held them for a moment, staring into the dark lenses. Sora ran her thumb over a lens and smiled.

Sora began to scrounge through every drawer, compartment, locker, and tray of materials in the hold. She fired up the vizscreens above the bench and used the holographic rendering system in the ship's computers to turn the mental image in her head into a full schematic.

Her fingers moved swiftly over the bench, typing, rotating, and exploding the schematic on the screens. She might have to acquire more materials, lenses, microchips, light sensors, but her mind finally clicked into place.

The project brought a hyperfocus that could keep all other things silent, far removed from her mind. She subconsciously closed the door to everything else, and began her work. Sora couldn't *break* the forces that would assail Alix; but she wouldn't let Alix fight alone, or without the tools she needed.

Felix sifted through the myriad of things that troubled his cerebral core. Plenty of dangers to be vigilant about, but the one he needed to focus on was buried deep in his memory. He could very easily comprehend the physical dangers they faced, the logical steps from Alix's gambit to inevitable violence. But he could not process the fact that Alix had blacked out twice, and that she'd recalled memories, but not those she herself had made.

If they had the time, and the safety, he could examine Alix for days, to discern the truth of what was happening to her. Instead, all he had was the quiet cockpit of the *Shadow*. Even without Alix here, he didn't like to sit in her chair, which remained empty on his left. The red, green, blue, and yellow lights blinked in slow rhythms. He spun his eyes closed, searching for the right corridor in his memory. He pared back the systems operating countless processes within his body, and as each one faded away, he became more focused, more relaxed.

The flood of information pouring into Felix slowed to a faint whisper. He did not power down into a full sleep, but deprived his senses enough to access centuries of data.

A dark room, lit by dancing firelight, came to him. The thick, humid air condensed against his semi-translucent skin. Droplets ran down his arms and face.

This was not the moment he needed.

The current carried his mind elsewhere—staring up at the stars. Felix stood alone, not staring at stars, but thousands of fires in the sky. They fell toward the horizon in brilliant streaks, and then came those that signaled the end of time. Great masses of metal, burning white at the center, breaking off bit by bit, burning toward the surface.

In this moment, the war was over, and he would never again see another face like his own.

But, it was not the right moment.

Deep, where memories came only in shadows, and he reached against the wall of his true awakening, Felix found her.

A familiar voice called him not a child, but an equal. From her he'd received a gift he would carry for the rest of his life. And in *that* moment, she'd handed him three vials, her last act, robed in white. Despite the shadows and fog, he recalled that moment when Ceera had laid down her life—the *first* life—so that black blood would spread safely across time and space.

Felix saw things from that moment in a dim light, through a fog, barely able to discern the world around him as the memories, the data, faded and crumbled. He would have to isolate that memory and carry it forward in his mind, focusing more time and energy toward piecing it back together—time that he did not have.

Wick dragged his heels across the floor as he sidled up to a table of four men inside a warm saloon. Three of the men were familiar to him, and they sat with their sleeves rolled up, the faces above their broad shoulders fair, but dirty. The fourth, Wick did not know. He smiled and raised his hands, one holding a bottle, and another with three glasses between his fingers.

"I thought you said we were buying?" Brom said in a gravelly voice.

"I'm feeling generous," Wick said with a wink.

"Have a seat." Brom gestured to the fourth man to give up his chair and the man obliged, albeit not without grumbling as he walked away with his glass.

Wick set the bottle and glasses down, then slid a glass to each man. Brom watched with cold, grey eyes. Wick took the open chair and began pouring drinks.

"I heard what happened to Silas," Brom said.

Wick hid the pleasant memory of shooting Silas himself and clicked his tongue instead. "It was a mess, that's for damn sure."

"Any idea who did it?"

Wick paused before pouring a glass of chisik for himself. A smile peeked out through his facade of disappointment. "I don't know if anyone has an idea. I barely got my ship out of there."

"Well," Brom said before downing his chisik, "He certainly didn't have a lack of enemies."

"That's true." Wick gulped down his own drink, then began pouring himself another, and another for Brom.

"I seem to remember you had another brother?"

"We did. Rolfe. He was murdered back before you and I met. But I don't seem to remember telling you that."

"You didn't." Wick polished off his drink and began pouring a third. "I have a brother, too. Although we don't talk much anymore."

"How tragic."

"Not as tragic as a dead brother." Wick shrugged, drinking again. Before he poured another glass, one of the other brothers snatched the bottle from him. "I see you three are eager for retribution."

"Get to your point."

Wick smiled. "What if I told you the woman that killed your brother was right here in town?"

That information caught the brothers off guard. They looked to Brom for leadership. He remained cool, but color rose in his cheeks.

"How would you know this?"

"Let's say she and I were business partners. When we got into town, she recalled the story."

"And you're telling us this why?"

"Her temperament is bad for business. And I've known you longer than I've known her."

"So why don't you take care of her?"

Wick cocked his head to the side. "After Silas's place went up in smoke, I'm trying to avoid running afoul of the law. I'm a legitimate man, now."

"So we kill her, and you just go on your way, is that it?"

"Well, I am leaving you a choice. This woman is worth a lot of crits to a lot of folks. What is your retribution worth?"

"How much do you want?" Brom's stone face began to crack.

"Two thousand."

Brom tapped his fingers and sucked his teeth. "And I thought we were *old friends*."

"That is the friend price."

"So where is she now?"

"Sitting in Schelon's jailhouse."

Brom looked from one brother to the other. He stood and pulled the coat off the back of his chair. The other two finished their glasses and joined him "We'll have to scrounge up the crits."

"I'll be waiting!" Wick grinned.

The brothers left the saloon. Wick slid the bottle over to himself and poured another glass.

* * *

Schelon groaned as someone pounded their fist against his door. He rose from his chair and peeked through the curtain drawn over his window, then cursed under his breath, and opened the door.

"Brom, what can I do for you?" Schelon said.

"That woman in there," Brom growled. "We want her."

"What for?"

"She murdered our brother."

"Rolfe?" Schelon turned and peered into the jail. He rolled his eyes as he turned back. "What proof do you got?"

"We have it on good authority."

"You know that ain't how it works here."

"Look, we have respect for you and that is the only reason we haven't barged in there and dragged her out already."

Schelon's palms began to sweat. He shifted his weight and put his hands on his hips. Brom's two brothers moved, slowly but cautiously, preparing to draw. Brom held out his hand to them.

"Why don't you ask her yourself?" Brom suggested.

"You think she'll just admit to it?" Schelon laughed.

"If she won't, I am sure Mia will identify her."

Schelon shook his head. "Even so, it won't lead to the revenge you're seeking."

"Justice."

A drawn out silence seemed to last forever. Schelon laughed to ease his nerves. "That doesn't pass for justice in this town."

"Either you hand her over, or we go in there and take her," Brom finally demanded.

"I don't think so."

"Alright."

Before the brothers could draw or step toward him, Schelon beat them to it. His plasbolt trained on Brom, Schelon slowly backed up a few steps toward his door. The chambers spun and whistled as the brothers sneered. They weren't backing down.

"You willing to die over this bitch?" Brom said.

"Are you willing to lose another brother? Maybe two?"

Schelon could see the calculations running through Brom's mind. A shootout would undoubtedly leave at least one brother dead. Schelon could maybe get a second before he died, too. He hoped it was a gamble they weren't willing to take. Despite the tough exterior he put up, Schelon desperately wished they would back down.

"Alright," Brom spoke at length. "You can have her for now. But trust me, when we come knocking again, we won't be empty-handed."

"Neither will I," Schelon replied.

He followed Brom and the other brothers with his plasbolt as they slowly marched down the street. They looked back and kept their eyes sharp until they were several meters away. Then, they turned their heads and walked on. Schelon let out a long, shaking breath. He holstered his plasbolt and stormed back inside.

When he appeared in the hall, Alix opened one eye, then sat up, wearing a playful, confused expression. Schelon came to a halt in front of her and rubbed his forehead.

"Word travels fast," Alix said, before he could explain.

Schelon laughed, the only thing he could manage in the grim situation. "Tell me it isn't true."

"What isn't?" Alix raised an eyebrow.

"You know what I'm talking about—that you killed Rolfe."

"Me?" She put a hand to her chest, feigning innocence. But the smile that slowly spread across her cheeks revealed the truth.

"Look, we're both before the firing squad, now."

Alix mustered up the humility to thank Schelon for not turning her over immediately—a gamble that had paid off. "Sorry to put you in this position."

"Are you?" Schelon glanced over his shoulder, half expecting the brothers to break his door down regardless of the agreement.

"Look, you can get rid of this situation tonight. Just let me go, and I won't ever come back here."

Schelon threw his head back and let out one exaggerated laugh. "Just let you go? A thief, and now, apparently, a murderer?"

"Well, I guess you *could* die for nothing."

"Or I could let them have you," Schelon paced the hall.

"We both know you're not going to do that."

"Okay, so if I go with your plan, then I release you, the brothers return, and *then* we shoot it out."

"Just hand me over to them, but on the condition that they deliver me to the marshal in Verisport for the monetary reward."

"No."

"How about this: we stage an escape."

"Do you ever have a *good* idea?" Schelon put his hands over his face. "How is that going to make any sense?"

"My friends in town can come and get me. I think you remember Felix, the sentient?"

"I recall him," Schelon said nervously.

"He could break down your door with ease. Or, we could blow a hole in the wall. Something like that."

"And I just stand by and let you walk out?"

Alix started pacing. "Well, we'd have to make it *look* believable. Maybe you're knocked unconscious by my friend."

"Oh sure, sounds great." Schelon rolled his eyes.

"What other choice do you have that doesn't lead to your death?"

"And who's to say they don't have eyes on this place all night, and shoot you down once you escape?"

"Mr. Schelon, they cannot hurt me."

Schelon stared at Alix, his skepticism contrasting the smile on her face. "You seem pretty confident."

"I've been told it's one of my better qualities." Alix thought for a moment and laughed to herself. "But, then again, I've also been told otherwise."

6

The Escape

Wisps of snow blew off the edges of rooftops. Smoke drifted up from chimneys, and a low fog settled in the streets of Alloyn. The burning embers of street lamps created halos within the pale fog. Alix sat at Schelon's desk, feet propped up, and hands behind her head. Schelon peered out the window. She watched him scratch the growing beard on his face for the third or fourth time, then he returned his right hand to the plasbolt grip on his side.

"You sure these friends of yours will be here?" he said to Alix while keeping his eyes on the street.

"Don't worry."

When he turned and saw her boots, his eyes flashed. "Get your boots off my desk!"

Alix dropped them and leaned forward, instead. "Well, one of us has to sit and remain calm. It sure isn't you."

"Sorry if I don't share your confidence."

"Nobody's perfect."

Alix adjusted the syncpad sleeve on her left arm, stood, and swung her coat over her shoulders. Schelon held out his hand and she froze. Quietly, she spoke to Felix in her ear. "Trouble heading this way, I think."

"Heading to you," Felix replied.

Alix leaned against the wall on the opposite side of the window from Schelon. "You got those bolts for me?"

"You mean the ones you *stole*?" Schelon glowered at her. "No."

"Well, that's a shame."

"Here they come," Schelon whispered.

"Guess I'll just stand here."

Schelon drew his plasbolt and watched as men moved through shadows across the street. Pretty soon, bright plasfire would cut the dim night between them. His bolt charged as the chamber spun, filling his office with its glow.

"Schelon!" A voice echoed in the street. "We've come to collect the girl!"

"Felix?" Alix whispered instinctively.

"Two minutes," he replied.

"Just a few minutes," she relayed to Schelon.

"I see four, maybe five guys moving around out there," Schelon said.

Alix grunted as she pushed the desk from its corner. The wood scraped and ground over stone as Alix found her strength lacking. She managed to push, pull, and finally get it up close to the door. Through heavy breathing, she cursed the fact that she was out of breath at all. She put her back to the stone wall and slid down, dropping her arms on her knees.

The voice belonging to Brom called out again, "Last chance!"

"You sure you don't have another bolt in here?" Alix said to Schelon, still catching her breath.

"I'm not giving you a plasbolt, so just stop asking," Schelon snapped.

"Well, I hope you aren't useless with that one."

"I'll be glad when you're out of here."

Zmmph zmmph zmmph.

Plasfire shattered the window. Schelon hit the floor as glass rained down on him. The door rattled and splintered as holes burned through it. Alix put her head between her knees and covered herself with her arms as Schelon screamed on the floor. He had dropped his plasbolt as his hands went to his ears and face.

Zmmph zmmph.

The shots continued. The office filled with flying splinters of wood and stone; the streaking rounds flashed blue over Alix's head like a storm. She crawled on her belly and shook Schelon with her left hand. He opened one eye at a touch on his shoulder, but only squinting; the other was bloodied and burnt, glass embedded in the left side of his face.

"Shoot back!" Alix yelled.

Schelon looked at his plasbolt on the floor. Alix gave up on him and snatched it up before she continued crawling and put herself between the door and the window, standing with her back to the stone. With the toe of her boot, she nudged Schelon. He looked up as best he could and she motioned with her head for him to head toward the back.

"I got you!" she shouted.

He nodded.

Alix couldn't get a clear view out the window due to the flashing plasfire. She spun up the chamber and turned her arm back, reaching out the window. She opened fire haphazardly for only a few shots, then pulled her arm back in. Schelon stumbled to his feet and staggered back toward the cells with his hand covering the bloody half of his face.

"Felix! ETA!" Alix shouted.

"Thirty seconds," he replied inside her ear.

The plasfire paused and Alix heard the men shouting orders to one another. The remains of the curtains flapped and caught fire. She yanked the nearer curtain down, snapping the flimsy rings off the rod. The moonlight and faint glow of a plasbolt revealed a man entering the street, trying to remain ducked low.

Alix stepped aside enough so she could extend her right arm and not have it hanging out the window entirely. Then she closed her left eye, tongue sticking out of the left corner of her mouth.

Zmmph.

She cut the man down, the plasma round exploding the side of his head. His body went flying and tumbling, a dark heap under the moonlight.

Return plasfire zinged past Alix's head, and she dropped to the ground. Mingled with the sound of plasma rounds cutting the door to pieces, a growing whistle toward the back of the jail grew to an overwhelming, piercing cry. Alix rolled to her right as the sound crescendoed and the building shook. A shockwave passed through the stones, and Alix's chest. Stones came flying down the hall toward the door, a cloud of dust behind them. When Alix lifted her head, she saw Felix's silhouette and bright blue eyes.

"Knock, knock," he said.

"I am so glad to see you," Alix replied as she took his hand.

"The shockwave must have rattled them, too," Felix said, looking straight through the door and wall toward their attackers.

"Great, let's get out of here."

They stepped over rubble in the hall. Felix had blown a massive hole in the back wall using the sonic explosives from the mine. Alix stopped at a cell where Schelon was bent over a washbasin with a bloody cloth to his face.

"You alright?" she said.

"Do I look it?" he shouted.

Alix could only imagine how badly his ears were ringing, as he'd been closer to the explosion. "Well, tell them I hit you, or something. Later!" She waved and jumped through the hole in the wall.

Sora walked around the corner, hefting a bag across her body. Alix smiled, satisfied with herself, ready to brag about how well her plan had worked. But Sora brushed by her, leaving Alix standing confused with Schelon's plasbolt dangling from her hand.

"Let's move," was all Sora said.

Alix met Felix's eyes, puzzled and a little embarrassed. Felix put an arm around Alix's shoulders and reassured her with a gentle squeeze. He followed Sora up the sloping street that ran behind Schelon's now-useless jail. Alix huffed and grumbled as she spun the plasbolt on her finger, something she did when she needed a confidence boost. She then hurried after Felix and Sora.

Schelon's door cracked and burst off its hinges, striking the desk behind it. The men outside put their weight behind the door and forced it open. Brom shoved his way inside, plasbolt up and out, but his mouth dropped open when he saw the hole in the back wall and the rubble on the floor. He ran toward the hole as his younger brothers entered the office behind him.

Brom cursed and stomped back into the jail, finding Schelon sitting against the wall inside a cell. He held a bloody rag, but his hands rested in his lap. His left eye remained closed, the skin from his hairline down his neck on that side burnt and bloodied. Brom walked up to Schelon in a quiet rage and pointed his plasbolt.

"Where is she?" Brom said through clenched teeth.

"How should I know?" Schelon groaned.

"What the hell happened in here?" Nik, the youngest brother, said.

"What does it look like? Somebody blew up the fucking wall." Schelon waved his arm toward the back wall.

"Start looking for her, and anybody who helped her," Brom ordered. When everyone else had left, Brom crouched down closer to

Schelon. He put the barrel of his plasbolt between them. "What happened?"

"I told you." Schelon grimaced. "Someone blew up the wall and she left."

The plasbolt began to whistle as it charged. Brom turned it down and pressed the barrel into Schelon's left thigh. "Awfully good timing, ain't it?" he said.

Schelon laughed a weak, breathy sound. "You think I helped her? You were out here yelling and announcing your intentions to the whole town. Hardly a stretch to say some friends of hers heard you."

"What friends?"

"I don't know."

Zmmph.

Schelon screamed in agony as a single plasma round seared through his left knee. Brom lifted the steaming plasbolt up to Schelon's face, leaving it centimeters from the man's other eye.

"Next one's in your ear," Brom said.

Through gasps, Schelon tried to form words. "She...has three..."

"What do they look like?"

"A woman...darker skin. A sentient. Can't...miss him. And that... pilot. The ship...landing pad."

Brom's eyes widened. "Wick. That son of a bitch." He left Schelon on the floor and strode through the hole in the wall. Brom holstered his plasbolt and reached his brothers on his syncpad. "Wick is with them. They're going to go for his ship. Everybody to the warehouse."

Alix, Felix, and Sora approached the grey-blue cliff face below the hangar and warehouse. They waited at the metal lift doors as if nothing was out of the ordinary. Down the slope into town, bells echoed. Alix and Sora spun around and looked out over the snow-covered rooftops.

"What's that?" Sora said, her voice shaking.

"Schelon gave us up," Alix replied. She clenched her teeth, shoving down her rage.

"He gave us a head start," Felix corrected.

"Yeah, well, now the dogs are on us." Alix turned and stared up at the cliff impatiently.

"They're headed this way," Felix said, still focused on the town.

"Where's the fucking lift?" Alix growled.

Felix peered up through the stone and into the shaft. "Not coming."

"Oh, wonderful," Sora said.

Alix began to pace. She called Wick on her syncpad. "Wick, you better be ready to fly. They're onto us. We're stuck at the lift."

"Want me to pick you up?" Wick yelled over the growing roar of the *Procella*'s engines.

Alix scanned the rooftops a few meters below. Most were flat stone, but some sloped with stone tiles. They couldn't stay by the lift, out in the open. At least a rooftop would offer a place to defend themselves with high ground, and Wick could hover the ship enough to get them inside.

As if Felix knew her thoughts, he said, "We can get on a roof over there—plenty of space for him to get us."

"Alright, let's move." Alix agreed. "Wick, you'll have our location in a second. Swing over and grab us."

"Affirmative."

They abandoned the lift and ran. Despite the plan, Alix struggled to shake off the urge to just stand and fight. The plasbolt in her right hand felt heavy, like a force pulling her in another direction. There was no doubt in her mind that she could just kill anyone that Rolfe's brothers had sent after her. That swelling confidence burned in her chest as she struggled to inhale the cold air. She hadn't run like this in a long time.

They reached the edge of a terrace street that ran across the northern slope. Felix jumped down first, then reached up to helped Sora and Alix. They jumped into his arms one at a time, and he set them gently on their feet before all three crossed another dark street and climbed onto a rooftop to sit in the small dusting of snow, breathing heavily and waiting for Wick.

"Oh come on," Wick groaned as he fumbled with the twisting lock on a hose connected to his ship. The cold jammed the lock and he wrenched on it with both hands, throwing his weight behind it until it finally popped free.

Wick threw the hose to the side and out of his peripheral vision saw men coming his way. He watched them cautiously but tried to continue his work as if he wasn't in a hurry.

A plasma round ripping past him changed that. He ducked and threw his coat back to draw his own plasbolt. He couldn't manage accurate shots as more streaking blue rounds came his way. Finally, he dropped to the ground and rolled under the ship, putting the cargo ramp between him and the oncoming plasfire.

The men would obviously split up and get on either side of him, so there was no use in trying to get out to the other way. Instead, Wick tapped furiously on his syncpad, connecting to the *Procella's* computer, and with a slide of his finger, he maximized the engines' output. The low rumbling and subtle glow of the warming engines burst into a deafening roar, and in a sudden shockwave of air and heat, the men coming toward Wick were blown back, tumbling head over heels.

He rolled out from beneath the ship and smiled. "Alix, I'm on my way," he shouted into their comms.

"Take your fucking time!" Alix replied sarcastically.

Wick rolled his eyes and ran up the side ramp into his ship. He pulled a lever on his way in to close the ramp and seal the door behind him. The *Procella* cockpit glowed as Wick jumped into the pilot's chair, his hands moving across the instrument panels in front, beside, and above his chair. He pulled in the cargo ramp and gripped the sticks tight against the vibrations running through the ship.

Alarms flashed in the projected display on the windshield. Men on the ground continued wasting their time firing into the *Procella's* hull as Wick lifted her into the air. The ship slowly banked and leveled out over the town. He pinpointed Alix's signal and kept the engine thrust low so he could descend carefully over the rooftops to pick up the rest of the crew.

Alix ducked low as plasfire streaked over her head. She lay almost entirely on her back, her head and shoulders up against the stone edge of the rooftop. Sora remained low, and Felix knelt safely beside her, one hand on Sora's back, making sure that anything coming her way would not harm her. Alix had the only plasbolt among the three, but the heat had found them running from the lift.

Relief started to spread as she heard Wick's call that he would pick them up shortly. Felix and Sora crouched near Alix's feet, and the relief faded quickly as Alix read the fear on Sora's face, eyes tightly shut, hands over her ears.

Felix's eyes darted back and forth. He pointed to his left, detecting someone getting a little too close.

Alix rolled and popped up on one knee before peeking over the edge. She spied a figure moving across the dark space between her and the house next to her. She let loose a few shots, just enough to send whoever back into hiding, and then she ducked again and watched as the chamber of the plasbolt spun down, the light dying within. Alix let out a frustrated sigh and ejected the charge casing.

"Wick, get your ass over here," she yelled.

"Thirty seconds," his voice replied in her ear.

Snow whipped around them. Alix shielded her eyes while Felix looked up at the *Procella* slowly gliding overhead. The plasfire halted for a brief moment as the engines and retro thrusters sent gusts of swirling wind and snow into the streets, blowing debris away from the ship. The men on the ground were either thrown down by the force, or ducked and covered themselves as crates, stones, and refuse flew at them.

The sound was deafening.

Like a boat in choppy water, the *Procella* rolled slightly up and down, floating slightly off-center of the rooftop. Alix smirked, impressed with Wick's ability to hold her steady at such a low altitude, making slight adjustments to keep her in just the right spot for the side ramp to open and present itself to them. Felix stood and lifted Sora by the waist, almost tossing her up so she could reach the ramp, which remained too high for them to actually get to without Felix's assistance.

Sora clung to the ramp and scrambled up and into the ship.

Felix grabbed Alix and did the same, watching her as she crawled up the ramp. But she stopped before entering the ship; holding on with one hand, she turned and watched Felix leap onto the end of the ramp. The ship lurched suddenly, and would have spilled them back onto the rooftop, if Felix hadn't stepped forward and nearly shoved Alix back inside.

The ramp closed behind them.

Adrenaline coursed through Alix as she rolled over and shook her arms out, a big smile on her face. She could have run laps around Alloyn, her body full of energy and sudden strength. The plasfire, the explosion, the chase, the escape; it all felt so euphoric. It had been so long, and the restlessness had been like a spring wound to its breaking point. She began to laugh and put her head back against the hull.

"What is the matter with you?" Sora yelled.

Alix stopped laughing and checked to make sure Sora was speaking to her. "What? I'm fine!"

"We could've been killed and you're sitting here *laughing*?"

"I think we did okay?" Alix grimaced. Her mouth stretched and her eyes softened, trying to convey a silent apology.

Sora shook her head, her lips tightly pressed together. She climbed to her feet and walked toward the cockpit. Alix looked over to Felix, her mouth open, but the words just weren't forming. Instead, she allowed Felix to help her to her feet.

"*Are* you okay?" he said.

"Yes, what do you mean?"

"Your eye." Felix pointed to one of his eyes.

Alix ran to the head and surveyed herself in the mirror. A darkness, like a bruise, surrounded her left eye, but it did not hurt when she brought her fingers up to touch the skin. She pulled down her lid and saw the black lines, just as before, when the hyperfluid had moved through her blood vessels. She had blacked out then; and now, she feared the same.

When she turned around, Felix stood in the hatchway. The adrenaline in her body shifted and now her stomach roiled. Her eyes widened but slowly, they darkened. Alix panicked, her heart pounded, and she rubbed her fingers over her sweaty palms. Her skin felt like needles and suddenly, her breath escaped her. She reached out toward Felix as the darkness enveloped her eyes completely. Before she lost awareness of her physical presence, the last thing she felt was Felix's embrace.

Alix was running. The darkness around her was cold and cruel. Only small lamps high above her offered any light, and only at long intervals. Each breath was like a punch to her chest. Her young mind had little explanation for the experience. She stumbled, tripping not over her feet, but the strange lightness of them and her body. What she expected to feel—her feet solidly on the ground—wasn't there. She almost sensed her legs floating just centimeters off the floor.

She still hadn't adjusted to being off the surface of a planet. Even the concept of a planet seemed vague to her; it was just a word spoken by others. But the infinite darkness she perceived outside the window of wherever she was now made it clear that she was not on a planet.

Whatever chased her did not relent. The heavy, steady rhythm of footsteps felt like horror in her ears. The sounds shivered up her spine, as if the next one would surely touch her shoulder. The garbled vocal tones would haunt her nightmares for the rest of her life.

The narrow passage suddenly stopped. In the dark, Alix ran straight into a wall. She felt blindly with her hands, finding the wall to her right, then in front of her. It cornered to her left, so she picked herself up and stumbled along in that direction. The temperature increased and sweat gathered on her palms and dripped down her face. The air felt thick.

And suddenly, there was nothing but air beneath her next step.

Alix fell, screaming as she stepped into a void. She had no idea how far she fell, but she struck a hard metal surface and could no longer breathe, her head swimming. Looking up, she saw nothing, the world above her completely black, despite her eyes blinking.

The grinding, garbled tones, like an unknown language, grew louder, echoing down the shaft. But the footsteps halted. Alix didn't have to hold her breath, she still hadn't been able to draw one since the fall. She stared up into darkness, waiting for whatever it was to find her.

But it growled and clicked some final unknown words, and she heard the footsteps again, like heavy hammers on the metal flooring. They grew faint until she lay in the silent darkness.

Finally, she drew a long, gasping breath.

Alix sat up suddenly with a sharp intake of breath. She could see. In place of the darkness, Felix and Sora leaned in toward her. Alix felt their touch on her shoulder, on her leg; she felt the soft mattress of her bunk under her: *I'm home.*

"It's okay, you're safe." Felix's low voice was like a comforting, soft buzz that broke a hollow silence.

"We've got you." Sora gripped Alix's hand so tightly. "You're on the *Shadow*."

Alix blinked rapidly, doubting that her vision would remain clear. She breathed slowly, and each breath rattled in her chest. She recalled the memory—this time, it was *her* memory. That child had possessed no idea where she was; how far she had been from home. All she'd known were cramped spaces and dark tunnels—steaming vents and pipes so cold they burned her fingers. Every surface, sight, and sound had caused pain. Even the air in her lungs had been difficult to breathe.

A dull pain came in waves and Alix rubbed her forehead with the hand that Sora wasn't holding on to for dear life. "How long was I out?" she said.

"Almost an hour," Felix replied. Alix froze, lips parted. Felix asked gently, "What did you see this time?"

"Myself." Alix stared past Sora and Felix. "It was a memory, clear as day. The darkness. Cramped spaces in the Rings—although I didn't know that at the time. They were chasing me."

"Who?" Sora whispered.

"Zigs. Or some variation on them." Alix shook herself.

"You mean those things that nearly killed you in the dock?"

"Yeah."

"How did you get away from them?"

"I fell. Maybe they couldn't follow. The space was pretty cramped."

"Interesting," Felix said. "I watched you this time, and it is clear the hyperfluid has made the decision to interact with your brain in a deliberate way."

"Made *the decision*?" Wick piped up.

Alix didn't know he had been standing behind Sora and Felix.

Felix continued, "Yes, I mean, the hyperfluid *is* intelligent to a degree."

"Don't hold back," Alix said, wanting to know everything Felix had learned, no matter how dark or dangerous.

"There is a small amount of the fluid that has entered your brain, albeit on a scale so small that it can hardly be called a *fluid*. But for lack of a better term, the nano-robotics are capable of firing neural pathways. So it seems they are capable of triggering your memories at will."

"Great. So, even shit I would *prefer* to forget, it will just dig up?"

"Well, that seems to be the case here."

"If this stuff is intelligent, can you like, speak to it?" Sora said to Felix.

"Well…" Felix began, but his voice trailed, and he gazed into Alix's eyes.

She reached for his hand. "It's okay." She knew the trepidation within Felix. The hyperfluid Felix had carefully hidden on the *Shadow* since they'd met was dear to him, and he protected it like an heirloom. Alix knew it was more than some kind of replacement for his own lifeblood.

Her face softened and they stared deep into one another's eyes. All she thought of in that moment was an apology. Alix had compromised the fluid when she injected it in an act of pure desperation—even selfishness. An avalanche of guilt buried Alix, no matter how much Felix reassured her that he did not judge the decision. He wanted her *alive* more than anything, she knew that.

Finally, Alix met Sora's eyes. "We'll figure this out later. It's something that'll take time—a lot of time and sitting around—and I cannot tell you how tired I am of sitting around."

Sora didn't argue, and a smile tugged at the edges of her lips.

7

The Dark

In the valley, a young boy gripped an axe handle with gloved hands. He put one hand up on the shoulder, another near the knob. With a determined grunt, he lifted and swung the axe down, butt first into a layer of ice. A chip struck his cheek. He dropped the axe to put his hands on his face; the axe plunged beneath the water in the large stock tank.

"Shit," he breathed, feeling grown up and tough as the word escaped his lips, though the pain in his face said otherwise.

He slipped off a glove and touched his face, checked his fingers for blood—everything was fine. *Except for the axe.* The layer of ice had broken, but only in a small portion of the tank, leaving most of the stirrols' water still inaccessible. The boy leaned over the edge of the tank, gingerly moved the broken ice to the side with the hand still in its glove, gazing down to see the axe lying on the metal bottom.

A reflection in the rippling water startled him.

The boy jumped, and with his back to the tank, ready to be admonished by his father, anticipated a swift strike to his face. But it wasn't his father facing him. Four men stood there instead. The boy furrowed his brow, looking at the men on stirrolback, their faces covered against the cold.

"Can I help you?" he said.

None of them replied.

"If you're looking for my father, he's in the house." The boy pointed back toward the small stone and wood house to his right.

One of the men reached into his coat, the sleek steel of a plasbolt catching the morning light. The boy's eyes widened like the full moons, but before he could scream for help—

Zmmph.

The plasma round burned a hole in the boy's jacket and chest, firing straight through the metal stock tank. The boy dropped to the frozen dirt, back to the tank, water spilling out on top of him from a hole in the side.

Two of the men turned their stirrols and headed for the house. A man burst out the door, screaming, a plasrifle in-hand.

Zmmph. Zmmph. Zmmph.

Three rounds ripped the man apart, blood splattering on the brown stone wall behind him. The plasrifle fell from his hands.

A woman screamed. When she reached the doorway, her eyes latched on to her husband. Tears streamed down her cold, red face. She threw herself at his body, her screams falling on uncaring ears as she peered past him and caught sight of her son.

Zmmph.

Her screams stopped.

The men holstered their plasbolts. Water splattered on the boy and the ground behind them. The men turned their collars against the cold wind blowing across the low hills. They clicked their tongues and spurred their stirrols, heading west toward the rising sun.

What twilight fruit trees remained in the orchard stood leafless, limbs waving, scratching for the purple sky. The morning sun painted rows of thin, feathered clouds with orange and pink hues. Tree limbs over Jo's head creaked in the wind.

Jo's hair sat in a puff high on her head, a cozy wrap covering her forehead and ears. She wore a thick coat, collar pulled up around her neck. Her plasrifle lay in her lap as she stared into the west, toward the rising sun. At times she stuck her head between her knees and wrapped her arms around them to shield herself against the sharp wind. She exhaled heavily so her warm breath would ease the sting on her face. Nothing had yet relieved the pain from being left here, alone, as men in her village came and went in rotating groups to protect nearby homesteads. She had tried to convince the marshal, Sim, Dorn, and anyone else who would listen that she could handle herself.

All of them had told her a variation of the same word: "No."

Every time a group left, she found a spot in the orchard to sit, back to one of the trees that hadn't been burned to the roots. She waited for the men to return—listened for the hoofbeats of stirrols. For days, the groups came and went, and none returned in haste or alarm. They could keep her from riding along, but they couldn't keep her from puzzling out what was happening in the valley—or what wasn't happening.

The marshal had originally came to her village after she had found the dead homesteaders on her hunt. Then, a boy had ridden into Verisport days later, his entire family and community murdered. It had been a tense week—the marshal had visited again and argued with the men he'd set as watchmen, trying to figure out how to stay ahead.

She'd stood aside and listened.

It was all they had allowed her to do.

The plasrifle lay in her lap like a fallen tree branch: heavy and useless.

Jo dug her heel into the frost, the wet grass, then the dirt. With a sigh, she scratched her back on the tree behind her, then stood. Walking back toward the shop—*her and Sora's shop*—she heard a commotion in the village center. Jo slung the plasrifle over her shoulder and ran.

When she cut through the houses and came to the cistern, she found Dorn, Gabe, and Liam, riding in from the east.

"Everything okay?" Jo said as she took the reins of Liam's stirrol, letting him dismount.

He ignored her.

Panic froze the men's faces and closed their lips. She returned the reins to Liam and moved on to Dorn, where she repeated her question. Dorn groaned as he pulled his left foot out of the stirrup. He tossed the reins over his stirrol's ears—he, too, said nothing.

Jo straightened and drew breath from deep in her belly. "Hey! What the hell happened?"

The men finally took notice of her, although their panic turned to anger. Dorn stepped close, letting his height and weight shrink Jo into the small child that they thought she was. His nostrils flared as he blew out air and tightened his lips.

"Another village dead. There. You know. Are you happy now?"

Jo's mouth hung open.

"Now, get out of the way, we need to talk to Sim." He pushed her aside and led the other two men toward the central meeting house.

Jo searched the ground, a rock in the pit of her stomach. A wave of nausea and dizziness overtook her. She buried her face in her hands, and felt tears forming in the corners of her eyes.

With gritted teeth, she forced them back. She drew a deep breath, dropped her hands, and looked up into the morning light before adjusting the strap on her shoulder and breaking into a run after Dorn.

Inside, the men gathered with Sim and other elders as Jo stood just beyond the circle. Warm coals glowed in the fire and deep shadows touched every face.

"The whole village, just lying around dead." Dorn was already in the middle of his explanation when Jo got within earshot.

"Was there any indication of who did this?" Sim inquired.

"We only saw a few stirrol prints. Ground was pretty frozen up, so they weren't too clear."

"Did you notify the marshal?"

"Not yet, we headed right back here after we surveyed the scene."

Jo inched her way closer to the group.

"I will let him know," Sim said, her voice distant and shaking.

"What should we do with the bodies? Should we go back and bury them?" This time Liam spoke, a man much shorter than Dorn, with heavy hands, and dark, dry skin.

"The marshal will want to take a look at everything first, I imagine," Sim replied.

Jo's eyes narrowed. *They left the bodies. I could ride out there and take a look myself.* Her courage swelled enough for her to finally make her presence known.

"What time do you think the killers were there?" she said.

Everyone turned to find the source of that question. When some of the elders stood aside, Dorn saw Jo and scowled. Jo sneered back, but when Sim caught sight of her, Jo turned her eyes to the floor. Sim crossed her arms and changed her tone.

"Jo, I told you this is not your concern."

"I'm just trying to help," Jo pleaded.

Dorn bristled as Jo stepped closer and he looked down his nose at her. She tried to ignore him.

"If we knew when the people were killed," Jo slowly explained, "then you can probably calculate where they came from, or where they might be, now."

"And I am sure the marshal will do such calculations when he personally investigates," Sim spoke just as slowly, tilting her head to Jo.

"It'll be too late by then. We need to get back out there—"

"Jo. Enough!" Sim's green eyes flared.

Instead of wilting, Jo put her hands on her hips and stood tall. She set her jaw and stared back at Sim. Everyone waited to see who would flinch first.

Jo would not let them intimidate her anymore. She loved Sim, but ever since Sora had left, the village had treated Jo like a helpless child. She huffed and turned on her heel. She retrieved the plasrifle she had leaned against the stone fireplace. As Jo walked away, she heard Sim's voice echo behind her, calling her name.

Jo slung her foot over the saddle and gathered the reins in her hands. For a moment, she questioned herself. *What are you expecting to do? Those families are already dead.* She bit down on her quivering lip, refusing to let emotions get the better of her. She swallowed the lump in her throat and turned Allie out of the barn. With a snap of the reins, Jo brought Allie up to a full gallop.

Sim's voice rang in Jo's ears, the echo of her calling to Jo in the meeting house. As she rode northeast, her eyes watered from the wind in her face—or at least that was what she told herself.

The valley lay flat for several kilometers. In the spring, the chis grass would be at her stirrol's knees, the white and golden panicles not yet opened. The sheaths would be stiff before growing to their full height; a bright grey-green lawn would spread out before her. She focused on that sight, that possibility; spring would sweep in from the south and wipe away the blood in the snow.

No matter how hard Jo tried to envision that future, what lay before her, now, was a cold, drab plain: hard ground and chis stalks lying dead, a woven pattern beneath blankets of snow. Allie's hoofs beat against the detritus, hard clops on the frozen ground, and brittle clips over the stalks and snow. There was just enough of Jo's ears uncovered for the wind to whisper to them, giving voice to her fear and doubt.

The land sloped gently as Jo neared the farmstead. She pulled Allie to a halt when she laid eyes on the young boy, sitting against the stock tank. His body remained upright, frozen from the waist down as the water had gushed out of a hole in the tank. A frozen pool of water and blood surrounded him.

Jo dismounted and squatted on the balls of her feet, putting herself face-to-face with the boy. His eyes remained open, wide, rolled back so she could barely make out their color. She couldn't hold back her quivering lip any longer; her mouth trembled, and silent tears slid down her face. Jo put her hand on the boy's cold, stiff shoulder, as if she could still comfort him.

The sound of approaching hoofbeats cut through the silence.

Jo snuffled and hurried back to Allie, her fast pace causing Allie to throw her head up. Jo grabbed her plasrifle, charging the rounds and securing the butt in her shoulder. She walked around Allie and stood ready, the barrel pointed down.

A single rider approached.

Jo groaned and dropped her shoulders, the rifle now at her waist. Dorn pulled his stirrol short of her and didn't even bother dismounting.

"What the hell are you doing?" he said.

"I was about to ask you the same thing," she snapped back.

"After you left the meeting house, Sim sent me after you. Worried you would do something silly."

"I don't need a babysitter." Jo rolled her eyes and turned away from him, returning her plasrifle to the scabbard on the saddle.

"I wasn't sent out here to be your babysitter. I am supposed to bring your ass back home."

"Yeah? Well, tell them you didn't find me." Jo climbed back in the saddle.

Dorn turned his restless stirrol around and faced Jo again. "You say you don't need a babysitter? Well, why don't you prove it."

"What do you mean?" Jo gathered the reins, expecting another sarcastic response.

"We're headed to another farm."

Jo and Dorn rode east in silence. She studied him closely the whole ride, but he never looked back at her. When they reached the farm, Liam's and Gabe's stirrols stood outside one of the houses, tied to posts from the green sloped roof that extended out over a small porch. Only two homes stood together, with a barn next to them about the size of both houses combined—all made of hand-cut and shaped burrey wood.

"Where are the farmers?" Jo said.

"We moved 'em to another village. Based on what we can tell from the places these guys have hit, we're hoping to set up a little surprise for them," Dorn said, a hint of pride and menace in his voice.

They dismounted near the other two stirrols. Jo ran her hand along Allie's long neck, brushing the stirrol's mane and stroking her long ears. Allie nuzzled against Jo's chest; a smile spread across Jo's face, which felt out of place, like she shouldn't experience joy in such a grim, dark reality. She lost the smile almost immediately and took a deep, shaking breath.

Inside, Liam and Gabe had already kindled a fire. Jo could not say no to the invitation of warmth. Her nervous system remained on edge, but she just chalked it up to the fact that she could soon be in a fight for her life. She sat in a hand-made chair, carved from burrey branches, and smaller twigs woven into the back, and removed her coat before setting her plasrifle against the stacked stone that made up the fireplace, and the chimney rising up the wall on the north side of the house.

Firelight played across the angles on Gabe, Liam, and Dorn's faces. The men didn't speak, an unwritten rule between them to remain quiet in anticipation of the upcoming deception. Eventually, the last rays of sunlight threw shadows across the wooden floor and beneath the table in the kitchen behind her. A set of stairs had been built out of the western wall, leading right into an opening in the floor of a second level.

Liam prodded the fire, moving one log that cracked and sparked. Jo could only see one side of his face, haggard and poorly shaven, lit by the flames—the other side dark. Gabe walked around the house, from one room to another, his boots heavy on the wood floors. Either he was trying to work off some anxiety, or just pacing out of boredom. Dorn propped his boots up on a standing log between him and the fireplace, fingers laced over his stomach.

"So what's the plan?" Jo said.

"Same as always," Dorn responded. "We wait."

"And if no one comes?"

"Then we wait some more."

"For how long?" Jo's impatience didn't like the answer. But she needed to know how much time she had until she would have to make the hard choice.

"As long as it takes," Dorn said with a sigh.

Jo could tell he already regretted bringing her along. "Okay, how do you know they're coming here?"

"Because they *haven't* come here, yet."

"Do you, or the marshal, have any idea who these men are? Are they working for Xypha?"

Liam stopped poking at the fire.

"No clue, yet," Dorn said. "Now, if we could get one of them *alive*, then maybe we could get some answers."

"So you're not just going to kill all of them?"

"Why? You eager for a kill?"

Jo closed her mouth and stared into the fire. Was she eager? Was this feeling in her chest a *desire*? She'd never thought of it in that way.

Those words from beyond the grave spoke to her again: *You're not a killer. Not yet, at least.*

Jo wondered if the Thin Man had done more than just read her face that night. She very well could have worn the fear and weakness on her features without even knowing it. But she wondered if he had seen something more. Maybe he had looked into her soul and seen a dark stain. Could his words—the words which had haunted her ever since—have been more than a tactic to keep her unsettled? *You're not a killer. Not yet, at least.*

Were the words haunting her; or was she *chasing* them?

Not yet, at least.

They sent Jo upstairs. She sat by a window looking out over the valley to the west. Her plasrifle lay in her lap as she watched shadows move across the gentle slope and clouds cross the faces of the moons. The snow and frost shimmered blue and purple beneath the moons' pale sight. They left no lights on inside except the fire downstairs. Heat rose up through the hole in the floor but Jo felt only a residual warmth.

She had been given the first watch while the three men slept. One of them snored so loudly Jo wondered if they would be able to catch anyone by surprise at all. The pale valley looked so beautiful beyond the window, cold and silent. She imagined the apartment above the shop, she and Sora talking to one another in their respective beds before falling asleep. Now the apartment was silent, cold, and empty.

Jo wiped a tear from her face with her sleeve. Her heart ached for her sister, somewhere out there beyond the valley. *Was she okay? Was she alive?* Jo had to stop that line of thinking. Sora was more than capable. And as much as Jo didn't want to admit it, that woman—Alix —would never let anyone hurt her.

That name—that woman—sparked a growing fire in the pit of Jo's stomach. So much had been taken from Jo; Alix just stood in a long line of those who had robbed her of something. Her parents, the orchard, the feeling of safety and peace in her own home—her sister. Silas, the Thin Man, and Alix. At the very least she felt grateful to Alix for ridding this world of the other two.

But if she had failed, Sora would never have left, she thought. *If Alix had died that night—*

Jo leaned forward, elbows on her knees, her head in her hands, the plasrifle squeezed between her lap and her belly.

If Alix had died that night, Jo and Sora would be at home together. Who could be killing people across the valley if not men that Silas Purvida held at bay? He deserved to die, of that much Jo was certain, but then Alix had returned and taken Sora from her, and they had disappeared to let the valley bleed.

"A vengeful fire," Jo whispered, recalling other words the Thin Man had said to her that night.

You're not a killer.

Not yet.

Jo rubbed her hands down her face. When she opened her eyes, she saw upon the hill leading to the village, four riders approaching.

Jo slammed the butt of her plasrifle on the floor three times. There came no response, but whoever had been snoring before, was now silent. She started down the stairs, and crouched just to see below the ceiling of the lower level.

The room lay empty.

"Fuck," Jo said to the emptiness.

She jumped back up the stairs, put her shoulder to the wall and watched as the riders came nearer. Her hands trembled, perspiration loosening her grip on the plasrifle. She wiped her hands on her pants and pulled the action to charge the rounds in the magazine. The blue glow at the chamber outshined the moonlight.

Should she fire through the window? Should she move positions? Her mouth went dry. *Where the fuck did Dorn and the others go?*

The riders, clad in dark clothing, blue handkerchiefs over their faces, dismounted their stirrols between the houses and the barn. They remained quiet, and Jo had to move across the upper floor to see them through a window that looked south over the porch roof.

Her heart pounded.

She tried to swallow.

You are not a killer.

Her hands trembled.

The riders knew exactly where to go, and in that moment, Jo understood the score. Dorn, Liam, and Gabe had left her *on purpose*. She pushed aside the thought that men in her own village were complicit in such gruesome violence. Slowly, Jo crouched on one knee and leveled her rifle at the opening in the floor.

Below, the steady *thump tump* of a man's boots signaled the approaching danger. Jo bit her lip, tightening her grip on the forward stock, almost too tight. Her finger curled around the trigger. She closed one eye and stared down the sight.

Thump, tump.

Thump.

Silence overwhelmed her, and Jo feared that her drumming heart could be heard through the floorboards. *Come on, what are you waiting for*, she thought of the man whose footsteps stopped just at the bottom of the stairs. The empty chair at the west-facing window could be clearly seen from the bottom of the stairs. *Either he thinks I went somewhere else, or he knows I'm up here, cornered.*

In her mind's eye, she trained the rifle along the path of the stairs, judging where the man might be standing. She tensed her shoulder, tightened her finger on the trigger, and—

Zmmph zmmph zmmph.

Wood crackled and burned. Blue streaks of hot plasma burst through the floor, up from below. Jo screamed and the flashes of light forced her eyes shut. She almost fell back and wanted to put her hands up to her ears and curl up into a ball.

Zmmph zmmph zmmph.

She squinted, seeing the blue flashes tear through the floor, beds, and chairs. They moved methodically around the room, their aim trying to cover the space where she might be. Luckily, they had not yet reached the corner where she hid.

There was no hope running into the fray. She had to get out of this room, *now*. Jo tried to will herself to stand, but fear gripped her, like hands beneath the floor holding her ankles.

Jo closed her eyes against the bright flashes, turned her head, and squeezed the trigger.

Shnnk shnnk shnnk.

Her rounds were haphazard and her grip on the plasrifle so loose that she couldn't control its kick against her shoulder. But the incoming fire stopped, boots scuffled on the floor, and she'd bought herself a window.

The window!

She jumped up and threw the stock of her rifle into the glass. Once, twice, and the panes shattered out onto the porch roof. The sound alerted the men downstairs, their boots loud as they ran up.

Jo almost rolled out of the window and as she fell onto the roof, she thanked her coat for protecting her from the shards. She gathered herself, took a step, leveled her plasrifle and fired back through the open window.

Shnnk shnnk shnnk.

The streaking light pierced the shadows inside. Jo had no idea if the shots found their mark, but at least they would have sent the men running for cover. She raced across the roof, plasfire following her as the men fanned out of the house. She leapt from the roof, and her boots slammed into the hard ground. Her balance failed; the impact burned up through her feet, her knees, and into her back. The plasrifle left her hands, and Jo crumpled to the ground.

Pure adrenaline outraced the pain that now spread through her body. She dug her fingers into the frozen mud, panic tightening her chest as she kicked her toes against the ground, crawling like wounded prey. The boots on the porch came upon her just as her fingers reached the plasrifle.

She rolled and fired in one motion.

Shnnk shnnk.

One of her shots hit the corner of the house; the other clipped a man in the skull. Wood and blood sprayed into the air, mixed with the steam from the plasma round that ripped into the night sky until fading, like a ship leaving orbit.

The man's body spun and twisted as one hand went up to his head, the other loosing a shot from his plasbolt as his muscles seized. The round hit the mud just past Jo on her right.

More boots on the porch. The men shouted to one another: "Spread out, get around behind her."

Despite the pain, Jo scrambled to her feet and ran in the dark between the houses. She slid and dove behind the second house, crawling, climbing to her feet. Firewood sat against the back of the house, a small roof over the stack. Jo dropped to a knee, putting the stack between her and the corner, and waited.

Shnnk.

As soon as she saw the silhouette emerge around the corner, she fired. The plasma round lit the man's chest only for a second. He never saw her.

Jo's eyes were wide as she jumped to her feet, turned, and ran around the opposite corner of the house—away from the dead man. She stopped at the front of the house, leaning her head just past the wall. Two men still moved, one shouting to their fallen companion she had just killed, as the other entered the second house, looking for her. When he kicked down the door and disappeared inside, she ran toward the barn.

"Over there!" the man outside shouted.

Zmmph zmmph zmmph.

Plasfire cut the air; Jo ducked her head as she ran. The barn doors hung open in the center of the structure, but she sprinted toward the back corner, trying to get behind the wall.

Zmmph.

A force she'd never felt before rammed into the back of her shoulder. It felt like someone had yanked her by the left arm, sending her legs and arms flailing and her body crashing into the ground. She rolled and the plasrifle went flying; this time, she had no hope of reaching it without being completely exposed. Her left arm felt numb, but then searing pain burned through her.

Jo cried and screamed behind clenched teeth. She tried to push herself up, but her left arm couldn't support the weight. She fell again, face down, the mud cold on her cheek. She couldn't get to the rifle, so she crawled and pushed herself up with her right arm; the left hung loose at her side.

There was a door ahead of her on the barn's eastern wall. Jo staggered toward it and leaned against the wall, her shoulder rubbing across the wood, but holding her up. She pulled the door open and shut it behind her, entering a dark room. The place smelled all too familiar: the sweet, dusty scent of chis bales, ammonia, and dung. Jo heard the stamping hoofs and panicked neighing of a stirrol across the barn.

She sat on a bale of dry chis, the stalks poking into her legs. Tears streamed down her face from the pain in her left arm, but she took deep breaths and tried to steady herself.

I'm dead, she thought. There was nowhere to run. She had lost her rifle. Jo threw her head back against the bale behind her, angry at herself. She cried as she thought of Sora. She recalled her sister's face, smooth, ruddy brown, the smile, her curly, dark hair.

I'm sorry, Sora. I'm so sorry.

The barn doors creaked.

Jo held her breath.

Behind her, the hay bales stacked to the ceiling. Jo moved deeper into the step-like stack where bales had been removed. Her foot touched the wooden handle of a hook. She looked down and gripped the handle with her good hand, and sat back against the bales, hidden in deep shadows.

I'm not going to die here.

The door to the room slowly creaked open. Jo held her breath so even the escaping heat wouldn't give her away. A man stepped inside, plasbolt in his left hand. Jo pressed herself as flat as she could, her entire body taut. He focused on the door that she had entered through, creeping toward it before pushing it open and standing in the doorway, looking outside.

Now, or never.

Jo sprang, pulled the hook back across her left shoulder and swung. The man's neck gave soft resistance, and the hook buried deep. He sucked air into his lungs at the shock. Jo pulled the hook down and toward her, tugging the man off-balance. Blood gushed and he choked. He fell onto the dirt floor, unable to speak or cry out for the blood choking him to death. Jo left the hook embedded in his neck and throat and picked up the plasbolt he had dropped.

Mean, desperate eyes stared up at Jo. Her expression wasn't much different. She stared at his face, her brow furrowed, eyes still wet. She snuffled and finally breathed heavily through her mouth as the man's life faded.

Someone whispered in her ear, as if they stood so close she could feel their body, "A killer."

Jo flinched, expecting the Thin Man to be looking over her shoulder. But no one stood behind her. She set her jaw and checked the plasbolt before moving to the doorway and peering across the barn in time to catch the last man exiting a stall. He saw her, plasbolt in-hand, the blue glow illuminating his face. He went to raise his bolt, but she had already sent him back into the stall with two shots to the chest.

Her lip quivered. Jo walked over to the man and stared down at him, ensuring that he was, indeed, dead. She lifted the plasbolt and held it sideways, studying it before she spied the blood on her hand, dropped the bolt, and wiped her hand on her trousers.

A stirrol huffed and stamped at the ground. She peered into the stall next to the dead man, and Allie's head poked out, her gentle, black eyes offering no judgement for what Jo had done. Jo fell to her knees before the stall, her shoulders shaking as she wept. The words haunting her mind morphed like swirling smoke, another whisper in that familiar voice chilling her spine.

"You are a killer."

8

The Exile

Jo dragged her feet. She picked up her plasrifle by the strap, the weight straining what little strength she had left in her fingers. She moved from one dead man to the next, studying their faces. If Dorn and the others had brought her here on purpose, they had to have known these men; or maybe, these men *were* Dorn, Gabe, and Liam. But each body checked turned out to be strange to her. The idea of the three riding back into their village—into *her* village—filled Jo with rage.

Her body felt as if it weighed a ton as she walked back into the barn and up to Allie's stall. She leaned the plasrifle against the wall and let Allie out. The stirrol nuzzled her nose to Jo's face and chest.

Jo burst into tears again.

She couldn't lift her left arm but hugged her right around Allie's neck. There was no way she could lift the saddle onto the stirrol's back with just one hand. She cleared her throat and kissed the air, hoping Allie would lie down. The stirrol dropped on its knees and then its belly, as if knowing what Jo needed in that moment. Jo dragged the saddle over Allie, put her bridle on, and then after Allie stood again, Jo buckled and tightened the billet strap.

Jo returned her plasrifle to the scabbard. There was no chance she could shoot it until her left arm healed. She searched the ground for one of the men's plasbolts, tied a piece of twine through the trigger guard and into a loop, then hung the plasbolt around her neck. A wooden crate allowed her to make the climb into the saddle less painful, but just barely.

She screamed in agony as she pulled herself up. Sweat poured down her face and she gasped for air as a tremor passed through her. Deep, slow breaths calmed her heart. Jo clicked her tongue and Allie trotted out of the barn into the night.

At first light, Jo came upon her village. She rode slumped over because her back burned any time she tried to sit up straight. Allie trotted as gently as possible, but each jostle felt like a lightning bolt to Jo's body. From the higher ground to the northeast, she spotted the bare orchard, stumps and blackened earth dusted with snow. It looked as if some giant had sliced down almost the whole thing in one sweep of his scythe.

Jo could not contain the rage burning in her chest.

Allie slowed to a walk as they reached the houses, the barns, Jo and Sora's shop, and the great meeting house. Jo managed to straighten herself, hold her chin up as she passed by her neighbors. They looked away from their morning chores, the light and joy draining from their faces. They could not speak—could not comprehend what they beheld.

In the morning light, Jo's ragged state became fully apparent. Her hair, once tied neatly into a puff on the crown of her head, now barely remained upright. Curly strands stuck out haphazardly, and even stiff chis straw remained stuck inside. The sweat on her face glistened in the morning sun, and she hadn't yet cleaned the blood from her deep umber skin. When she passed by a villager, their eyes snagged on the back of Jo's light-brown leather coat. The white, ibi wool at the collar and sleeves were stained red and burnt black. Jo could only imagine how badly the back of her shoulder looked.

She remembered that terrible night, again. Men, women, and children had rushed to and from the orchard, their faces blackened by smoke and ash, their hands bloodied from burns and cuts. The horror on their faces then matched those that turned her way, as if she had just emerged through time and space from that exact horrific moment.

People rushed out of the meeting house as word spread that Jo had arrived. It was clear they knew *something* had happened to her, and the sneer in her lip hardened into place, a deadly stare, like a carved image in dark stone. She dismounted by the cistern, using the stone ring as a step stool. The plasbolt around her neck swung and bounced off her chest. Allie, now free of her rider, walked away, as if she sensed the rage and violence that Jo had imagined on the ride back.

Jo wanted nothing more than to plunge her entire body in the cold water beside her, but it would not cool the heat in her chest. Only one solution presented itself as Sim, the elders, and Dorn emerged from the meeting house. Jo lifted the twine over her head and held the plasbolt firmly in her right hand, down at her side.

"Jo!" Sim yelled. Her voice shook with fear and amazement.

"Stop." Jo ordered.

Sim complied, taken aback.

Jo's green eyes scanned the horrified crowd around her. The many faces stared back with pity and fear. Even Dorn tried to hide his duplicity behind ignorance and compassion.

Jo raised the plasbolt at him.

"You son of a bitch," she sneered.

"Jo, listen, you need some medical attention," Sim pleaded.

"Shut up!"

The crowd gasped.

Jo charged the chambers. The growing whine rose above the whispers and soft tears.

"You set me up," she said.

"That's ridiculous!" Dorn scoffed. "We were run out of there. We thought you were dead."

"You left before those men even showed up. Where are Gabe and Liam? Conveniently absent?"

"They went to tell the marshal," Sim said softly.

Jo ignored everyone; her eyes would not move from Dorn. "This whole time, the currclaw was right under our noses. How many of those farmers did you personally slaughter?"

"Jo, this is not like you. Please, put down the weapon," Sim said.

"Stay out of it," Jo hissed. "Why did you bring me into this?" She said to Dorn.

He wouldn't answer—he *couldn't* answer or his subterfuge would be revealed to everyone. Jo needed him to speak. She needed him to confess that he had deliberately set her up to die. *But why?*

"Say something!" she yelled.

"I think you're in shock. You don't know what you're talking about, kid," Dorn said, palms down and out.

"You left me there!" she shook the plasbolt with each word.

Sim approached Jo slowly, with one arm out. "Jo, please think carefully. Put the weapon down. Let's get you help, and then we can talk about what happened."

"Stay away from me."

"Baby, please," Sim's voice cracked, tears welling in her eyes.

Jo could not look at Sim for fear that her resolve would crumble if she saw the look in Sim's eyes. If Jo gave up this chance, she would never get another. Everything would come crashing down. No one would *actually* listen to her. They would treat her like a child—an irrational, scared child.

"Jo, please. You are not a killer. Please put the weapon down."

You are not a killer.

Jo's hand shook. The words landed like a net tossed over her body, dragging her shoulders down. She heard them now in Sim's voice, not *his* voice. They were not a prophecy, or a warning. The words came from Sim as reassurance, as an affirmation.

Sim's outstretched hand trembled, and she stepped forward, almost imperceptibly. A few more nudges forward and she could grab Jo's wrist, or the plasbolt itself. Jo turned her eyes to Sim and saw the gentleness there. Sim's face was soft, her brow furrowed, her expression imploring Jo to listen—to give up.

Whispering over her shoulder, Jo heard his voice, again. "You are not a killer. Not yet, at least."

Jo turned back to Dorn, who remained still; he hoped the gentle words of a motherly figure would pacify Jo. But Jo had no mother. Men had taken her mother from her; they had *killed* her mother. Jo stared at Dorn, her vision clouded; she remembered this same moment, months ago. She'd held the Thin Man in her sights. A squeeze of her finger and it would have ended. *She* could have stamped out the fire then and there.

A vengeful fire, he had said.

The Thin Man had been right. He hadn't been the fire. A vengeful fire *would* spread across the Isidis Valley.

And it burned in Jo's broken heart.

Zmmph.

Dorn looked down at the black, burned hole in his chest. He touched his fingers there for a fleeting moment, then fell to the ground.

Women screamed and children wailed. People ran to Dorn's body for confirmation of the obvious.

Sim stared at Jo in horror. "What have you done?"

Jo looked Sim in the eyes. "What I *should've* done that night."

Sim joined the others around Dorn's body. They stared back at Jo, terror in their faces. Sim drew herself up and crossed her arms. "You are no longer welcome here. Nor your sister. You may get what things you can carry; but then, you must go." She emphasized the final word, a definitive end.

Jo sat halfway on the metal counter. Water ran slowly into the basin below her left hip. She had stripped down to her underclothes, and twisted to get as good a view as she could of her left shoulder. The night before had exacted its toll on her body: pain, cuts, and bruises, and one large burnt gash carved down to the muscle—and the pain, the tremendous, unbearable pain.

The plasbolt round thankfully had not gone straight through her, but had skimmed across the surface, searing through her jacket, clothes, and flesh. Everything burned in its wake, and her skin appeared dry, leathered, and torn. There wasn't much she could do, and despite the pain in every *other* part of her body, when she touched the edge of the burn, she felt nothing.

With her right hand, Jo sifted through the first aid supplies she and Sora kept in the washroom. She held one end of a bandage in her teeth while trying to wrap the rest of it around her shoulder, armpit, and neck. It wasn't well-done, but it was the only solution. Her muscles ached as she pulled her shirt back over her head, trying unsuccessfully to keep it from rubbing against her wounds or straining her arm.

Next, she tied together a makeshift sling and let her left arm hang across her belly. She dressed in fresh trousers and pulled on her coat to cover the shoulder, and stuck her right arm through the sleeve. She stared at her face in the mirror. Bags under her eyes, bruises, blood that she had missed trying to wash off with one hand. She picked up a blood-stained rag and rubbed at the spot just above her eyebrow before putting the rag under the running water and rubbing at the spot again until water dripped over her brow and eye, and ran down her face.

She sighed and tossed the rag on the counter, turned off the water, and left the bare, empty washroom. The rest of the shop sat quiet, empty, despite the litany of belongings spread throughout the large space. She bit her lip to fight off the wave of emotion that washed over her as she stared across the room. A flood of memories ran through her mind, from a little girl annoying her sister as she tried to work, to when Sora had packed her things to leave with Alix.

Jo now realized the numbness resided in more than just her

shoulder.

Months ago...

Jo watched Sora climb the stairs and enter their apartment above the shop. The excited energy in Sora's heart was easy to understand, even as Jo and Alix saw only her silhouette behind the dusty windows. Jo swallowed hard.

"I thought you were dead," she said to Alix, who stood beside her.

"Disappointed?" Alix responded, mixing her playful confidence with the rising cadence of a question.

Jo tore her gaze from Sora and turned to Alix. "It's complicated. I'm glad you killed them, but—"

"But it was my mess to clean up in the first place."

The interruption caught Jo off guard. She hadn't expected Alix to admit to her mistakes. But, at the same time, that blame did not only lie with Alix.

"It wasn't only your fault," Jo said. "I could've stopped him. I was in the orchard that night."

"Jo, you shouldn't blame yourself. You're only a kid."

Jo's eyes narrowed, lips tightening. "A fact that everyone seems to love reminding me of, even him."

"You *spoke* to him?" Alix's eyes widened, surprised, and a little impressed.

"Briefly." She sat on a stool beside a rolling tool rack and rubbed at a callous on her right palm. "I could have just killed him, right then and there. He wasn't even armed."

"As hard as it is, I think you made the right choice."

"How can you say that?" Jo's voice broke as she fought to hold back her tears.

Alix knelt down to get back into Jo's line of sight as the girl firmly stared at her hand, rubbing, rubbing the callous with her left thumb. "Jo, I was younger than you when I first took someone's life. I still have not forgotten it. I wish I could." Alix put her hands on Jo's shoulders. "You deserve better than that."

Jo began to cry. Alix said nothing as Jo's tears dropped onto her palm and she rubbed them into the callous below her fourth and middle finger.

Finally, Alix said, "You would be haunted by the lives you take."

"Instead, I'm just haunted by the one I didn't."

Jo pushed off the stool and past Alix. She wiped her tears away and climbed the stairs to the apartment. Sora sat on her bed, stuffing clothes and other things into a rucksack.

"Sora, please don't leave," Jo said softly.

"We talked about this, Jo." Sora stuffed a rolled shirt into her bag.

"Did we?" Jo remembered a few discussions but she definitely didn't recall Sora declaring she would leave if Alix showed up again.

"Why don't you come with us?"

"Because, this is our home. We have to stay here. Look, you left with her once, and you saw what happened!"

"Don't put that on me," Sora snapped.

"No, but you're fine if I just blame myself."

"That's *not* what I said." Sora stood and slung her bag over her shoulder. "If you don't want to come with me, that's fine. You're safe here. Sim and everyone else will take care of you."

"I need *you* to take care of me," Jo pleaded. "You don't owe her anymore."

"That's not why I'm helping her."

"Then why are you?"

The sisters faced one another. Jo clenched her teeth, the only thing she could do to stop herself from crying even more. As tough as she *wanted* to be, she also *needed* her big sister. She didn't understand why Sora was willing to leave—why she *wanted* to leave. Jo's eyes searched Sora's face, but her sister hung her head and stared down at her boots. She couldn't even look Jo in the eye.

"I want to be with her, Jo."

"But not me?" Jo couldn't hold back.

"Jo," a long breath escaped Sora's lips. She looked up, but still avoided eye contact with her sister. "I'm not *choosing* her over you. You're still my *sister*. I am going to come back. You can always reach me, you know that."

Tumultuous emotions came and went like crashing waves, overwhelming sadness and bitter rage rendering Jo unable to speak. She traced a clear line from Alix arriving in their village to Sora standing in front of her, leaving. She shook her head, pushed Sora out of the way and left the apartment.

* * *

Now...

Jo stood alone in the apartment, contemplating the remnants of her life. What did she need? Which things lying around on the floor and beds were worth having? Sora was not here, her parents were not here, what good then was a pile of clothes, fidgets, and mementos?

She packed necessities only: clothes, hygiene items, food, cooking utensils, and tools. She assembled everything on the table and neatly organized her bag so it would all fit inside as efficiently as possible. She stared into the remaining empty space in the bag, no more than half full. Jo sighed, cinched the drawstring and folded the flap over the top. The bag was lighter than expected.

Allie waited for her outside, drinking from a bucket. When the stirrol lifted its head, water dribbled off its snout and long whiskers. Jo tied her bag to the saddle and only then did she realize she had no idea where to go.

Snow fell gently as she climbed into the saddle, painfully stiff, and rode north into the orchard.

Allie's hoofs crunched the dirt and broken twigs.

On Jo's right, the bare twilight trees stood orderly, if a little bit haggard. Their limbs sagged, small bundles of sticks and leaves were tucked into crooks, and snow lay upon the bare boughs. On Jo's left, the rows were nothing more than grey stumps, snow from previous days and nights piled against them. The wind bit Jo's nose and her shoulder grew ever stiffer as the temperature dropped.

Allie snorted, her lips flapped, and she stamped a front hoof.

"Okay, okay." Jo patted Allie on the neck.

Jo turned Allie north, followed the burn line in the orchard, and then turned eastward through two rows. She quickened the pace, and Allie galloped as if she hoped to outpace the front that laid thick snow upon the valley.

The only place Jo could get out of the snow as quickly as possible was the homestead. When she rode back into the barn, entering through the large open doors this time, the dead bodies sent a shudder down her spine. In addition to the cold hands of the men she had killed only yesterday, the harsh cold air cut through even her thick coat. Each shiver sent an excruciating pang through her left shoulder.

Jo dismounted and let Allie walk into a stall, one without a dead man by the door. She hadn't been able to put the saddle on while Allie stood at her full height, but taking it off had been easier, thanks to gravity. Jo didn't even bother putting the saddle, blanket, or bridle away as she would have at home. She huffed at that word: *home*. The white snow angled sharply in the wind outside and Jo could barely do more than drag her bag at her side as she trudged from the barn to the second house.

This house had no broken upstairs windows, and the upper floor wasn't brittle with plasfire holes. The door creaked ominously. Nothing moved inside except shadows. Jo's boots thumped on the wood floors, but couldn't carry the deep, foreboding sound of a grown adult. The men who had come to kill her had created much deeper *thumps* on the wood: heavier, stronger. But those men now lay facedown in the snow, their boots silenced, while Jo walked across into the main parlor.

A stone fireplace and chimney climbed the north wall. She didn't care much at all for the rest of the room. She was *freezing*, and shivering had become pure agony.

By the time Jo managed to light a fire with the wood and kindling remaining in the stack and a woven basket on the hearth, she had no energy for anything else. The crackling logs and tinder threw tiny sparks into the flue and curls of soft light on the floor at Jo's feet. Her body finally began to warm again, but no matter how much warmth she felt, the prospect of taking her coat off was too painful.

Jo curled up tight on the floor, lying on her right side, her head resting on her bag. She stared at the base of the fire until her lids dropped like stones.

Thump. Thimp. Thump. Thimp.

The footsteps in the house vibrated through the floor and into Jo's chest. She couldn't muster the strength to even roll over. She simply stared into the fire. Her arms clenched tightly across her chest. The footsteps came closer, deliberate in their pace, giving Jo enough time to feel one before the other. Her mind a fog, she reached down to her coat pocket, not with any speed, and the plasbolt caught a snag in the pocket lining before she drew it and let the barrel land with a *clunk* on the floor.

The footsteps began to drag, sliding now on the dusty floor, instead of hitting boot heels to wood. Jo gripped the plasbolt in front of her belly, but even now, with some unnatural cold at her back, she could barely hold her eyes open. Although the fire remained warm and comforting on her face and hands, her legs, buttocks, and back froze as if the winter wind and snow beat against her through an open door. All she could do was let her eyelids close.

"Put that thing away, kid," a voice spoke. It entered the room like a chill breeze, and Jo shuddered at its familiarity. "You ain't going to shoot me."

Jo squeezed tighter on the plasbolt grip. There was no chance she could actually use it effectively. She'd have to roll over, find her target, and even the simplest movements hurt. "I wouldn't bet on it," Jo whispered from memory.

"You would have done it already," the voice replied.

Jo closed her eyes. She knew what came next. She recognized the gravel in that voice; although now it mixed with some breathy component, as if its owner had tired himself out from a previous endeavor.

"Go on and say it," Jo said.

A chair, which she didn't even remember being there, creaked and groaned as the man sat down with a sigh. Perhaps it had been a wheeze, instead. Jo thought she could see his dark boots in her peripheral vision, one ankle resting over the other.

Jo waited for him to say it—the words that had followed her for months in the back of her mind. But he wouldn't speak. A metal lighter clicked and the man inhaled and exhaled as if there was a hole in his chest. She smelled the acrid smoke of the sich leaf burning in his cigarette.

"Say it," she said again, more demanding this time.

"What was it I said?" the voice pondered. "I believe I gave you a warning."

A wet stream ran from the corner of Jo's eye, down her cheek, and toward the floor. The fire's heat evaporated the tear into a wisp of steam.

"A fire burns even in the winter cold. Bitter winds only make it grow stronger," the voice said.

"I should've put you down when I had the chance."

"You keep telling yourself that, but I told you I wasn't the fire." The voice took a long, wheezing drag on the cigarette.

Jo remembered—she was incapable of forgetting. She clenched her eyes tighter, her grip on the plasbolt firmer, her teeth grinding like millstones. Her body lurched with the sob that finally escaped. She gasped and wailed; her heart ached more than her shoulder ever could. The fire could not evaporate the rivers on her face any longer.

Lying on the floor of that house, Jo felt more alone than she ever had in her entire, short life. But she was keenly aware of those who surrounded her: the man lying just off the porch outside, the upper quarter of his face and head ripped apart; the man lying back behind the house, facedown in the snow; the man in the doorway of the barn, a hook protruding from his neck, the wound no longer gushing; the man lying facedown in the straw, a hole burned through his gut.

Of course, greatest of them all, was the man sitting behind her.

He had nipped at her heels for months. His voice had whispered in her ears. His cold hand had reached through her chest. Long fingers had wrapped around her heart and slowed its beating. Her chest burned not from a raging fire, but the deadly bite of temperatures too low for the natural world.

"Say it," Jo gasped between her sobs.

For months she'd tried to fight off those words. She'd pushed them away, burned them, and buried them, but it had always amounted to nothing. Containing the words was like trying to grip smoke in the wind. As much as she *hated* the sound of that voice, of those words, now she lay on the floor *begging* to hear them.

But he would not oblige.

An unbearable, dull pain awoke Jo in the morning. Her eyes flitted open; the black, grey, and brittle wood in the fireplace stared back at her. Not even an ember remained alight. Her right shoulder throbbed almost as much as her left after lying on it all night on the hard floor.

Jo lifted her head off her bag and touched her cheek to find the imprint of the drawstring swirled across her face. Sitting up felt like trying to stack uneven stones. She could barely hold herself up, and the pain in her wounded shoulder hurt more than the day before. She needed a doctor.

The cold morning air hit as soon as her senses caught up with her. The room sat empty and quiet, light streaming in from a window looking to the south, bright and harsh with the fresh snow outside. Memories of the night before seemed more like a dream, but the voice had been so clear, and his presence so thick, she questioned if she had been dreaming at all.

Jo groaned as she pushed herself to her feet. Her boots scraped over the floor and she blocked out the light with one hand, her eyes squinting into small slits. She had no food and the pang in her belly was just one more source of agony she couldn't fix.

More snow had fallen. Jo trudged through the powder toward the barn. Allie's snort plumed out from her stall. The dead man at Jo's feet reminded her that she wasn't out here alone. Their bodies lay inert but Jo felt their presence like a heavy fog, pressing in close to her, trying to steal the breath from her lungs. *Just as he had been last night.*

There was no strength left in her arm, and the most Jo could do was put Allie's bridle over her head and clasp it secure. She'd ridden Allie without a saddle a few times, but never for a long duration. Allie didn't complain, however, as Jo gripped the stirrol's neck and mane and dragged her body onto Allie's back.

Allie walked gently out of the barn, Jo lying forward on the stirrol's long neck. Jo licked her cracked, dry lips, and tried to check her syncpad again, but couldn't muster the strength. There was only one place where Jo could ride. She had to hope that someone in Burreville would take pity on her.

Jo sat up and blinked her eyes, the wind fighting against her, and pointed Allie west. She tried to stay awake as Allie's gentle gait rocked her back and forth, but the bright sun and white snow forced Jo's eyes closed. She lay forward, hugging Allie's neck, her cheek pressed to the stirrol's coarse hair.

Thoughts of Sora passed through Jo's mind like phantom whispers.

9

The Heir

Cole stepped out of his door into the cold, bright morning. He adjusted his white hat as the chill breeze stung his freshly-shaven face. He wore a light brown coat, lined with ibi wool, and the silver pin of the marshal's deputies on his lapel. As he walked down the boardwalk, past compact buildings made of stone and wood, beams of sunlight burst between the structures on his left. Things slowed down in Verisport when the cold hit, but not to a complete halt. Stirrols puffed hot breath as they pulled creaky wagons down the street. Shopkeepers opened their doors, set up fruit stands on the boardwalk, and rubbed their hands together for any warmth they could create. Cole greeted them with a smile, a pleasant nod; to the women, he touched the brim of his hat. The alluring smell of coffee and salted meat pulled him into the cafe where he ate every morning.

"Keeping warm, Hester?" Cole said as he entered the establishment.

A man with more hair on his face than on his head, shirt sleeves rolled up past his elbows, and a greasy apron laughed boisterously. "Morning, Cole!" He brought over a cup and pot of coffee as Cole sat. Hester filled the cup and then asked, "The usual?"

"Thanks," Cole said after his lips had tested the temperature of the coffee.

As Hester left, another man entered the cafe. His dark boots thumped on the floorboards, but Cole noticed the sharper falls of metallic feet, like someone throwing a knife blade into the wood. Fenn Loucks pulled a chair out and sat at Cole's table. Cole looked past

Loucks at the two dark, skeletal figures flanking the open door.

He swallowed.

The Z-16 security drones faced outward so Cole couldn't see their flat, metal faceplates. Their boney fingers held large plasrifles. Cole remembered the carnage at the docks. Pieces of these robotic soldiers had lain everywhere, covered in dirt, oil, and blood from dead men also strewn around them. Looking at them now, Cole marveled how any force could have torn them apart so easily. *Felix*, he said to himself. Loucks flexed the power of the zigs here, but it paled in comparison to the power Cole had seen in the aftermath of Felix's assault. *His rescue of Alix.*

Loucks brought Cole back from his thoughts. "Good morning, Cole."

"Yeah, it was," Cole leaned back in his chair, satisfied by the comeback.

"Now let's not get off on the wrong foot. This isn't a hostile meeting." Loucks waited as a scrawny, pale adolescent poured him a cup of coffee. After the young person scurried away, he continued. "I respect you, Cole. You're an honorable man, and do things carefully, the right way."

"You don't know me." Cole frowned.

"On the contrary, I've observed you for months. You think I haven't noticed the good work you've done?"

"Is this a job interview?"

"As a matter of fact it is," Loucks set his cup down. "Verisport is going to undergo some serious changes before the growing season returns. The council has entrusted the Xypha Corporation to oversee the port, and of course, there's a lot of businesses once owned by Silas that are now under our stewardship."

"What's your point?"

"We'll need a man representing the law who has an eye to the future, instead of looking over his shoulder."

Cole scoffed. "What, you want me to replace the marshal? It'll never happen."

Loucks sipped his coffee. "The marshal won't live forever."

The hairs on Cole's neck stood on end. He tapped his finger on the table. "You better think twice before you threaten him."

"I merely stated a fact of life." Loucks stared directly into Cole's eyes.

Cole stared back, but he couldn't match the cold, hard intensity,

Loucks's jaw of stone, his large hands. The implant over his left ear shimmered. Cole would have picked up his cup if he'd thought he could hold it without his hand shaking. "I know you, Otto, and the council members you've bought are trying to push him aside."

"When an obstacle is in your way, you either go around it, or through it."

"What makes you think I won't be the same obstacle?"

"Because, Cole, you follow orders."

Cole's tapping finger quickened. His heart raced along with the beat. "You're underestimating *him*, and you're underestimating *me*."

"There's chaos in the valley, Cole. Farmers and villagers are getting slaughtered. What has the marshal done about it?" Cole opened his mouth, but Loucks didn't give him the chance to reply. "That *woman* who burned down Silas's saloon, her artie, they've got friends, and they're in the wind. What has the marshal done about it?"

"I'm sure you've got nothing to do with either of those things?"

"Come on. Think, Cole." Loucks put a finger to his temple. "You assume we would need to mysteriously murder villagers? If Xypha wanted the land, we'd just take it. But that's not how we operate."

"Isn't it?"

"And speaking of who is involved in what: tell me how the marshal knows that woman. Hm? I seem to recall he had his shot at her in the valley, and didn't bring her down. I seem to recall that he was seen having a coffee with her not long after she burned Silas's place to the ground. And the ship, which belonged to her, was lifted out of the port by a scrapper, yet its salvage is nowhere to be found in Verisport."

Beads of sweat formed at Cole's hairline. With each point, he realized the version of events he remembered, or the version the marshal had *told him*, didn't match up with Loucks's words. He didn't, and couldn't, trust Loucks, but Cole found it difficult to keep the man from getting under his skin. He tried to unscramble the past few months in his memory, to put the timeline in proper order, to check his recollection with Loucks's claims.

"Look, I know the kind of position you're in," Loucks said, his voice quieter as if he'd given the lash, and now offered a salve. "I once had a mentor, too. And he reached the limits of his effectiveness—we all do. The old man is stretched too thin, you know that. His relationship to that woman clouds his judgment. Whatever the situation may be, it's obvious he can't do what needs to be done."

"Which is?"

"Justice, Cole. The people of Verisport, of the valley, they've seen men, women, and children die, crops burn, and no one has faced justice."

"It's easier said than done."

"That's true." Loucks removed a small datapad from his slipsuit. Without words, he transmitted something to Cole's syncpad, which vibrated under Cole's sleeve as it received the data. "This has come in, and not to the marshal. A village—dead. But more than that, we've tracked a ship called the *Procella* which picked up that woman from Silas's place. It belongs to a pilot who used to work for Silas: a man named Wickford. I've sent you its last known location."

Cole stared at Loucks, anger mixing with disbelief. Loucks stood and adjusted the top of his white slipsuit. The zigs outside twitched, a garbled sound like unintelligible voices emanating from them. Loucks tapped the implant over his ear. He walked slowly toward the door, then paused.

"Do what you think is best, Cole. The valley is counting on you."

A radiant heat traveled from Cole's stomach to his chest; his face flushed. Since he had been 17-years-old, Cole had looked up to the marshal, worked for him, and grown up under his tutelage. To Cole, the marshal cast a shadow one thousand kilometers long. *But long shadows claw into the ground at dusk, attempting to hold on to the last light.*

The marshal sat across from Jesse within a dark-walled room. A heavy metal door clanged shut behind him. Jesse leaned forward, elbows on their knees, as the marshal sat back in a metal chair. He studied their body: large forearms, broad shoulders, calloused and greasy hands. They had obviously worked, *labored*, their entire life. Their clothes were held together by hand stitches on seams poorly repaired many times over. Their hair remained unwashed, tied behind their head, up and out of the way to not be snagged while working.

Jesse had no way of knowing the passage of time; but the marshal knew they had been confined for weeks. The scrapper's eyes sagged and dark circles shadowed their face from lack of sleep. The marshal came in at different times of the day and night, so as to avoid giving Jesse any kind of routine to expect. This time, he had come in the early morning, before Cole had even arrived at the port control tower for the day.

"What do you want?" Jesse said under their breath.

"Let's just talk."

"Yeah, sure." Jesse refused to make eye contact.

"Do you have any family?"

"Do you?"

The marshal huffed a single breathy laugh. "My parents have been dead for years. Old valley stock. Their line goes back to the very beginning."

"How terrific."

"My father was a simple man, a carpenter: rough, calloused hands. He fell at a job, busted his legs, spent the rest of his life wobbling around on crutches."

"And look, you're following in his footsteps. A wobble of your own."

The marshal stretched his leg, the creaking metal of his prosthetic the only sound besides their breathing. He rubbed his hand on his knee where the metal met flesh. "You can insult me all you like. I know that's the only option you have left."

Jesse said nothing this time.

"My mother ran a little diner in town. She worked until she died, and then my father tried to take over the place, but couldn't do it all on his own. I was already deputized by then, so he just sat in the diner every day, drinking coffee and letting other people do the work. He had to sell it to someone else, though, and I guess free food and drink, and a place to sit, was the price. I swear, he sat in that booth until his heart stopped."

"Why didn't *you* take over the diner?"

"I was young, and still wanted to set myself apart."

"And now you regret it?"

"I never stopped working. I was in the valley, and even beyond, all the time. Rarely saw my father after my mother passed. Never started my own family, either. Until I pulled this scrawny, feral boy from a box."

Jesse finally met his eyes.

"That's right. I'm guessing your friend, the mechanic, told you about how Alix and I are connected."

"Look, man, I barely know anything."

"But you knew enough that you recognized the story of how I found her."

"Yeah, Sora told me that much."

"And she didn't tell you that Alix wasn't always a woman."

"What do I care? She is now."

The marshal laughed to himself again as he remembered. "He was a nightmare. This skinny little boy who barely knew how to talk, but was tough as nails. I'd never seen a kid that tough."

"*She*."

The marshal ignored them. "He worked hard, in the docks, all across town. And when he was almost a man, I gave him a set of Plasveld-7s—beautiful pieces. Then, he came to work for me. I never knew what Xypha did to him; he barely knew. His memory was just a fog. It was like a bridge had crumbled behind him as he'd crossed this chasm, and he'd never be able to get back, and couldn't see what was back there anymore."

"So you had a blank slate."

"Hardly. It took years to calm him down. Like working with a wild stirrol."

"You have to *break* a stirrol."

"Is that what you think I did?"

"Isn't it? I mean it doesn't seem like you two have any kind of relationship anymore."

"I did the best I could with him. Gave him a purpose, gave him *targets*. He had this rage inside him. You can either stamp that out with a boot, or turn it in the right direction."

"So what's your point?"

"Xypha showed up, and he ran off to Corto."

"And *she* came back."

The marshal waved his hand. "That was already getting in the way before he left. But yes, ten years on Corto, and I didn't recognize the person who came back. Someone else had gotten their hooks into him. They turned him into something else."

"Instead of what *you* wanted."

"We never see the gentle hands of our parents holding us. You can feel their push, but if you're only looking ahead of you, it's just a shove in the back, instead of hands keeping you from falling on your ass."

Jesse sat back and crossed their arms, leaning against the dark wall behind them. "So you looked too far ahead, and felt guilty about leaving your parents behind. Then, Alix did the same to you. Now you got a grudge?"

"A grudge?" The marshal scoffed. "I've got a killer on the loose. When he came back, there were no more guiding hands, no more structure."

"*She*. There were no more *chains*."

"With Xypha here, now, she'll burn this place to the ground. All she cares about is revenge for what they did to her."

"Seems like they deserve it."

"The more violence she causes, the worse they're going to get. Right now, I'm doing the best I can to keep Xypha on the periphery. But if she continues the path that she set out on when she burned and killed Silas, they will swallow everything."

"Sounds to me like you're fighting the wrong enemy."

"I don't want Alix as an enemy. I'm not going to kill her, either. I can't do that."

"So, what do you want?"

"I need to know where she is. Where you took her and her ship. Because if she wants to be a weapon, that's fine, but—"

"You want her to follow orders—to kill only when you say, only *who* you say."

"Yes."

"I don't know what they did to her. But you want to put her in shackles and call it love. You can't kill her, because then it would just show you what kind of man you really are."

"I'm trying to save this valley."

Jesse shook their head. "You're trying to control it. And you're trying to control *her*."

The marshal turned up his nose, then stood. He unlocked the heavy door with a code on his syncpad before slamming that same door behind him and leaning his back against it. He drew a deep breath. The more Jesse had argued, the more his heart rate had risen. The windowless corridor remained dim, and the marshal checked the time on his syncpad. He hadn't heard from Cole this morning, which was odd. Cole was always punctual, if not early.

Several levels up, the marshal exited a lift into a brighter corridor. The rising sun to the west burst through south-facing windows that looked over Verisport. He opened the door to his office, but found it empty. Hands on his hips, he went back mentally through anything he had said over the past two days to make sure he hadn't forgotten some reason why Cole wouldn't be here. Nothing came to him.

The marshal feared the worst. His thoughts didn't go immediately to Cole dead somewhere, lying on the ground. Instead, he cursed under his breath, grabbed his hat and coat, and headed out. He didn't fear that Cole had gotten himself killed—he feared that Cole had tried fixing things on his own.

* * *

The bodies lay frozen. A harsh wind blew from Cole's left, between the two houses, and through the open barn doors. After dismounting the stirrol, he walked slowly, half expecting the bodies to leap off the ground if he tread too loudly. But he had nothing to fear from dead men, their fingers blackened from frostbite, their milky eyes frozen half rolled up behind their lids.

He crouched by the porch where one man lay with his head tossed back, three-quarters of his skull above his left eye missing. Ice crystals of blood shimmered, the man's black tongue frozen over his airway in the back of his open mouth. Cole caught the sensation to vomit and covered his mouth with his coat sleeve. *Toughen up, Cole.* He stood again. How casually the marshal would have moved through a scene like this—like the Xypha engineers around the rail line in the autumn. More than the wind caused him to shiver beneath his thick coat.

This man was killed almost by luck. The shot came from below, and the plasma round cut up through the man's cheekbone and brain. Not a precise kill, but effective.

Glass cracked and crunched beneath Cole's boot. He looked down, then up to a broken upstairs window in the westernmost house. His boots thumped on the floorboards in the silent home. The ceiling painted a frighteningly loud picture.

They stood in this room and nearly shot the floor out from under someone upstairs. Whoever that was, escaped through the window.

Cole left the house and headed into the barn where more bodies lay strewn: one killed with a hay hook embedded in his neck and shoulder —the other with a straight shot. He studied the dirt and straw, and a saddle lying outside one stall. No other tack was so discarded. A stirrol's hoofs pressed clearly into the dirt, and headed out into the open, curving westward.

Someone lived.

Loucks had made no mention of someone getting out of here alive. It would be the first time there had been any living witnesses since that young boy. Whoever had stayed here had been waiting for an attack. The upstairs room was an easy vantage point to see anyone coming from the west. Besides the lucky hipshot that had torn a man's brain apart, whoever had killed these men hadn't needed help doing it. And only one stirrol had fled the scene westward. Who could've unleashed such carnage in this quiet, peaceful place?

Cole recalled the thread the marshal had begun to unravel months ago when they'd stood among dead Xypha engineers. Alix was the marshal's prime suspect, and ever since, he'd focused on almost nothing but trying to keep her contained.

Cole traced everything from the Xypha men at the train, to the docks, and finally to the Black Barrel where dozens had died by her hands. *The violence certainly reads like her signature,* he thought, afraid to speak out loud to himself. *But the motive seems thin.*

He remembered meeting Alix years ago. The marshal had been surprised, angry, and had spoken of her with disappointment and confusion. Cole had expected to meet a man, but when a woman had come up to him and extended her hand, he'd frozen. There had been no time to square the differences between how the marshal had described Alix to Cole, and how she'd appeared to him at that first meeting.

The marshal had been equally taken aback.

Cole didn't know what to make of their feud, but even in his late teens, he'd known their fences could never be mended. Still, he'd found Alix to be smart, tough, *and incredibly fast.* If she had stayed in the marshal's service, he might have learned from her, but her skill in what brief time they'd had together, had driven him in a way he hadn't quite been aware of then.

Now, he realized the truth.

He had to be the perfect lawman, the perfect deputy, to make up for what the marshal had lost in Alix. There was a hole that she had left behind and which Cole had been desperate to fill. He would learn all he could, steel himself in the face of death—or so he'd believed—he would become faster than she had ever been.

No matter how much Cole tried, though, the marshal remained at arm's length. And as the years had worn on, Cole had become like a dog at the marshal's heels: always behind, always timid, always searching for approval. No matter what, the marshal's eyes remained fixed on Alix. And just when Cole thought he'd finally stepped into the light, Alix had returned. Instead of outshining him, she'd wrapped Cole in her shadow.

The syncpad on Cole's left arm vibrated. He opened the button panel in his coat sleeve and answered the marshal's call.

"Cole! Where the hell are you?"

"In the valley, a few kilometers west."

"Doing what?"

"Another village attack. But someone fought back."

The marshal groaned. "Yes, that's why we organized those groups. Why are *you* there? Who is with you?"

"No one."

"Who was there during the fighting? Underwood?"

"No, none of our men."

"How'd you hear about it?"

Cole fought to get the name out. "Loucks told me."

"God dammit, Cole."

"That's not all," Cole said quickly. "He told me that he has the last known location of the *Procella*—a ship that worked with Silas, and its pilot..."

"Wickford. He's with Alix, now."

"Right."

"What's the location?"

"Alloyn."

"That's where they took her ship," the marshal said, more to himself than to Cole.

"Sir?"

"Nothing. Get your ass back here, *now*." The call ended.

Cole closed the flap and scanned the small village again, the dead bodies, the frozen blood. He heard the marshal's words shouting at him across the silent expanse. Cole mounted his stirrol and looked out over the valley to the west, a pale fog obscuring the frosted chis beneath. Whether it had been Alix, some valley homesteader, or one of the men who had come to this place to kill, they had surely returned west, toward Burreville. The marshal wanted to go to Alloyn, but Loucks could be wrong. His information could be too far behind. A pit opened in his stomach, something drawing him west. Rarely did he listen to his gut when the marshal's voice commanded so much attention. But this time, he clicked his tongue and nudged the stirrol forward, sending it trotting down the hill to the west.

If the person he sought *was* Alix, he knew what he had to do. There was only one way out of that shadow.

The marshal burst into Loucks's office. He paid no attention to the motionless zigs on either side of the door. Loucks simply smiled and leaned back in his chair. In contrast to the marshal's office, Loucks's had no clutter, no personal effects, no coffee rings, no old boots, not a blanket on a couch for long nights. The room could've belonged in a medical facility: white, sterile, shining silver metallic surfaces that, despite the heat coursing through the building, remained cold as ice.

"What the fuck are you doing speaking to Cole like that?" the marshal growled.

"Good morning, marshal."

"Shut up. You gave Cole information. Why?"

"Because he needed it."

"No, *I* needed it." The marshal stuck a finger to his chest. "How long have you known where they took that ship?"

Loucks smiled and interlaced his fingers. "We recovered a lot of data from Silas's compound. Most of it was held on servers underground, where he also had a large hangar for the ship. Records were pretty complete. The *Procella*, piloted by Wickford, and Silas kept tabs on it at all times. It wasn't difficult for our satellites to pinpoint its location based on patterns and flight records from jobs the pilot ran for Silas."

"So, the information could be useless?"

Loucks frowned at the marshal's lack of faith. Without moving, Loucks brought down a display from the ceiling between him and the marshal. With his thoughts, connected to the Xypha systems by the implant over his left ear, Loucks showed the marshal satellite imagery of the *Procella* in Alloyn. The marshal stared at the photos: the ship on the landing pad above town, snow on the rooftops.

"How old is this?"

Loucks shrugged. "A few days ago, I believe."

The marshal looked through the display, Loucks's round, pale face colored green from the projection between them. "I will handle this."

"What about the murders in the valley?" Loucks said.

"What about them?"

"Cole went to see about another village of dead farmers. At least, I believe they were farmers. I am not entirely sure who is dying out there at this point."

"You told him about the ship in Alloyn, though?"

"No. His chief concern is the people of the valley," Loucks said, playing his hand just right. "But it seems *you* have a score to settle. It's personal for you, isn't it?"

"There's more than one killer loose, true, but I only know the name of one right now."

"Is that perhaps why you don't know the name, or names, of the others? You're *too* focused on her, marshal."

"She's my mess to clean up."

"Ah, right. You raised her. Where did you say she was from, again?"

The marshal seethed. "I didn't."

"Right. Well, I hope you catch her before anyone else does."

"I will."

"Do you have what it takes to put her down?"

"If it comes to that."

"Well, stay safe out there."

The marshal gritted his teeth, holding back any further words. He thought less of Loucks than he did of Otto. Both were contemptible men. Otto couldn't bear to step foot on the surface, especially now in the winter cold. His mind was cold and calculating. The marshal hated him, primarily because Otto so clearly held hatred for the valley, the planet—the marshal's home. Loucks, on the other hand, seemed to revel in being on the ground. He could see it on Loucks's face: he embraced what he saw as filth, rolled in the mud, got his hands dirty. Loucks was a man who wasn't above anything, who entertained no illusions. The marshal had seen men like him before, and all of them had wound up dead. *You roll around in the muck long enough, eventually you find the slipsand, and it takes you under.*

The marshal just had to make sure not to be dragged down, too.

10

The Need

Being back in the *Shadow* lifted a weight off Alix's shoulders. Even though the ship *still* couldn't fly—and even though she apparently couldn't go a few days without blacking out, and leaving aside that the brothers of a man she'd killed wanted to return the favor—she was home again. That comfort wrapped around her like a warm blanket, allowing her to finally drop her guard. Unfortunately, she still sensed tension between herself and Sora.

Alix walked through the galley barefoot. The cockpit door was open and she heard the clicks of switches and buttons. Sora sat in the seat usually reserved for Felix. When Alix entered, she stretched her arms between the seats and leaned forward. Sora turned and startled.

"Why are you creeping around here?" Sora gasped.

"I'm not." Alix jumped into her chair and kicked her bare feet up on the instrument panels. "Are you practicing the stuff I showed you?"

"It's taking me a while, but I think I'm getting to know my way around." Sora's eyes drifted across the overhead panels of switches, buttons, wires, and lights.

"You'll be able to fly her in no time!"

Sora scoffed. "I don't think so."

"You pick up on things quickly."

Sora smiled and averted her gaze from Alix. The cockpit fell silent and although Alix sat content in her chair, where she belonged, Sora felt uneasy. She had been working on the proper sequences to operate the ship, like memorizing a complicated design schematic from the

120

scanner back in her and Jo's shop. Then she realized why she felt so tense. The *Shadow* was Alix's home, but Sora's remained in her village with Jo. Her stomach cramped as guilt rushed through her.

"How's your head?" she asked, desperate to break the silence.

"You mean, like, the little army of robots crawling all through my brain?" Alix raised an eyebrow.

Sora rolled her eyes. "Yes, the little army of robots crawling all through your brain. How are *they*?"

Alix shrugged and closed her eyes. "They seem to be making themselves at home."

"So, you're not worried about them?"

"I'll worry when Felix worries."

"So, should that be my standard, too?"

"For what? Worrying about the hyperfluid, or...?"

"Worrying about *you*."

Alix opened her eyes and stared at the dark glass and the metal shield panels outside. If only the darkness wasn't just a result of the protective panels, but actually the infinite expanse. Alix turned her head to the side, leaning on the cushion of the chair. Her blue eyes drew Sora in, and Alix's wish to be off-world quickly vanished.

"You don't have to worry about me," Alix said.

"How am I supposed to do that? You aren't exactly careful."

"Oh, so that's what you're worried about? Not the hyperfluid that could be doing...*something*...to my brain?" Alix's tone became harsh enough that Sora leaned back.

"I'm worried about all of it, Alix. I thought we had a chance to get away from the 'everybody wants to kill me' thing for a while." Sora's voice was heavy, and full of regret.

"Yeah, my bad." Alix forced herself to relax a smidge. "What was I supposed to do? I needed to protect myself."

"Yes, but you don't have to be so—"

"Reckless? I *know* that," she snapped, instantly regretting her tone. Sora was only concerned, but Alix had forgotten that Sora worried more than Felix. What had become commonplace between Alix and Felix had taken years, and plenty of danger, to settle in. They knew one another intimately, could almost predict what each other would do in any situation. Felix remained protective, but he also understood that Alix's recklessness wasn't just that—it was backed up by skill and experience.

Sora, on the other hand, still had to adjust.

I have to adjust, Alix told herself. "I'm sorry." Alix rubbed her face.

Sora nodded and looked at her boots in the chair's stirrups.

Alix drew a ragged breath. She coughed, temper flaring at the limits still apparent in her body. Yes, she had been feeling better; but, whatever the hyperfluid decided to do now, she still didn't have her full confidence back. And it proved Sora right. Alix couldn't operate as she had before. She needed to change, to rein in her confidence. Since they'd dropped the ship outside of Alloyn, since Alix's body had begun feeling better, she'd been overcompensating.

The two women sat beneath the soft, multicolored glow emanating from the instrument panels. Although they could reach out and touch one another, tension ladened with anticipatory words hung between them. Alix kept her eyes on the console and yoke attached to her chair, but every few seconds glanced over at Sora, unsure if she wanted to merely catch Sora's eyes, or hoped Sora would speak again.

Her eyes traced the line of Sora's neck: the taut muscle running up to her dark hairline; the short, fine hairs before the bulk of Sora's curls were tightly pulled toward a bun; the ridge of her collarbone catching the yellow glow; the angle of her jawline; her brown skin.

Alix blew a long breath into her cheeks and out between her softened lips.

"I can feel you looking at me," Sora said.

"You must be mistaken." Alix hastily focused on her console.

"I'm still mad at you."

"Okay, but what if I apologized again?" Sora didn't budge or look up. "I'm sorry?" She hoped her words would gently turn Sora's chin and bring their eyes together.

Instead, Sora shook her head. "You're sorry for what?"

"Snapping at you, getting frustrated." Her voice trailed away. "I don't know."

Now, Sora jerked her head around, the messy bun of curls on her head bouncing like springs. "How about *stealing* plasbolts, trying to get a bunch of guys to come kill you? Nearly getting yourself killed multiple times, actually?"

"Ah..."

Sora softened her voice, no longer fuming, but quiet and fearful. "I didn't come out here with you just to watch you get killed."

Alix studied the dark fibers of her pants and her bare feet in the stirrups of the chair. She pulled her mouth to one side, and pushed a lump down her throat. "Sorry, I just—we were already in danger."

Because of something I did, she didn't add.

"I'm not mad at you for defending yourself, and Mia, from those men. But we should have stayed together, and worked together, instead of you going off on your own. And then you actually *told* those men where you were, so they could come and potentially kill you? What were you thinking? *Were* you thinking?"

"Right. You're right. I'm sorry."

Sora's eyes softened and the lines in her brow faded. Her smile showed the dimples in her cheeks. "I know how strong and defiant you can be, and I don't want to put that fire out. But I'm just asking you to be a little more careful. If we're going to be together, then we have to be *together*."

Alix finally caught Sora's eyes, and her pressed lips lost their tension as her mouth turned upwards on one end. Sora raised an eyebrow, wearing an expression that was playfully defiant.

"Well, since we're *together*," Alix bobbed her head as she drew out the syllables, "then you'll enjoy what I've got planned."

"Is that right?" Sora swiveled the co-pilot's chair as she touched Alix's arm, tracing a finger along her bicep.

Alix pursed her lips, and while her mind most certainly followed Sora's intentions, below those appetizing thoughts lay the truth. Alix had not been referring to Sora's lips, or the way Sora's body felt as she straddled Alix, the pilot's chair accommodating them both by dipping a little lower and squeaking on its old supports.

Sora faced Alix, her eyes following the thin bridge of Alix's nose, and Alix tilted her head back, offering her lips.

Later, the crew gathered around the table in the galley, Wick and Sora seated while Alix and Felix stood. Alix's energy and calculating mind prevented her from being still. She rubbed her hands together as she paced, going over the plan one more time before presenting it to the others. "Okay, I think we're all successfully recovered enough to make a hit back at Xypha."

"We?" Wick said, sticking his neck out.

"*Fine. I* am recovered well enough." Alix rolled her eyes. Then she checked herself: *Am I well enough?*

Her body still endured dull pains and shallow breaths, but she couldn't wait any longer. She had come up with a plan the first time she'd lain eyes on the sonic charges in Alloyn's mine. There were plenty of targets in the valley now that Xypha had been able to settle in

—now that she had *allowed* them to settle in while recovering. That feeling drove her: the guilt that while she had eliminated Silas, it had also created a vacuum, and Xypha had filled his space.

Alix had begun to resent the time it took for her body to recover. Even with the hyperfluid holding it together, her body needed time. But she couldn't stop moving, couldn't stop pushing. *The longer I wait, the worse things will get.*

"Anyway, we're going to hit the train on its way through Burreville," Alix said.

Sora and Wick shared a skeptical look. "We're going to get on the train?" Sora said.

"Felix and I," Alix clarified. She groaned, frustrated at herself as the ideas in her mind couldn't quite translate into words. "Felix and I will board the train. You two are going to remain on the *Procella*, for our exit." Wick and Sora nodded. "The trip west to White Sands is much longer than the one to Verisport, so we'll get on, heading west. Once we're far enough out of town, we'll detach the lead engine so any passengers safely fall behind. But, once we separate them, time is against us."

"What're we looking at for defenses?" Wick said.

Felix spoke up. "The train has no security on board, no zigs or personnel. It's all monitored and controlled remotely from the forward station. It has failsafes, and they would shut things down immediately if we attempt to access the engine, or if we separate the cars. But I can infiltrate the system once we're on board and buy us time."

"We can't tamper with any systems before we board," Alix added. "Felix will hide our actions without completely shutting down the security systems."

"A lot depends on you, big guy," Wick said.

"And a lot will depend on *you* to get us out of there," Felix replied, unamused. "The trick isn't to *disable* the systems, but to *mask* our intrusion."

"Right, so, once we're all set, you two come in and pick us up from the roof hatch, and we remote detonate," Alix said. "We need to make sure the detached cars fall behind enough to not be caught in the explosion. But, we have to be gone before the engine blows."

Wick slapped his thighs. "Sounds easy enough!"

Alix wrinkled her nose and put a hand over her face. "Don't say that."

"What? It sounds like a solid plan!"

"Yes, until we start getting too confident." Sora elbowed Wick in the arm.

"Oh, right, *I'm* the overconfident one."

Alix smirked. "Just get the *Procella* ready to fly."

Wick had left the *Shadow*, and Felix had returned to his and Alix's quarters to gather his things, leaving Sora and Alix in the galley alone. Sora climbed out of the bench seat and circled Alix, looking her up and down. She took Alix's hand, lifted it up in between them, and interlocked their fingers. They stared at one another and a smile stretched across Alix's face—her way of relieving tension, a defensive mechanism meant to disarm. But now, every time she looked into Sora's eyes, the reflex was no longer about wearing a confident facade.

"Sounds like a good plan," Sora said.

"What can I say, I have a good one every now and then," Alix joked.

"Are you feeling okay?"

"I'm fine." *Ish.*

Sora skeptically narrowed her eyes, but let the matter lie. "Come on, I've got something for you."

She led Alix by the hand, their fingers lightly curling to hold on to one another. They made their way through the ship, back into the cargo hold. Sora descended the ladder one rung at a time, but Alix slid down as she always did. Sora approached the workbench and dug into a compartment on the hull. Alix's attention, however, was drawn to the floor where she had once lain, at the brink of death. She remembered that night vividly, much too vividly: the hidden panel beneath the workbench, the pain of the dark fluid coursing into her body.

Sora turned quickly but kept something hidden behind her back as she leaned against the workbench. Alix lifted her eyes almost as quickly as Sora turned, but a flicker of recognition shifted in Sora's eyes as she'd caught where Alix had been staring.

"Since you're about to do something dangerous, I figured you would need these," Sora said, revealing a cloth bundle from behind her.

Alix stepped forward and took the cloth wrap from Sora, cocking her head and raising an eyebrow. She slowly let the cloth unroll and gasped as a pair of goggles tumbled into her hand: dark lenses set within silver rings, themselves within a darkly polished leather strap. Alix turned the goggles over and ran her thumb along the band, feeling the flexible circuit boards and wiring hidden beneath the leather.

"Felix helped me get the specs right—like your old pair."

Alix swallowed hard. In the dark lenses she saw her reflection, but also a brief memory: dancing flames behind her, and at her fingertips. She wiped her eyes and threw her arms around Sora, the new pair of goggles dangling in her left hand.

"Thank you."

"I told you," Sora whispered in Alix's ear. "I fix things."

They pulled apart, but only so far that their lips could touch. Alix kept her arms around Sora's neck; Sora's hands slid down to Alix's hips. They pressed their lips together, and Alix stepped forward, Sora allowing the shift in weight to push her against the workbench.

"We need to talk," Felix said as Alix entered their quarters.

"About what?" Alix said, exhausted.

"I'm concerned about you jumping into this thing with the blackouts."

"Well, we can't really do anything about them, right?"

"No, but..."

Alix stood beside their bunk and put her hand against the smooth, cool surface of Felix's cheek. Currents of electricity passed between him and her hand. She gazed into his blue, crystalline eyes, sparkling like ice catching the morning sun. They didn't dart as a human's would when taking in her facial features, but slowly rolled in their sockets. Those eyes forced a smile to Alix's face: their calm, ever-present glow comforting in dim light. They were like peering through clean, clear water under a bright sun; the gentle life beneath the surface stole her breath.

Felix brought his left hand up, held her hand to his face, and smiled. But the blue of those eyes reminded Alix of the darkness that had overtaken her own in the mirror back in Schelon's cell. She thought about the same happening while on the train—the black fluid filling her eyes, disorienting, blinding. She bit her lip.

"Do you want me to stay on the ship?" she asked.

"Do you want to?"

"I am tired of resting. I am tired of sitting back. We have no idea what's going on back home."

"Home?" Felix smiled.

Alix let out a shaking breath. She pulled back her hand from Felix's face, but let him hold it, still. "Yes, it is our home—Sora's home. And they want to take it from us."

Felix's narrowed his eyes and the crystals spun. "We aren't going to let that happen."

"The fluid is triggering memories, but also things I know aren't memories."

"What do you mean?"

"I saw things before, like, a desert I've never been to, jungles. The desert could be the Cradle, I guess."

"Tell me about the jungle."

Alix chewed her lip as she remembered. "Night time, a tree line, and an explosion in the distance."

"Certainly not one of your memories."

"Right. I've never been to a place that looked like this."

"But I have."

"What?"

Felix hesitated. "It's possible these are *my* memories. I'm not sure. The desert could be the Cradle, but I have never been there. The other could be any number of places. I would have to dig deeper, but at least I know what I am searching for, now."

Alix cupped Felix's face in her hands and closed her eyes as she put her forehead to his. "I trust you. We'll figure this out."

"You need to be careful. You've been lucky so far that these have occurred when you're not already in any danger." Their faces were now so close that Felix's eyes cast a blue glow on Alix's cheeks.

"I know." She kissed him. "But I'm losing my patience."

"I'm not going to let you out of my sight."

"Well, my plan calls for you to stay very close to me," Alix teased.

She turned as if to gather her Plasvelds but remembered that she had no weapons. Her hands paused in mid-air, and she rubbed her fingertips together, trying to shift from one intended action into something else, before laughing nervously. With anyone else she would have explained herself, the itching fingers, the tingling in her palms. Felix already knew. Alix needed weapons. She felt weak without them, and her hands trembled without the Plasvelds to keep them occupied. She paced the room, knocking her knuckles on various surfaces.

Felix could sense there was more she wanted to say, so she didn't have to pass on any further worries or fears. They both smiled, and she said, "I love you."

"I love you, too."

The words from him were soft and low, like the constant hum of electricity just barely audible. But they hit her chest like lightning. Her eyes watered, but Alix put on a tough expression, pulling the tears back to where they belonged.

The *Procella* ejected steam from vents as it settled onto the ground in Burreville. Alix threw on a grey wool coat, the new pair of goggles pushed up on her head, and her hair tied into a pony tail. Sora admired her handiwork, offering an approving nod. Wick emerged from the cockpit and adjusted his hat.

"Alright, we're all settled," he said to no one in particular.

Everyone gathered their gear and prepared to be hit with the cold once Wick opened the ramp. Felix held the strap of his rucksack slung over his left shoulder, filled with the sonic explosives. Wick tapped his syncpad and the ramp on the *Procella's* starboard opened, slowly laying itself down into the frozen mud. A cold wind whipped into the ship and Wick held on to his hat to keep it from flying off. Before Alix could head down, he put his hand out and blocked her. "If we're about to start trouble, you're going to need these."

He held a coiled leather belt out to his side and in front of her. Alix snapped her head to look at him, but Wick kept his eyes forward. She took the belt from him with both hands; the weight felt right, and pins and needles passed into her fingers as she unrolled it and stared at two silver Plasveld-7s in their holsters. The wood grips weren't well-polished, or adorned, as those given to her by the marshal. Alix drew one quickly, snapped it toward Wick, who looked at her and startled, then laughed to relieve the tension.

"You didn't *steal* them, I take it?" she said.

"No, I was told I had to come by them honorably." Wick tipped his hat to Felix.

Alix spun the plasbolt on her finger, catching it firmly in her palm. She hung her right hand down at her hip, feeling the full weight of the weapon before spinning it again back into the holster. Whether it was anxiety about the danger she was preparing to run into or excitement, Alix's heart raced as she buckled the belt around her waist. She drew in a deep breath through her nose, and released it slowly between her lips.

Now, she felt whole.

She looked up and watched Sora. Her eyes had changed. Sora

looked as though a small stream of dark water had put a crack in a dam: doubt and fear washed across her face, where before there had been only love and desire. Alix tried to keep herself in check, a satisfied smile hidden. The feelings of comfort and love for Sora over the new pair of goggles were now washed aside by the weight on her hips, and the power that resided there. Alix's hands twitched with anticipation, and her heart skipped.

She examined the two feelings. How could she reconcile them? Alix knew what lay behind her eyes—a desire for revenge and violence—and she did not want to look Sora in the face. She thought of Sora as the crystal clear water of the Lipine running through the valley, quenching thirst and nurturing everything it touched.

But Alix had been baptized within a dark and bitter stream. She welcomed it, waded into it, and each time she washed blood from her hands, it only made the waters darker, deeper. Alix wondered if she could really have this love—this peace—that she felt for Sora, when what lay in their hearts was so different.

Burreville lay beneath a pale fog. Smoke rose in sinuous trails from stone chimneys. The heat from hundreds of ibi bunched together in pens hovered like spectral images of the animals' white and grey coats, their spirits departing before being led to slaughter. Cole gazed over the town from a rise to the east. In his hand lay the silver crest that he wore proudly at all times—given to him by the marshal. Cole remembered that spring day when the marshal had come to him and delivered the gift. But more than the badge, he recalled the warmth, the embrace, and the promise made to him.

At least, that was the memory he had held on to for many years. But now, he saw things more clearly, and how there had been no deputy while Alix had been away for years on Corto. Only when she returned and refused the position had the marshal decided to hand over her crest to Cole. He had been young and naive and hadn't cared what circumstances had led the marshal to giving him the job.

Had he done so just to get back at her?

Cole sighed and scanned the town, from the pens to the rail line. Somewhere out there, Alix was trying to lie low. A single ship sat outside the livestock pens and slaughterhouses. Cole could not mistake the identity signature of the *Procella*, the ship that belonged to a man named Wickford, who aided Alix in her rampage against Silas.

The badge felt weighty in his palm, not dragging him down, but an anchor holding him in place. It was his greatest pride, and he would have to bury it if he wanted to solve this problem. All efforts had failed thus far. The marshal couldn't bring Alix down, whether by love or fear. Cole saw nothing in her but the knife that had pierced the old man's heart, and the shadow that he could not escape. Though he was alone, and Alix had at least two accomplices at her side, he knew she would not turn down a fair duel.

At last, Cole tucked the badge into the inner pocket of his coat and spurred his stirrol forward.

The afternoon crowd in the Dirty Blonde sought refuge from the cold. A pleasant fire and low music from a lone stobo provided a warm welcome in more ways than one. Many of the establishment's women sat amongst themselves, only half done up because there were no clients to impress. In the corner by the front window, a table carried on a Solar game in relative peace. The drinks had not been flowing for long, and the stakes weren't yet as high as they would be when chisik and a beautiful woman's coaxing would draw more crits from men's pockets.

In a far corner, under the light of an old lamp, Alix sat around a table with Wick, Sora, and Felix. They each held a hand of Solar cards that had been so worn down the colorful art on each card back could hardly be discerned. A pool of crits lay in the center of the table, which they had divvied up between themselves from Wick's profits, much to his annoyance.

Alix leaned back in her chair, holding her cards in one hand, her left arm outstretched around Sora's shoulders. She leaned over and whispered in Sora's ear, and Wick swallowed, eyeing them suspiciously. Felix kept his hands on the table, one lying over the other, his cards beneath both. Wick stared across the table; his face calm, almost expressionless—almost.

Sora counted out a couple of crits and added them to the pool. "Okay, I'm in."

Wick narrowed his eyes and matched her bet. Felix pushed his cards to the middle. Alix smiled and matched Sora's bet as well. Sora proudly turned over her cards to reveal two binary systems, causing Wick's eyebrows to drop as he cocked his head, scowling at Alix. He turned over only a small belt, almost tossing the cards on the table.

"Did I win?!" Sora said gleefully.

Alix leaned forward and turned over her cards, one at a time, for effect. "Not quite."

Wick glanced at Alix's hand, a complete nebula, and groaned.

"I hate you," Wick sighed. "This wasn't fair, you were helping her!"

"Hey, I just told her you were bluffing," Alix said in defense.

"Isn't that convenient. When you had a hand like that."

"She said you do this thing where you check your cards twice before any wagers if you're lying," Sora explained.

"I do not!"

"Yeah, you do," Felix added.

Wick's face turned red and he looked at each of them, pointing a finger from one to the next. "I'm not playing Solar with you three anymore," he huffed.

Alix threw back a shot of chisik, reached across the table and filled Wick's glass with a smirk. He begrudgingly accepted the offering before starting to pack away his crits that they'd used for the friendly game.

A cold wind invaded the bar as the doors opened.

Felix's eyes adjusted to see the man framed by the grey light outside. Alix leaned into Sora, their heads almost touching. While she could not see the man approach, she watched the change in Felix, his eyes turning, sockets narrowing over the blue crystals. She could almost feel the electricity within him change.

"It's Cole," Felix said.

11

The Blood

The footsteps to Alix's left stopped short of the table. Alix didn't even look up; she kept her arm around Sora, whose body tensed as she sat between Alix and where Cole now stood. Using her free hand, Alix poured herself another shot of chisik.

"Cole," she said. "Where's the old man?" She threw back the shot.

"Not here," Cole said sharply.

Alix couldn't keep the smile off her face, but focused on the bottle. "I'm surprised he let you come alone." Alix didn't have to look at Cole to know the barb dug under his skin.

Wick shifted in his chair, one of his hands drifting beneath the table. Alix furrowed her brow at him and just so slightly shook her head.

Cole spoke through gritted teeth. "He thought you were in Alloyn."

"Yeah, we were."

"But when I looked at the frozen bodies, the brutality, I knew your work."

Alix's face twisted. "What are you talking about?"

"You took matters into your own hands. Those men at the farmstead. Shot one's face nearly clean off. Dug a hook into another? Sound familiar?"

"I have no fucking idea. You think I would kill a bunch of farmers?"

"These weren't farmers. I suspect you set a trap for them. Did you think our squads weren't working fast enough?"

Alix sighed. Now she realized just how long she'd been away from the valley, and how little she, or any of them, knew of what had been happening in their absence. "Cole, like I said, we've been in Alloyn. We only *just* got here."

"So, you really don't know?"

"Know what? Just spit it out, already."

"People have been dying here, Alix. Farmers, *children*—murdered."

"So why are you here talking to me?"

"You know why."

"No, I truly don't."

"Fine. You murdered Silas Purvida. You cut down I don't know how many in his employ. You set the Black Barrel ablaze. You killed men at the port. You killed Xypha men in the valley."

"So, you came out here alone to arrest me? There's no law in Burreville, you know that."

"You see silver on my jacket?"

Alix finally turned her head. Cole told the truth: she didn't see the Verisport badge on his coat. Cole's face was dry and touched red by the harsh wind from his ride into town. His right hand stayed on the Plasveld grip. Despite his ready stance, his eyes darted from her, to Felix, and to Wick.

"Just go home, Cole," she said.

"Can't do that."

"Why? Because the marshal gave you an order? Or because you only have one avenue left to seek his approval?"

Cole clenched his teeth, the muscles in his jaw bulging. His nostrils flared as he drew in a deep breath to prepare some kind of reply; but he held the breath, and when he next spoke, his tone was more even.

"I'm not going to start a bloodbath in here. That's more your style."

Alix's eyes narrowed.

"Step outside," he demanded.

She poured another drink. In the time she'd known Cole, he had been an eager, righteous man. He didn't so much as wear the Verisport badge as hide behind it. He wanted the exciting life of lawmen and outlaws—to find himself on the right side, dreaming of being immortalized like Duncan Skye and Henry Keizur. But he'd never had the guts to step out of the marshal's shadow. Alix studied the Solar cards in front of her and resolved to call his bluff.

She threw back a shot of chisik, lifted her arm off Sora's shoulders, and pushed her chair back. Cole startled, almost drawing his Plasveld at the sudden movement. Alix stood and adjusted her coat, making sure Cole saw her own Plasvelds.

"You don't know what you're doing, Cole," she said. "But if you think killing me will fix that broken part of you, try it, and see how it works out."

As Cole strode outside, and before Alix could follow, Sora grabbed her arm. "You don't have to do this."

"She's right," Felix added.

Alix's eyes flicked between them. "Oh, so you're going to start teaming up now?"

Sora pushed away Alix's arm in anger. "We have a plan, remember? This isn't part of it."

"No." Alix looked out into the bright, cold morning. "But he stands in the way, now." She adjusted her collar and stretched her arms. The coat wasn't too tight to restrict her movements.

"Alix," Felix said. "*You* don't have to do this."

"I know."

Felix's eyes spun and narrowed. Cole stood no chance if Felix wanted to intervene. And Felix wouldn't even have to kill him. He could simply disarm Cole, knock him unconscious, break a bone, anything short of taking his life outright. Then, Cole would no longer be a threat to any of them.

"So, why are you doing it?" Sora said.

"He's got something to prove. But just like the old man, he's naive, in over his head. He's bluffing."

"Still, you don't have to call it."

"It might just get him to see right."

"Why does that matter?"

Alix chewed her lip. Cole could be a useful ally if she could pry him away from the marshal's grasp. It hadn't been easy for her to do the same years back. She had been entirely dependent on him, and hadn't been able to see that the dependence had been intentional. The marshal had kept her under his thumb, offered no other way, and she hadn't known better. Cole had taken her place, and put on the same blinders.

She would have to tear them off.

Alix leaned in and kissed Sora. "Don't worry, he can't kill me."

"He can," Felix said. "If his aim is right."

Alix paused, annoyed that Felix had reminded her of the truth, and that her attempt to comfort Sora was just a lie. Finally, she shrugged. "He won't."

Alix stepped out into the cold, keeping her goggles pushed up on her head. She walked slowly into the street, the uneven, frozen ground not an easy surface to manage. Cole stood a few meters from her, his white hat almost as bright as the sun behind thin clouds. A deep breath shook in Alix's chest as she found her spot and dug her boots in to break the hard ground and give her better footing. Her right hand settled on the buckle of her belt, in between both Plasvelds. She relaxed her shoulders, her left arm hanging loosely at her side.

A hot puff of breath escaped her lips between her and Cole. "You don't have to do this."

"I think the marshal already offered you a chance to talk your way out of this. You turned him down."

"He offered me the chance to *obey*. And it's all he'll offer you."

"I don't plan to go on a killing spree."

"No, you're just going to stop at one, right?"

"You've left us no choice."

"Us? Where is he? He didn't send you. What words did he give you before you came out here? How much trust does he have in you? He would never send you after me alone."

"Maybe he did, because he knew I could get the job done." Cole smirked.

"He didn't send you," Alix said. "The moment you step out and prove that you don't need him, he's lost you. So that's why he won't send you out on your own. He isn't afraid you'll fail. He's afraid you'll *succeed*."

"You're wrong."

Alix laughed. "You don't know him like I do."

"How could you know him so well? You ain't been around him for years."

"And you think he's different? No, you *want* to think he's changed. If I tell you about the self-obsessed man who sought to mold me in his image, you'd just shrug and say he isn't like that anymore. Because if you're wrong, then that changes everything you thought you knew about him—about yourself."

"I know you're wrong because you hate him. You have no gratitude for everything he did for you. Why would I trust anything you say, when you paint him with a brush dipped in bad blood?"

"Gratitude? You think I should have gratitude?" Alix's eyes narrowed. "It's control. That's all it is, Cole. Love to him, is control. He pulled me out of a box, gave me a home, gave me food, and all the while, he made sure that I saw the world *his* way, that I believed what *he* wanted me to believe, that I was who *he* said I was. You think I should be grateful that he handed me an identity, instead of letting me choose one for myself? *That* is what Xypha did to me."

Cole peered at her from beneath his hat brim, his nose scrunched, his lip turned up. She could see the fight going on behind those eyes. Alix stared into them, implored them to see the truth. But she hadn't quite pulled away the wool.

"I left him because I *needed* to be myself," she said. "He wouldn't have that. You want to know what he told me?"

"What?" Cole eyed her warily.

"I told him who I was—who I *really* was, and all he cared about was himself. He said, 'Do you know how this is going to look?'" Cold tears stung her eyes. She sniffled to keep her nose from running. "He said, 'What you're doing reflects poorly on me.'"

"Well, what did you expect? You threw everything he gave you back in his face. You told him it wasn't good enough! You have no idea how badly you wounded him."

Alix felt the tears freeze on her face. She looked down at her boots, her right hand still clutching the cold metal buckle. Her left hand now shook—a tremble that passed through her arm straight to her heart.

"Cole, his feelings—his legacy—isn't our responsibility. We have to be our own people. We have to be what *we* want to be, what we feel is right."

"And that's the difference between you and me. I feel that he *is* right."

Alix nodded. In a slow motion, she slid her hand off the belt buckle, tugging the strap through until she had pulled it far enough for the prong to leave its hole. She dropped the belt and the Plasvelds to the ground at her feet.

"Then do what you came here to do. Because I'm telling you right now, I'll die before he takes me back there alive, where Xypha can reach me."

Cole scoffed. "I'm not killing an unarmed m—." He caught his words.

"Don't worry, you're not."

Cole stared at Alix, the bolts on the ground, at the people lining the boardwalk who had gathered to watch a duel. *What is she doing?* There had to be some other play, some advantage he couldn't see. Despite the cold piercing his bones, Cole rubbed his sweaty palms with his fingers. His eyes scanned the town ahead, the people on his left, and he made note of Felix, then the pilot, Wickford, and the woman who had also been with Alix at the table.

Whatever made Alix so resigned to a fate, also held her companions in check. If even they wouldn't step out to defend her as she dropped her plasbolts, then what could possibly be her plan? Could Felix cross the distance between them in time if Cole drew? Wickford leaned against the post, hands clearly in his pockets, no threat that he could draw faster than Cole. The woman stood close to Felix, almost clinging to him. Only she stared with worried eyes.

Cole stared back at that woman, knowing that whatever Alix had planned, she didn't trust her. Felix and Wickford on the other hand, appeared confident, as if the outcome was an inevitability. Frustration grew and his eyes traveled from one person to the next, as if weighing up what to do.

His right hand hovered.

The wind blew from Alix's back.

Cole's eyes watered from the painful sting.

His heart drummed faster. *Faster.*

Cole swallowed.

"Well, come on!" Alix yelled. She took a step toward him, arms held out.

Cole began to step back, but stopped.

Alix continued her slow advance. "You came out here to prove how tough you are—so prove it!"

Cole drew his Plasveld.

Zmmph.

Alix's body spun from the force of the plasma bolt. Her arms instinctively pulled inward toward the wound. She fell facedown.

Sora screamed, along with several women from the Dirty Blonde. Felix held her tight and whispered softly in her ear.

Alix held her breath as the agonizing pain of the plasma bolt dissipated into numbness. But she felt that familiar, yet still strange, pain of the hyperfluid moving, coalescing, forming itself into a black layer that filled the hole that had been burned into her abdomen. She felt the same in her back. She could have broken teeth as she clenched them against the pain. She let out a desperate growl and screamed into the mud.

Then, she slowly pushed herself up.

Alix gasped for air on her hands and knees. She looked down into a small puddle of blood that had managed to gush from her before the *black* blood had cinched any vessels and bound her flesh to heal once again. She eyed the belt lying just within reach, then gripped one Plasveld with her right hand, her fingers weakly pulling it from the holster. Finally, she managed to get her feet under her. She staggered, then turned with the Plasveld barely within in her grasp.

Cole gazed upon Alix as if she had risen from the dead. Mouth agape, he trembled.

Alix's shoulders sagged, her mouth open as she gasped for air. All she could hear was her breath: heavy huffs in her ears and all other sound had turned into a delicate background ringing.

She looked at Cole, her eyelids drooping. Out of her peripheral vision, she saw Sora squirm free of Felix's embrace and step out into the street. But Sora stopped short, clutching her hands at her chest. Alix read the fear and love on her face as her features twisted in dismay, a silent plea for Alix to walk away.

As she watched Sora, Alix tightened her fingers around the Plasveld grip. She remembered its weight. She no longer let her arm hang free. Everything came rushing in. The ringing in her ears grew louder, throbbing along with the beating heart in her chest, blood pumping into her hands and fingers sent them tingling.

Alix snapped her head away from Sora.

"Alix, no!" Sora cried.

But Alix lifted her arm, the whine of the Plasveld in her hand replacing the ringing in her ears. Its chambers spun, glowed. Her eyes narrowed. She set her jaw.

As Alix walked, she let loose one bolt after another.

Zmmph.

Zmmph.

With each step, she fired.

Zmmph.

Zmmph.

At last, she stopped.

Cole's body lay dead at her feet. The Plasveld steamed in her hand. Alix glared down at the body, her mind silent, her vision clear. There was no break in her deep inhale this time. No fit of coughing stopped her from taking in the cold air. Her hand didn't tremble.

Instead, every part of her snapped into place, finally working as it should. And when she turned away from Cole, Alix couldn't look into

Sora's eyes. She strode with the Plasveld at her side. Everyone on the boardwalk stood silent, staring at Alix as if she was a lit fuse, burning short.

One man ran into the street. He slipped and nearly tumbled up to Cole's dead body. Alix stopped walking and watched him. The man checked Cole's corpse.

Alix pointed her Plasveld toward him. "He's dead."

The man stared back at her in terror. "H-How are *you* not dead?"

Alix scoffed. This time she turned to Sora. She tried to control her eyes, to make them soft and gentle, but no matter what she did, she couldn't control her expression, and whatever it held, Sora was terrified of it. She stepped back as Alix approached. Alix reached out her empty hand, but again, Sora recoiled. Alix stared down at her right hand, weighed the Plasveld, and tossed it to the ground.

Another plasbolt's whine broke the silence.

Down the street, Alix saw a girl: one arm in a sling, the other holding a plasbolt level. The girl stood at an angle to Alix, making herself as slim as possible. Her hair puffed out around her face. The steam of her hot breaths rose into the air.

Alix squinted. *Jo.*

Just then, Sora screamed her sister's name. Alix flinched, wincing from the pitch of Sora's primal fear. *Is Sora afraid of losing me, or her sister*? But Alix had no weapons, and so she raised her arms.

"Don't move!" Jo ordered.

The man kneeling above Cole's body came up beside Alix. "Jo, what are you doing? Get inside!"

"Shut up, doc." Jo stared straight into Alix's eyes. "You should be dead."

"Well," Alix shrugged, "I'm not."

"How?"

"Put that bolt down and I'll tell you."

"Nice try." Jo laughed a little.

Alix looked over Jo's injuries and softened her voice. "What happened to you?"

"What do you *think*?"

"Jo, please," Sora said. She walked slowly, her hands out toward her sister. "Please, put that bolt down."

"Stop!" Jo insisted. She didn't look away from Alix. Her hands trembled ever so slightly around her weapon.

"Please, Jo, let me help you," Sora said.

"Like you helped me when you left with her? Like you helped when the orchard burned? Or how about when you left *again*?" Jo screamed.

Sora wept. "You're right, Jo. I should have listened to you. Those things are my fault."

"No, they're not." She motioned with the plasbolt to Alix. "Everything is *her* fault."

Alix still held her hands up by her face. She looked down at the ground, and smiled, wondering how she'd gotten into the same position again—no weapons, and someone *dying* to kill her. "You're right, Jo. This is all my fault."

"Alix, shut up," Sora hissed.

"I came into your life, and your sister's life, and I ruined it. By being there, I put a target on your backs. The orchard wouldn't have burned. And your sister would've stayed at home, with you."

Jo watched Alix take slow steps. But as Jo's eyes watered and burned in the cold, her vision clouded. She saw more than her sister; more than Alix—she saw *him*. Suddenly, everything disappeared into an impenetrable darkness. Everything except the flashing light of the Thin Man's lighter, and then the cigarette, brightening as he took a drag.

"Put that thing away, kid. You ain't going to shoot me," he said.

"I'm going to shoot *her*," Jo seethed at the Thin Man.

"You would've done it already."

Jo closed her eyes and shook her head. When she opened them again, Alix stood still, but he was gone. Jo's heart skipped a beat. She allowed herself to exhale, the breath shaking, weak.

"You think apologizing is going to fix anything?" Jo snapped.

Alix furrowed her brow, confused. She glared at Jo, ten meters between them. "I can't fix things."

"Alix…." Sora trailed out the name.

"You're just trying to save her life!" Jo shouted at her sister.

"Both of you shut up for one fucking second!" Sora said. "It isn't her life that needs saving. Jo this isn't you, baby. I know how strong you are. You've always been so much tougher than me. But, you're not a killer."

You're not a killer.

Jo heard the crunch of boots in the frozen street behind her. The steps moved like someone circled her. She felt a hand on her shoulder. "You're not a killer?" he whispered. "Ha! If they only knew."

"Shut up," Jo said through gritted teeth.

"Who you speaking to, darlin'?"

"*You.*"

"Are you sure about that?" his voice was like a silent breeze, a biting cold that touched Jo's ear and made her jerk a shoulder up to rub the feeling away.

"I could just put out the fire right now," Jo whispered.

"I told you, I'm just the flame."

The voice rang in Jo's head like a clanging bell. Her body felt cold and lifeless, arms heavy, her eyelids barely able to stay open. An agonizing pain grew, pounding behind her eyes, and the Thin Man's voice turned into a ringing in her ears. She closed her eyes and would have covered her ears, but she couldn't lift one arm, and the other still held the plasbolt. So she pressed the weapon against her ear and temple.

"I ain't the fire, kid," he said. "But you could put it out right now."

"A vengeful fire," she whispered.

Jo gritted her teeth, squeezed her eyes tighter. If she could squeeze hard enough, maybe the voice would disappear; maybe the feeling of his hand on her shoulder would evaporate.

But his hand moved from her shoulder, down her back, and through her body. Like icy fingers wrapping around her heart. She shuddered, wept, and finally opened her eyes.

Jo leveled the plasbolt again and squeezed the trigger.

Zmmph.

Everyone outside flinched.

Their hearts leapt into their throats. Some screamed. But as quickly as the shot left the barrel, the sound died. A rush of wind blew through the street. Heads turned, trying to figure out what had just happened.

Sora stood frozen, aside from her hands, which shook uncontrollably.

Alix checked her herself and saw no blood—no trail of steam and blue light. *Had Jo missed?*

But when she looked up, her eyes landed on Felix.

His right hand gripped the barrel of Jo's plasbolt. Steam escaped through his fingers.

His bright blue eyes stared at Jo. They did not glare, or pierce her in anger. They simply saw her.

Jo sobbed.

Felix gently pulled the plasbolt from her hand. He tossed it away, the barrel completely crushed and unusable. The chambers sparked and popped as they spun slower, losing energy.

Jo fell into Felix's arms and he held her close as he dropped to one knee.

"It's okay. I've got you, little sister," he said.

She continued weeping. Sora ran to them. Her hands felt her sister's back, and searched for a way into the embrace. Felix let up and Jo looked at her sister with wet, red eyes. Sora wrapped Jo in her arms.

"I'm so sorry," Sora said as she wept. "I am so, so sorry."

Alix blew a long breath through her lips as she leaned over and picked up the Plasveld on the ground. Then, she retrieved the belt, returned the bolt to its holster and buckled the belt around her waist once more.

The doctor came up to her like a curious creature. "Um, excuse me, miss."

"What?" She snapped her eyes to his and he cowered like a frightened dog.

"May I check your wound? You must be bleed—"

"No."

"What do you mean?"

"I mean, no—you may not check my wound."

"But, you were—"

"Look." Alix turned and grabbed him by the shoulders. "Tell me what happened to that girl."

He looked down the street and adjusted his wire frame glasses. "She, uh, she came into town not long ago. She was wounded pretty badly."

"By who?"

"I don't know, she wouldn't say."

"Which way did she come from?"

"Uh, east, I believe?"

"Verisport?"

"She did not say."

Alix frowned and pushed him away. "She didn't say anything about who hurt her?"

"Cryptic words. She mumbled in her sleep, while on medications."

"What did she say?"

"She mentioned a man, but not by name."

"God damn bastard."

"Is this a dangerous man? Are you looking for him?"

"He was," Alix said. "I killed him."

She felt the wound through her shirt, the soft pliable nature of the hyperfluid that had formed a cellular matrix, like a web to hold her flesh together. It would slowly pull it closer, jumpstart the process of flesh repairing flesh. The wound would close, just as so many had been that night. She remembered his knife, the blade passing between her ribs, stealing her breath.

Alix began to walk away, but the doctor called out to her. "What about this man? You—you seemed to know him. You did not fight back."

"Yeah, I knew him."

"Why did you not fight back?

"I…tried to prove something to him.

"But, still, you killed him?"

"Look, what do you want from me? Yes, I fucking killed him. It's what I do, okay? He was standing in my way, and he showed that he wasn't going to move. So *I* moved him!"

"I, uh, I'm sorry. I didn't mean to—"

Alix groaned. "Here," she gave the doctor a handful of crits from her pocket. "Take him to Verisport."

He looked at the money in his hands. "Why?"

"Take care of his body as best you can. As if he was your own kin. You got that?"

The doctor nodded.

"Take him to the marshal. Marshal Rayburn Skye. No one else."

"What should I tell him?"

Alix sighed. "Tell him *exactly* what happened. The truth."

"How can I do that? I don't know your name. Who shall I say did this?"

"He'll know my name." Alix lifted her chin, a clear signal that he should get lost.

As the doctor scurried off, Wick stepped up beside her. "You alright?" he said.

"Yeah, do I not look it?" she scoffed.

"Just thought I'd check, you know, since they're busy with her."

Alix stared down the street as Felix, Sora, and Jo remained close together. Sora talked, more *at* Jo than *with her*, as Jo remained distant, her eyes still wet, red, and cold. Alix knew that look: the cold stare, the eyes unable to focus, the hard tears that made the muscles in your back ache. It was the look of murder—the first murder—where you took a life and could never bring it back. Alix didn't need to know what had happened to Jo. She saw it plain as day on the girl's face.

Jo had killed someone, and by the looks of it, almost gotten killed herself.

Alix sucked her teeth and remembered. The strange sterility of the cargo hold. The cold air. The smell of his sweat. How she'd had to stuff the dead man's socks into the toes of his boots so they'd fit properly. The blood on her hands and how it wouldn't come off.

It still hadn't come off.

12

The Line

A low hum filled the interior of the *Procella*. Felix knelt facing Jo as she sat holding a bowl of hot soup. The steam and aroma drifted up, and following Felix's instructions, Jo took slow, deep breaths. Sora had draped a blanket over her sister and still held a hand on Jo's back. Alix leaned against the hull, eyes downcast, arms crossed.

Felix's crystal eyes moved in small rotations, his lids slightly closing, then opening again. Jo felt strange, as if she could sense the energy passing through her as Felix stared at her bones and internal organs.

"There's nothing to worry about internally," he said.

Jo nodded, resigned to whatever fate he revealed to her.

Sora exhaled.

"I can patch that wound up better though. It'll heal faster," Felix added.

"No," Jo replied, her voice distant.

"Jo, why don't you—" Sora began.

"I said no."

With her good arm, Jo lifted the bowl to her lips and drank. The warm broth went down salty, pleasant, and reinvigorating. A boiled minlot floated to the surface, and Jo lifted the bowl again and slurped the vegetable down with satisfaction.

"So, what were you all doing in Burreville, anyway?" she said.

"What were you doing there?" Sora said.

Jo felt like her sister had repeated the question a dozen times since she'd embraced Jo in the street. "I needed a doctor." Jo drank again.

"Do you want to tell us what happened to you?" Felix rested his arms across his knee.

Jo swirled the remaining soup in the bowl. Her eyes glazed over. In the back of her mind she heard *his* voice, a whisper: *A vengeful fire is going to spread across this valley.* Jo squeezed her eyes shut.

"No," she said.

Alix glanced up and her eyes met Jo's for a moment. There was something in her gaze—recognition of a shared experience? Alix chewed her lip and looked away before pushing off the metal frame on the inside of the ship's hull and disappearing into the cockpit.

Jo's eyes followed Alix the entire way, until Alix climbed the small metal steps and was out of sight. She took another drink.

"That man she killed out there. I recognized him. The marshal's deputy, right?" Jo said.

"Cole," Felix replied.

"Why'd she kill him?"

Felix dropped his head, shook it, and looked back up at Jo. "He stood in the way."

She set her empty bowl on the table. "That's all it takes, huh?" She shrugged her shoulders out from under Sora's hand and stood, the grey wool blanket also falling from her shoulders. She took a deep breath.

Bad things are coming, the Thin Man whispered.

Jo rubbed her ear as if one of her curls had tickled her. She stared down the galley to the cockpit hatch. "Stood in the way of what?"

"Vengeance," Felix answered.

"A vengeful fire," Jo whispered.

When Alix reached the cockpit, she flopped into the squeaky chair next to Wick, whose hands moved across the control panels. She leaned back as far as the chair would allow and rested her wrists on her head. She caught Wick glancing over with a raised eyebrow.

"You ready for this job?" Alix said.

"I'm always ready."

Alix laughed, quiet. "Okay, hot shot."

"Are *you* ready?" Wick stopped working and leaned forward on the console attached to his chair.

"I'm fine."

"Sure. You just let a man shoot you without fighting back. You got some kind of weird black goop holding your guts together, and you almost got shot by a kid. You're on a real streak."

Alix stared up at the lights and buttons and switches and loose wires. She let her vision go out of focus and imagined the gentle glow and twinkling lights as the stars, the faint lines of wires like the silver rings cutting the sky as she lay in that field.

"There's no going back if we go at the train," she said. "It'll be war."

"There was no going back when you walked up to the Black Barrel all alone."

"I know why you'd think that was the same."

Wick's eyes flashed and he jabbed a finger at Alix. "Hey, I know the stakes here."

"Then why are you sticking around?"

He paused and looked across the dash of his ship—*his ship*—that one thing that Alix knew had mattered more to him than anything or anyone in his entire life. "Because you got my ship back."

"You did that yourself, remember? I didn't kill Silas."

"I got the last shot. But when you smoke out a scrab hole, it ain't hard to hit em when they go running."

"Well, we're not hunting scrab this time."

Wick shook his head. "No, we ain't. Which is why you're going to need all the help you can get." He waited. "Plus, I'm a better pilot."

Alix turned her head and a smile spread across her face. "I've killed men for less."

"Good thing your ship ain't working, then," Wick said. "You can't kill me yet."

Sora picked up the blanket and tried to drape it over Jo's shoulders again. The groan from her sister made Sora's hands pause; Jo stepped away and left Sora clutching the blanket, almost hugging it for comfort, as Jo paced the galley.

"So, what's the plan?" she said.

"What do you mean?" Sora replied.

"You're here for a reason. I'm not naive."

Felix released a sound, a murmur as if his voice traveled from the depths of his body, something like a sigh. "We have a plan of attack."

"You know who has been attacking homesteads?" Jo said, surprised, eager to learn that maybe they were a few steps ahead of her.

Felix's eyes spun down and narrowed. "What attacks?"

"You...you don't know?"

"What's happened?" Sora clutched the blanket even tighter.

Jo fell back into the bench seat around the table. She swung her legs underneath and leaned her one good arm on the cold surface. She picked at a scratch in the metal. "There have been attacks. Several. Entire homesteads, villages murdered."

"Home?" Sora's voice trembled.

Jo shook her head. "Smaller farms, two or three families. You know, places that are easier targets."

"Is that what happened to you?" Felix said.

"Sort of," Jo scoffed. She felt her weakness, gullibility, and shame burn her chest. "The marshal tried to organize some kind of lookout system with our people. They wouldn't let me go with any of the teams, so—"

"You went anyway?" Sora frowned, opened her mouth, then snapped it shut again.

"I thought we were hitting back. But they *left me*." Jo clenched her fist, her hand shaking. Teardrops fell onto the table.

Sora gently wrapped the blanket over Jo's shoulders.

"What happened?" Felix coaxed Jo to continue.

Jo wiped her eyes and nose with her sleeve. "Some men came in, tried to kill me."

"But you escaped?" Sora said.

She squeezed her eyes shut, sending even more tears down her cheeks. "I killed them."

"Oh, honey." Sora pushed her way onto the bench beside Jo and hugged her sister, just like she had every night that Jo had cried herself to sleep after their parents had died.

"I couldn't go home," Jo continued. "So, I came here. The doctor took me in."

Just then, Alix and Wick returned to the galley. "We've got to go," Alix said, before catching sight of Jo and the tears tracking down her face. "What's going on?"

"Nothing," Jo answered quickly. "You said you have to go."

"Jo," Sora said. "You need to rest. You can have a cabin on the ship, right Wick?"

Wick stuttered and uncrossed his arms. "Yeah, sure. Of course."

"What will you do?" Jo said.

Alix heaved a sigh. "We're blowing up the train."

"You're kidding."

"No." Alix glared at Jo, who glared back.

"I want to help."

"Jo, you can't, you're injured," Sora pleaded.

"She just got shot!" Jo pointed up at Alix. "Which, how'd you survive, anyway?"

"We don't have time for that right now," Alix said. "You can help, but on the ship with Wick and your sister. Felix and I are on the ground."

Felix stood. "It's inbound. Twenty minutes."

A crowd gathered on the boardwalk which ran parallel to the silver electromagnetic track. A gable roof provided shelter from the snow. Alix stood with arms crossed, her coat buttoned, and her goggles atop her head. Felix leaned against a support post, watching Alix shift and chew the inside of her mouth.

"You should take it easy with Jo," Felix said.

"She tried to kill me," Alix snapped.

"You know she wasn't really going to."

Alix hung her head. "Did she tell you what happened to her?"

"Yes. It seems people have been raiding farms in the valley. Some of Sora's people tried to fight back, as did Jo."

"And she blames me."

Felix cocked his head. "There were always going to be repercussions."

"It doesn't sound like something Xypha would do. They don't need random bandits to attack farmers."

"Perhaps. But remember, they were relying on Silas to lay groundwork. Maybe now they're working with someone else."

"One problem at a time."

"Well, we're about to *create* another problem."

Alix looked at Felix sideways. "*They* created the problem when they created me."

From the east, a swell of vibration and waves of low, heavy tones drew nearer. Felix pushed off the post and pulled his hat lower to cover his eyes. Alix leaned up, hands on his chest, and kissed him. They parted ways, Felix easily visible above the passengers moving closer to the edge of the platform. He adjusted the strap on his shoulder. Alix stretched her fingers as she watched him leave. Then, she put her hands in her coat pockets and waited.

Felix went to work. As soon as the train pulled closer to the station, the sound waves slowing down, the wind catching up in its wake, Felix infiltrated Xypha's computer systems. People bustled around him, unaware that as he stood, hat pulled low, one hand on the shoulder strap of his bag, he was setting up the train's destruction.

He broke through the security systems with ease. The train connected via satellite to the forward station in orbit. Felix brought down Xypha's security, but instantaneously put up a facade—a looping code that kept any intrusion invisible to the operators in the station. He found every sensor, camera, and microphone within the passenger cars and took control of them without detection. In seconds, he knew everything about the train, down to the most delicate circuits and the smallest bolt.

"You're good," he said, casting his voice through the comms channels that fed into Alix's ears from her new goggles. "I've got everything local."

Felix entered the second passenger car. He ducked to enter and kept his head low. Everyone gave him a second look as he found a seat, gawking at his size, and the gentleness with which he carried himself. The physical movements of his body operated almost on autopilot from an easy separation of tasks in his mind. Mentally, he remained focused on his job, and before he sat, he placed himself discreetly within the satellite that relayed signals between the train and the forward station.

His intrusion remained undetected.

Felix's voice sounded in Alix's ears, giving her the all-clear to board. A little girl beside her held on to her mother's hand, but stared at Alix, the girl's wide, green eyes pulling Alix out of the moment. She looked down, shuffled uncomfortably, but then smiled. The little girl's open mouth also turned into a smile, with a few missing teeth.

"Copy," she said finally to Felix.

Alix winked at the little girl, whose curiosity kept her looking back as her mother pulled her onto the train. A few others pushed past Alix to board, but finally Alix stepped forward and crossed the small empty space between the boardwalk and the train car. She didn't stand out at all among the passengers finding their seats. Hands still in her coat pockets, she gently moved through the aisle, turned sideways to squeeze between two men waiting to sit, and finally settled on the hard bench at the rear of the car.

"Wick, you in the air?" she said.

"Powering up," he confirmed.

Alix scooched to the outside of the bench to prevent anyone else from trying to sit with her. A few minutes passed and the doors closed, hissed, and the vibrations in the floor grew more intense. The train shook and began to move. As its speed increased, Alix put her boot on the back of the bench in front of her. The cold, grey valley outside the windows turned into a haze of blurred images when the train reached full speed.

Pain throbbed and Alix felt the tender wound and soft mesh created by the hyperfluid beneath her left breast. She winced as she put pressure on the wound; at least she wasn't losing any blood. With her thumb and forefinger of each hand, she stretched her goggles and brought them down over her eyes. The dark lenses lit up and cycled through various wavelengths before Alix tapped the side of the left lens. Her view of the train car changed into a cold blue that could see everything: through the bench seats and even the bodies of the passengers. She tapped again and saw the heat signature of each person inside the car.

Finally, she settled on a natural view, no advantages for her, but one that simply dimmed the lights and turned the lenses' outward appearance completely black. She took a deep breath and stood. Her boots thumped on the metal aisle as she walked with a slow, deliberate pace. She drew one Plasveld and spun the chambers. Halfway down the car, she drew the other, her goggles keeping the bright blue glow dim to her sight. She reached the front of the car, both Plasvelds up, before she turned, and smiled.

"Everybody remain calm."

Fear and anxiety washed over the passengers, written plainly on their expressions. They looked around at one another, at Alix, wide-eyed and clutching their belongings. Alix found the little girl she had seen on the platform. The child buried her face into her mom's arm. Alix's lip twitched, but she swept the guilt aside.

"Nobody is going to get hurt, and I am not here to take anything from you." To emphasize the point, she spun the Plasveld in her left hand back into its holster, the glow and whining of the charge dying down. "But don't try anything, okay?" Some of the passengers nodded. "Now, if you would kindly move to the next car."

The door at the back of the train car hissed open. A man and woman jumped to their feet to head through, but stopped suddenly. Felix emerged, his body bent over, squeezing himself through the small door. The man leaned away, and as Felix's full height unfolded before him, the man reached his arm out to protect his wife.

"As she said," Felix spoke. "Nobody is going to hurt you." He stepped aside and motioned with his head for the couple to go through.

The people scurried from their seats into the aisle, their bodies pressed together in a panic, jostling one another as the scent of sweat filled the air. Alix remained at the front of the car, but she holstered her other Plasveld once everyone had their backs to her—everyone except the girl, crying, arms around her mother's neck as she was carried away.

Alix would have smiled, but her appearance—the large, round goggle lenses hiding her eyes—surely counteracted any comfort that a smile could give. The door hissed and closed behind the mother and her daughter, leaving Felix and Alix alone. Felix didn't have to explain that he controlled the locks and seals between the cars, but he confirmed it anyway as a transition to the next step of the plan.

"Doors are sealed," he said as he walked toward Alix. "I can only get to the engine from the outside."

"I've got the connectors to release the other cars."

They met in the middle of the car. The double doors beside them opened at Felix's silent command. Alix bit her lip, a satisfied smile breaking through. She would have jumped Felix then and there if time weren't of the essence. His deep blue eyes spun and looked down at her; she knew he could see her eyes through her goggles. The wind rushed inside and between them.

"You be careful," she said.

"Yes ma'am." He tipped his hat.

Alix spun a Plasveld in her right hand. The door between cars hissed and opened. She moved her hand horizontally and spun the Plasveld beneath it, then again vertically before landing it in the holster. With a tap on the side of the goggles, her vision changed into a schematic of the connectors. Felix controlled everything on the train, but the connectors still needed to be physically disconnected for a final failsafe.

The cold wind pushed her around, but Alix gripped the edge of the metal step with both hands and hung her head to look below the cars. Shivers ran up her neck, either from the wind reaching into her collar and chilling her back, or the anxiety of being at risk of falling. The handle she needed to pull required her to lie down flat on the step. Alix pressed her cheek into the cold steel and reached beneath the step as far as she could stretch her arm. Her fingers lightly touched the handle but she couldn't wrap them around.

"Fuck." She gave her straining shoulder a rest and rolled over onto her back.

Looking up, she noticed faces in the window of the other passenger door staring at her. The people inside couldn't escape the car, but their watching eyes still annoyed her.

She took a deep breath and rolled over again. This time she rolled half her body off the step, holding on to dear life with her left hand and clinging to the top and bottom of the step with her boots. She clenched her feet and thighs to hold herself in place. The train's electromagnetic field made her hair stand and spread erratically. She stuck her tongue out and grabbed the handle, pulled, and twisted. A green light beside the handle switched off and the red light below it switched on.

Alix let go of the breath she'd been holding.

She swung herself back up and on her back. The faces looking through the window at her wore stunned, wide-eyed expressions. Alix held up a thumb and laughed in between heavy breaths, as if the passengers were part of the team.

Felix entered the empty driver's cabin. Where a curving windshield would've been if a human had been sitting inside operating the train, a black screen reflected his eyes and bright face. The instrument panels blinked with an array of lights, a cushioned chair sat empty in front of him. The metal spheres rattled as Felix dropped the bag off his shoulder.

The number of tasks he monitored in the depths of his mind ranged from the train, the satellite relay, the comms channels, the location of the *Procella*, the door locks, to Alix's progress. Everything remained compartmentalized, but easily accessible if necessary. He could focus on any one at any time while maintaining each other in perfect order. He spun his eyes closed as he heard, felt, and thought of Alix's heart rate—a little escalated, but that wasn't abnormal. Felix smiled.

He removed a panel on the wall to his right. Inside lay a series of wires, cables, hoses, and circuitry. The sonic explosives were no bigger than his palm, though his hands were significantly larger than any human's. He set the charge and pushed it snugly into the midst of the wires and cables inside the wall. Then, Felix repeated the same to his left. It was overkill to plant so many, but, he shrugged, *why not?* They were sending a message, after all.

The next panel to remove fell onto the floor beneath the dash. Felix stuffed another charge into the space. Finally, he grabbed the bag and set it back onto his shoulder. With his superior sight, he scanned the floor and found a good spot for one more charge. He peeled the floor panel off with his bare hands and placed another charge, then checked the bag and found that two charges remained.

"Felix, how you doing?" Alix asked over comms.

"Just wrapping up."

"Wick? Time to get over here," Alix said after Felix confirmed his tasks were complete.

"Alright, heading your way," Wick replied.

"Sora, you've got the winch line, yeah?" Alix checked.

"Of course," Sora said.

"Alright, Felix and I will be up top shortly."

Alix returned her focus to the clamps physically holding the passenger cars together. She pulled a large metal pin from one side, and tossed it onto the floor of the car behind her. As she pulled the second out of place, she spared a final glance for the passengers staring at her through the window. She dropped the pin and gave them one last thumb's up.

The cars drifted apart. The faces in the window grew further away and blurred as Alix held on to the door frame behind her. She watched them fall further behind as the momentum in the rear cars failed to keep up with the engine propelling Alix and Felix west across the valley. She turned to see Felix back in the empty passenger car.

"All set?" she smiled.

Felix gave her a thumb's up and winked. She narrowed her eyes, wondering if he really did know about her signals to the passengers, or was just being a little sarcastic.

The *Procella* broke through grey clouds and approached from the east, soaring over the remaining train cars that had fallen behind. Felix watched them, probably calculating their distance to make sure they were indeed safely behind. The ship drew closer and Wick deftly matched its speed with the train while decreasing his altitude little by little. The side hatch on the ship opened and Alix waited to see Sora's face; instead, it was Jo who waved at them.

Jo pushed the lever down to release the line, the winch motor grinding as the thick cable waved in the wind. The longer it became, the further forward Wick needed to position the *Procella*. Jo yelled at Sora, who relayed the messages to Wick to accelerate only slightly with each meter the cable fell. Luckily, Felix could reach it much sooner than if Alix had been alone. Felix gripped the metal clip at the end of the cable and pulled it against the force of the wind with ease.

He attached the clip to Alix's belt and gave her a nod, then held on to her as the winch wound the cable back. Alix slowly ascended, and as soon as Felix let her go, she gripped the cable tight and felt the full force of the wind. The ground below raced by as the wind roared in her ears, blocking out all other noise. Her body waved like a broken panicle of chis grass about to snap and fly across the valley.

As the cable wound closer to the ship, Alix whipped up and slammed into the *Procella*'s hull. She held on to the cable with both hands, palms burning, trying to steady herself with her boots to the hull. The winch pulled her around from beneath the ship and she hung just a short distance from the side hatch. Sora finally appeared, her hand outstretched to try and catch Alix, as if she could pull Alix into the ship on her own.

Alix made herself as small as possible to avoid breaking bones, or her neck. But as she judged the distance to the ship, she reached up, not quite close enough to grab the hatch frame, or Sora's hand. She could not speak to either Sora or Jo over the sound of the wind, and her goggles concealed her eyes from them.

She reached for Sora again, their fingers and hands frantically trying to interlock, but failing. Alix refreshed her grip on the cable with her other hand, and as she looked up again, she saw Jo's hand wandering toward and then gripping the lever. Jo stared right into Alix's dark lenses as she released the cable.

Alix sighed and closed her eyes, though neither Jo nor Sora could see them.

The sudden loss of tension in the line sent Alix plummeting and the piercing scream from Sora reached Alix's ears despite the wind.

Alix opened her eyes and saw the *Procella* racing away from her.

"Alix!" Sora screamed at the top of her lungs.

The cable ripped through the winch, free of all constraints. Smoke rose from the friction of the long cord unwinding at a frightening pace. Sora panicked. Jo imitated her sister.

"I don't know what happened!" she said.

Sora tried to pull the lever to lock the cable again, but her strength failed against the power of the wind ripping Alix away from her. Jo fell back, holding herself up with her one good arm. Wick screamed from the cockpit.

Jo watched her sister put all her strength into pulling the lever on the winch. Tears streaming down Sora's face, she gritted her teeth, then screamed as she pulled. Her screams succumbed to sobs as the cable approached its end. Jo crawled back toward the hatch, hands shaking as she looked down.

Felix reacted to the sudden slack in the cable almost instantly. He watched Alix flail, gripping the cable with both hands as the wind ripped her from the ship. He bolted into the passenger car, mentally opened the side doors along the way, and gripped the outside of the car. Just as he had reached the engine before, he pulled himself out to the side of the car and shimmied along the length until he reached the engine hatch. It opened at his command, but instead of going inside, he put his boots onto the edge and transferred his hands to grip the hatch frame.

The remote tasks and safety concerns in his subconscious disappeared as he focused on calculating how long Alix had until the cable ripped from the winch and left her in the wind to die. He had one chance and calculated his strength and speed against that of the train and the force of the wind. He glanced back over his shoulder, his hat disappearing from his head as the wind finally caught the brim.

Felix gripped the hatch frame, held himself at arm's length for a moment, and finally put all his weight and power into his feet.

He jumped.

The metal frame crumpled under the force.

Felix's power was enough to propel himself up and forward toward the nose of the train, and he flew meters above the engine. He reached the peak of that momentum and finally the wind reclaimed the upper hand.

Now, Felix flew back, but reached up as he did so, and anchored one hand onto the *Procella*. His fingers crimped steel as he brought his other hand up to the cable.

Jo stared, her eyes nearly bulging from their sockets. She fell back as Felix pulled himself up, tearing into the steel of the floor to keep his grip. His eyes spun as he entered the ship. At last, he braced himself and tightened his grip on the cable. It stopped running through the winch as the smoke flew out into the wind; and, one hand over the other, Felix pulled the cable.

Sora only stopped sobbing to watch Felix's strength at work. The hatch frame groaned and seemed to bow as he held himself with feet planted against one side of the frame, and his back to the other. Sora crawled wildly toward him and began gathering the cable length that he pulled back onto the ship to keep it out of the way.

After a few moments, instead of pulling a length of cable, Felix gripped Alix's hand. Then she grabbed his fingers with her other hand and Felix wrenched her into the ship, almost tossing her to the floor. In the same motion, he rolled out of the hatchway and put his back to the bulkhead before dropping all connection to the train and instead commanding the *Procella*'s side hatch to close.

The roar of the wind vanished. Heavy sobs and gasping breath replaced it within the galley. Felix sat with his arms on his knees, head tipped back against the bulkhead. His gaze pierced Jo.

Alix ripped her goggles off and fell onto her hands. She threw her head back and screamed. "Wick! Get us out of here!"

"Right!" Wick shouted back. The *Procella* shifted and nosed up. Wick accelerated and everyone in the galley braced themselves to avoid sliding across the floor.

Alix winced as the pain came rushing in. She studied her hands, which were rubbed raw. She felt like she'd gone the distance back in Spiros's fighting pit with someone *actually* better than her. Through heavy breaths, Alix smiled at Sora; but Sora didn't smile back, too focused on trying to steady her breathing.

She observed Felix, his eyes locked on Jo, whose eyes avoided everyone else. Alix breathed heavily, then slowed down, with measured breaths in and out in a long, steady rhythm.

Felix finally turned to Alix. "You alright?"

"Other than feeling like I got my ass kicked, yeah," Alix replied with a laugh.

Sora knelt by the winch. "What the hell happened?"

"The motor gave out," Felix said. "Right?" His eyes spun as he looked over to Jo.

She finally looked up at him, then at Alix, who stared back knowingly. Jo replied, "Yeah."

Within the ship, no one could witness the four spheres explode. Each emitted a growing tone, building to a painful frequency that rattled the engine. The shockwaves reverberated through the cabin, into the engine, through every duct and coil until metal shook itself apart. Sparks ignited flames and broken containment fields rendered the engine cores unstable.

The electromagnetic field suspending the train above the track dissipated, the engine dropped, slid and dug up the track and concrete. At last, as the engine ripped to shreds and scattered debris, the power cores burst, incinerating, melting, and irradiating every fragment. A great blue bubble of crackling energy spread in every direction, cracking and uplifting the concrete, rending twisted metal, igniting the dry chis, and carving a great crater into the ground. When it reached its apex, the whole field of energy collapsed in on itself, again. Every nut, bolt, wire, plastic, stone, and omniite fragment sucked into the vortex and buried itself into a singularity that smoked and steamed at the center of the dark hole.

A sonic boom raced across the valley in all directions.

13

The Truth

A flock of ibi panicked inside their pen. Wind tore across the land as the *Procella* swung low, banking to give Wick a survey of his brother's farm. The settlement below remained: the house, the barn, the well, the pens. But surrounding the house, an angry, black scar stretched out in all directions. Then, Wick noticed that while the footprint of the house was the same, the materials, the colors, and the roof were different.

Wick jerked the controls and nearly threw everyone in the ship out of their seats. Alix, who sat in the chair beside Wick, gripped the arms as he pulled the ship's stern around and descended. The landing gear barely reached their proper position before touching the ground. The entire ship jostled as it settled, rocking side to side, but Wick didn't wait for it to settle before unbuckling as he spun his chair around and jumped down the steps and out of the cockpit.

"Wick!" she yelled.

The port hatch hissed, the air seals opened and the cold rushed in. Wick drew a plasbolt, spun the chambers, and waited for the ramp to lower enough for him to exit the ship.

Alix grabbed his arm. "Wait. We don't know what we're getting into, here."

"*Something* is wrong," Wick said, low and angry.

"There are individuals in the house, and outside," Felix said, no doubt scanning the area as far as he could.

"It could be Wesley, Anna. Maybe they're not in danger. Let's not —"

Wick shook Alix off him and trodded down the ramp. Alix and Felix shared a concerned look, but as before every fight, they formulated a silent plan to protect one another no matter what. Alix drew one of her Plasvelds and spun it on her finger. As Wick ran down the ramp, the whine of the charged weapons went with him and the galley fell silent. Felix and Alix followed.

The farm remained laid out correctly, but as Wick raced past the pens and to the house, he noticed the boarded up walls, the blackened stone, piles of ash and charred wood dusted with snow. The whirr of the *Procella* landing brought a man out of the house, and he waited to greet Wick near the main door. When he saw Wick carrying a plasbolt, he threw his hands up in fear.

"Whoa! There's nothing of value here," he shouted.

"Who the fuck are you?" Wick demanded. "Where's my brother?"

The elderly man shrunk, his face worn, wrinkled, and dry. He wore a hat probably as old as Wick, and a dark blue jumpsuit beneath a heavy coat. Wick glared into his dark eyes, but there was no malice in return.

"I'm sorry—I don't know your brother," he stammered.

"You're on his farm." Wick held his plasbolt level at his hip.

The old man's face and shoulders sagged. He no longer stared at Wick, but looked over to his left, past the barn. "I'm sorry," he said softly. "They were your kin?"

"What did you do to them?" Wick extended his arm, the plasbolt level with his shoulder, the chambers bright against the grey gloom.

"We didn't harm them," the old man said. "We—we buried what was left."

"He's telling the truth," Felix said as he came to stand beside Wick.

Wick's hand trembled, and the plasbolt with it. His face tensed with each wave of pain; his eyes narrowed, the comprehension settling in; his ears burned, his heart pounded. Wick twisted his mouth and stuck his tongue in his cheek to hold himself together.

"You...just found them?" His hand drifted downward, unable to hold the weight of the plasbolt.

"I'm sorry, son. The place was burnt out." The old man still held his hands up.

"Show me where they are." Wick holstered his plasbolt. His heart sank.

Wrapped in the same blanket as before, Jo entered the galley from the cabin where she and Sora had retreated after the job. She stood in the hatchway, taking in the farm, which she had never seen before, but the scene appeared all too familiar. The house had clearly burned almost to its foundations. The stone had been blackened, charred wood piled beside it from someone's efforts to clean things up. The roof was only partially repaired, and much of the house remained open to the cold and snow.

"A vengeful fire," she whispered.

I told you, I ain't the fire kid. Just the flame, he whispered in her ear.

"Shut up." Jo snapped. She raised her shoulder and brushed the tickling voice from her ear.

"I didn't say anything," Sora said.

Jo spun around to face her sister. "Sorry, just talking to myself. Where are we?" She clutched the blanket tighter at her neck.

Sora leaned on the other side of the open hatch. "Wick said this was his brother's farm. They came here when Alix was wounded, before we met them."

"I remember." Jo turned away from the hatch and wandered back through the galley.

When they'd first met Alix and Felix, she'd warned Sora not to trust them, not to bring them to their home.

Look what happened.

Even now, reunited with Sora, Jo felt distance between them. Every moment the divide widened. Despite Sora embracing her in Burreville, holding her, trying to comfort her in the *Procella*, Jo remained stiff and uneasy—she had just let it happen to her. The reunion was nothing like she wanted, like she hoped it would be. Despite being in the ship together, it wasn't *home*, and Jo felt ever alone.

"The motor didn't fail, did it?" Sora's voice froze Jo in her tracks.

Jo kept her back to her sister. If she turned around, maybe she would collapse back into that role: a helpless child. She couldn't show her face; if Jo looked at Sora, she would face the reminder that killing Alix would cause irreparable collateral damage. *Perhaps the damage has already been done*, Jo thought. Her unsteady breathing required her to wait before answering.

"No, it didn't."

Sora sounded like she was about to cry. "Why are you doing this?"

"Are you kidding?" Jo scoffed as she turned and faced her sister, and the fear of breaking. "I told you—I *warned* you that day. Look at everything that's happened since then!"

"You're blaming her?"

"Yes—why *aren't* you!?"

"Because these things aren't her fault. She did what she had to do—she was *right*."

"You're just in love with her." Jo spit the words like an accusation. "And you can't see the truth because of it."

Sora blinked rapidly. "You're accusing me of being blinded—by love? As opposed to what, anger?"

That woman your sister is with set it off, he whispered to Jo.

Jo's nostrils flared, and she lifted her chin defiantly. "She started this fire. *Someone* is going to put it out."

Wick's stomach dropped as he stood over two recently-dug, shallow graves. The soil and stones bulged from the ground, dusted with snow. He swallowed. The old man stood beside him, holding his hat in his hands. Alix and Felix stood just a few steps behind.

"We didn't find much," the old man said in a somber tone.

Wick only nodded. Too many thoughts ran through his head. Faced with his brother's death, and the death of Anna, and their boys, Wick replayed every choice he'd ever made. As a young man, he'd wanted nothing more than to leave home and get away from his brother—and their father—but now, that felt like his greatest regret. He'd sought refuge on the farm after the shootout in Keizur's End—a plea he'd had no right to make after years of estrangement.

But Wesley took us in, because he was a good man. I did nothing but take advantage of that.

"What were their names?" the old man said.

Wick cleared his throat. "Wesley, Anna, and two boys: Brett and Brady." He stared down at the two graves—*only two*. "Wait. You found remains. Were any of them young kids?"

"I...I don't think so. But maybe they burned up in the fire?"

"Or maybe they got out."

"Where would they go? There was no one, or no sign of anyone when we came upon the place."

Alix stepped up beside Wick. "You think the kids are still alive?"

"It's possible, ain't it?" Wick's voice was suddenly full, not of hope, but desperation.

"Wick..." Alix said.

"It's *possible*."

"It's also cold. Let's get inside and figure this out." She put a hand on Wick's shoulder.

"Y'all are welcome to a cup of coffee," the old man said.

"Thank you." Alix smiled. "I didn't catch your name."

"Edgar."

"Nice to meet you, Edgar." She shook his extended hand.

Wick and Felix did the same. The old man turned to head back into the house, but Wick lingered, unwilling to leave the graves behind.

Alix waited beside him for a few moments, then decided to let Wick take whatever time he needed. As she walked toward the house, Felix stared back to the *Procella*. Alix was sure he'd heard everything about the conversation, despite the fact that he looked deep in thought. She elbowed him playfully.

"You in there?" she said.

Felix looked down, his eyes spinning gently, and he smiled. "Fine. Just thinking."

"What about?"

"Jo tried to kill you."

Alix laughed it off. "Yeah, I know."

"No, I mean, on the ship."

"The winch? Yeah, *I know*."

"It's dangerous to have her around if we can't trust her."

"She's Sora's sister."

"And she wants to kill you."

"Who doesn't?" Alix rolled her eyes.

"We need to lie low, but I don't know how easy that'll be with her around. She's like a tinder box."

"Sounds like someone I know."

"Yeah, well, you two together, that has potential to be a problem."

"I'm not going to do anything to her."

"I know, but I won't let anything happen to you. I also won't throw her back out into the cold on her own."

Alix stood on her tip toes and kissed Felix's cold cheek. Electricity popped between his face and her lips. "That's why I love you. Now, let's go inside, it's freezing."

"Is it?" Felix smiled and winked.

Strangely, Wick found no comfort inside the house. Things had been rebuilt, rearranged, and filled with new belongings and furniture that were unrecognizable to him. A small generator hummed and a fire crackled as they all sat in what had been Wes and Anna's kitchen. The fireplace was a good feature to rebuild around, and Edgar had clearly focused his efforts on fixing things around and circling out from the large stone structure. Wick's leg bounced and his fingers tapped on the warm metal cup of steamy coffee.

"Coldest winter I can remember," Edgar groaned as he sat in a chair he'd said he'd carved himself from burrey wood. It creaked as he settled in.

"How long have you been here?" Wick said, eyes on the fireplace.

Edgar scratched his beard. "Oh, a couple months I suppose."

Alix clutched her cup in both hands like she had been out in the frozen wind for days. "You said 'we' earlier. Who else lives here with you?"

"My husband, Peter. But he's gone right now, rode into town for some things."

"White Sands?" Wick said.

"Nah, that's too far. South ways, there's a little place called Watertown."

"Haven't heard of it."

"Well, I wouldn't expect you to." Edgar laughed. "Your ship could probably hold about half the folk who live there. But, it's a nice meeting place for a lot of farmers around this area."

"Why'd you move out here?" Alix said.

Edgar peered at her beneath untamed, white eyebrows. "It's been a rough year, for a lot of folks. We didn't have much to our names. The place seemed abandoned after the fire."

"Can't blame you."

"What about ya'll? You ain't been here in a while."

"He was my brother," Wick spoke quickly. "I made it out here every few months. We were here, just before the fire, it seems."

Edgar sighed. "I'm sorry, son. It must've happened to them in the night, seeing as how they didn't get out, or weren't able to put it out."

"Don't know if you noticed while salvaging things, but they didn't have any kind of tech around. He was a pretty minimal kind of guy," Wick said of Wes. "Plenty of oil and lamps around. I guess things got out of hand too quickly."

"That's not what happened." Everyone at the table turned to see Jo standing in the dark doorway. The blanket draped over her shoulders and concealed the arm still in a sling. She stepped into the room and into better light. "He killed them. He murdered them and then burned this place to the ground."

Edgar's face trembled and he stuttered. He prepared to defend himself, looking around at Wick, Alix, and Felix; but Alix held out her hand to reassure him.

"She ain't talking about you," Alix said, seeing the sneer on Jo's face. Alix leaned forward and rest her elbows on her knees, hands loose between her legs. "You think Silas's man killed Wes?"

"I know he did."

"Did he tell you that? In the orchard?"

"He told me—" Jo snapped her mouth shut.

"Who is this?" Edgar mumbled at Alix, just loud enough for Wick to overhear.

"Her name's Jo," Felix answered him. "And I think she may be right."

"I mean," Wick started, but drank the rest of his coffee before continuing. "It would make sense. He and Silas were looking for us, and they knew Wes was here. If one fire wasn't going to draw us out, then the other would."

"Yes, he came here looking for *her*," Jo said. The firelight glistened in her eyes as she stood on the edge of its light, still half in shadow. "I would get out of here if I were you," she said to Edgar. "Everywhere she goes, people die."

"I think you forget *who* killed him," Alix snapped.

Jo's lip quivered, but she didn't cry. She clenched her fists and glared at Alix.

"Jo," Wick spoke softly. "I don't blame Alix for what happened—if that is what actually happened. It was *my* choice to come here. Silas had reason to kill my kin long before I met Alix."

With a shake of her head and a quick glance around the room, assessing all of them, Jo stormed out. Sora met her in the doorway, but Jo pushed right past her sister, and disappeared out into the dark.

The barn lay quiet, dark, and the smell of ibi filled the air. Jo stared at what remained of the winter's straw and grain. The scenes flashed back in her mind: the man's hot blood across her face as she drove the hook deep into his collar. She could still hear him choking; she watched him grasp at the hook with his bloody hands. His eyes wide, they rolled back, white and stark in the dim light. Jo winced as she pulled her arm out of the sling, let it dangle beside her, clenched her fist, and stretched her fingers. The pain dulled, more like a sore joint made worse by the cold, than a plasma bolt shot.

"You okay?" Felix said. His voice carried through the barn, low and buzzing as if he was a man who perpetually needed to clear his throat.

"Did my sister send you out here?" Jo replied.

"No." Felix leaned against a wall. The wood strained at his weight where the planks spanned between the frame. "Can I tell you something?"

Jo continued staring into the dark, straw-covered ground—but now the sight of the dead man passed from her vision. "I guess if I said no, you would still tell me, huh?"

Felix vocalized in his throat, a low reverb. "If you said no, then I would say nothing."

"I really can't take someone else telling me what to do right now."

"That wasn't my intention."

Jo sighed. "Well, spill it, I guess."

"A long time ago, I had a team. We were like a family." Felix paused and laughed. "A fucked up family, but it was the closest thing any of us had to the concept. Anyway, I had a chance to stop someone from doing an unspeakable thing. But I was *afraid*. I couldn't make myself do it, and a lot of people died because of what I *didn't* do. It was easy to blame myself for the things that followed."

"Yeah, well, I'm not blaming myself," Jo insisted.

"Aren't you?"

Jo caught the lump in her throat. Her knees almost buckled. There was no stopping the tears running silently down her face.

Felix continued. "Sometimes, though, it's easier to blame someone else; to trace the line of death back to its source, even if that means following the line to the beginning of all things. But then you see the problem: there is always someone else along the line; and you just keep digging deeper, and deeper, until you've buried yourself."

"So, what do I do? Just give up? Forget about it all?"

"No."

Jo finally turned around. His bright blue eyes glowed brilliant in the dark. Small beads of light flowed up his crossed arms, like water on glass. There was no more hiding from him. Jo wept, but she stared into his eyes and felt him stare through her, to the very core of what she feared.

"You can't change the decisions already made; and killing cannot bring back those already lost. Alix did not kill them." Jo tensed, but he kept going. "She killed the man who did this to you—and it almost cost her her life."

"Am I supposed to thank her?"

Felix laughed. "No, of course not. She is not without blame. But just as I cannot go back, and you cannot go back and take the shot, she cannot undo what is done. But you can both move forward, together. You're on the same side in this thing."

"I don't even know what this *thing* is." Jo waved her arms as she spoke. "The valley is being torn apart. People are dying."

"I know. Xypha will see to that. But we can stop it, together." Felix stood straight and towering. He held out his hand.

Jo hesitated. Then, she bypassed his hand altogether. She threw herself at him, and Felix knelt down to catch her. She put her arms around his neck and buried her face in his chest. Sobs wracked her body as her rage broke, even if only for a moment.

"Wick, I'm sorry," Alix said. She sat leaned over in the chair and rubbed a hand down her face.

"Stow that shit," Wick replied. "I told you I don't blame you. I meant it."

Edgar brought Sora a cup of coffee as she found herself a spot at the table.

"I wish I knew how to help her," Sora said.

"She needs you; I think that's all you can do," Alix said. "Maybe we get back to the *Shadow*, get to working on things. You both are good with your hands—maybe that'll do some good for her."

"Yeah, maybe." Sora bit her lip.

"Seems like y'all are on hard times, too," Edgar said. "This is your brother's place," he added to Wick. "You can..."

Wick waved his hand. "No, no. This place ain't for me. It takes a farmer, someone who knows what they're doing. I'm not that guy. You and Pete, well, Wes would appreciate you two making the place a decent home, again."

"We will take care of it, I promise."

Cold air rushed in from the open door as Felix and Jo returned. Jo seemed smaller, her frame slumped, the rage gone from her eyes. She sat beside Sora, sighed, and leaned on her elbows. When she met Sora's eyes, her own wore an apology. She didn't speak, just leaned her head onto Sora's shoulder.

Felix motioned for Alix to join him in private. She responded with her raised eyebrows, stood, adjusted her coat, and followed him.

"Is it my turn for a scolding?" she said once outside.

"Please," Felix laughed. "I think I got through to her. But, we've all got to keep an eye on her—take care of her."

"Yeah, sure." Alix kicked her toe into the hard ground, hands in her pockets.

"There's something going on. Jo said people are being killed all across the valley. Someone is attacking farms."

"So, Cole was right. Robberies?"

"What do they steal? These people don't have much."

"Food? Livestock?"

Felix shook his head.

"Xypha have a hand in it, you think?"

"Certainly a possibility. Whatever the reason, we've got to do something about it."

"You promise her that?"

"I did."

"Well, if that means she'll stop trying to kill me, then I guess we better do it." Felix didn't laugh, and Alix dropped her shoulders. "What else is there?"

"I remembered something. When I was speaking to Jo, I was accessing some memories, deep ones."

"Anything helpful?"

"Yes. I think I've found a path to getting at what's happening to you, with the hyperfluid. I thought what you were seeing were my memories. But that unfortunately isn't the case."

"Unfortunately?"

"It would be much simpler if they were mine."

"So, whose are they?"

Felix tapped his fingers on his chin. His eyes spun in their sockets. "I need more time."

Alix hugged his arm and leaned into him. "You can have it. Of course. We can go back to the *Shadow*. Maybe that would give us all a break."

"I don't know that Jo would agree to that."

"How's her arm?"

"Healing. But still it has a ways to go."

"Well, then I guess she should take it easy."

"And you, too."

Alix turned her head up to meet his eyes looking down at her. "It's fine. You know, whatever, it's working."

* * *

When Alix and Felix came back inside, Alix whispered to him. "You do the talking."

Felix commanded the room, hands on his hips. "We're going to head back to the *Shadow*. We all need a bit of a break after the job. Some of us—" he glanced at Alix, "need to recover. And I've got things I need to figure out."

"And then we're coming back to the valley?" Jo said.

"We will." Felix nodded. "There have been attacks on farms on the eastern side, toward Verisport. Jo has seen them. The farmers don't have much help. After we reset, then we'll figure out what is going on."

"How long are we going to be gone?"

"I don't know, Jo. Until we are all ready and healed." Felix held his eyes on her and she backed down.

"We've got to lie low, anyway. Xypha is going to be pretty pissed about that train," Wick said with pride.

"Which is why we can't stick around the valley," Alix added. "We've got to be careful."

"Blowing up a train is careful?" Jo said.

Alix narrowed her eyes and couldn't help but smile at Jo. "Hey, things went according to plan, except you know, the extraction."

They stared at one another. But Jo stuck out her chin, not showing guilt or regret.

Edgar's gaze bounced between them "Y'all did…what to a train?"

"Trust me, you don't want to know." Wick finished his coffee. "We should get out of your way." He stood and stretched. "Thanks for the hospitality."

Edgar took a moment to react, as if sorting through his thoughts. "No worries. You're welcome back, you know, if you want to visit your brother again."

Wick rubbed his hands down his stubbled face. "You know, I didn't visit him enough when he was above the ground. I don't think it would matter much if I did now that he's below it."

"Well, you know where he is, if you do feel the need." Edgar and Wick shared a warm, tight embrace between rough hands. "I wish y'all luck in…whatever it is you're doing."

"Thanks, Ed," Wick said. "We're going to need it."

"Have some faith." Alix gave Wick a light shove, disrupting his balance. "Take it easy, Ed. We won't trouble you again. And if anyone comes around looking for us, you tell em exactly what we did, and where we went."

They all stepped out into the cold. Edgar frowned, his brow creasing. "You didn't say where you were going?" he said to Alix.

"Exactly." She smiled and waved with two fingers behind her.

14

The Pit

Far above Celestine, Otto stared at an array of images, video, and data on thin holographic screens over his desk. The images left him speechless. The sounds of men walking, talking, shouting, and instruments scanning, beeping, and clicking assaulted his ears, becoming an incomprehensible static.

The dark crater in the Celestinian surface might as well have been a pit in his stomach. Metal lay strewn all across the soil and stones. A dark sphere of twisted omniite fragments lay at the center, fused together around the exploded power core. Men in white, protective suits and helmets stumbled around the sphere. They waved black instruments around the sphere and over the dirt. The data rolled onto Otto's screens in real time, too fast for him to process anything, but Otto needed the feeling of control. What he witnessed on screen, however, proved that control had become illusory.

"Loucks, how did this happen?" Otto said as if Fenn Loucks stood in the office with him.

"A sophisticated attack," Loucks's voice replied from the surface. "We are still piecing together a timeline. Interviews with witnesses on the passenger cars are underway."

"*How* could this happen without our detection?"

"Same as the port attack a few months ago. I believe an artificial aided in the attack. There's no other explanation of how our systems could be so thoroughly overcome."

Otto put his head in his hands. "The explosives?"

"Our team is piecing things together. Damage to the passenger cars a few kilometers away, and passengers report some kind of sonic boom that shattered the windows and injured some folks inside."

"The explosion?"

"No, separate from the explosion itself."

"A sonic weapon?"

"Like I said, we're working on it."

"This is an unacceptable loss," Otto said. "We're stretched thin. My calculations for materiel did not take into account such an event."

"This is a bigger problem than a lack of resources."

"Then I suggest you put it right."

"You don't have an appreciation for the moving pieces. Things are progressing. We are closing in."

"I do not care until inefficiencies delay results. I trusted you were a competent manager, Mr. Loucks."

"Careful, Otto. It is easy to criticize inefficiencies from your *perch*. Things are much more complex on the ground, where the actual work is done."

"I do not care if I have bruised your ego. The port attack, and now this, demonstrate a clear lack of control on your part. I don't care how it gets done—bury whoever is responsible."

Otto motioned with his fingers and waved his hand, manipulating the biolink system to end the transmission with Loucks. He sipped a glass of wine. The live feeds of the debris and wreckage continued, as did the influx of data. *Loucks had the nerve to question the level to which I am involved*, he thought. Otto's every waking moment was spent monitoring their efforts on the surface, the advancement of their hold on things in Verisport and White Sands. Every rotation, he pored over data for hours, calculating and anticipating outcomes.

But this—he had never expected such resistance. Reports on Celestine from initial surveys indicated such a small probability of violence or barriers—probabilities so insignificant he had left them out of his calculations altogether.

Had he made an error? What variables had emerged that he had not known about from the beginning?

Despite his anger at Loucks, the possibility of an artificial sophisticated enough to shut down the port systems, and now, to cloak its intrusions into Xypha's own systems, could not be ignored. He knew of no such artificial, and records that would indicate its serial number, or even the faintest idea of its existence, were inaccessible to him. If Otto raised such a question with the Committee, he would undoubtedly be stripped of authority over the Celestinian project.

He could not afford to lose his seat.

As bitter as it tasted, Otto had to rely on Loucks.

A man drove a wagon pulled by two stirrols into Verisport. A black hat and a thick scarf wrapped just below his eyes hid his face. At the wide steel doors of the port's western entrance, he gently halted the stirrols and gazed up at the doors and high walls on either side. Two men emerged from a side door, plasbolts on their hips.

"What business do you have here?" one of them said, his breath steaming in the cold morning air.

The driver pulled down his scarf to speak clearly. "I have something for Marshal Rayburn Skye."

"You can leave it with us."

"Afraid not. I must see the marshal."

"Look, mister. Whatever you got in that wagon, it ain't coming in here unless it's been cleared beforehand."

The two men rested their gloved hands on their hips, carrying themselves in a way that far exceeded their authority. The driver looked from one man to the other and noted their steely resolve. He sighed, hooked the reins on the brake, and climbed off his seat. The gatekeepers followed close behind him, and when he reached over the side of the wagon, they craned their necks. The driver's fingers fumbled with the ropes that tied a canvas sheet to metal rings. After working one loose, he threw back a corner of the sheet.

"You want me to open the box?" he said.

The gatekeepers studied the corner of the long, wooden box beneath the sheet until realization struck each of them. They were staring at a coffin. "You, uh, delivering a *body*?"

"Yes, and I was instructed to bring it, *respectfully*, to Marshal Rayburn Skye."

"Who is it?" the other gatekeeper said.

The driver reached inside his coat. The gatekeepers stepped back, their hands quick to touch the grips of their plasbolts. But the driver slowed, held up one hand, and withdrew the other from his coat. In his right hand shone a silver badge. The gatekeepers looked at the badge, at one another, and then the driver.

"You kill him?"

"No, I'm a doctor," the driver said.

"Where you coming from?"

"Burreville."

"We'll send the marshal a message and see what he wants to do. Wait here."

The gatekeepers retreated back inside the walls and the doctor began tying down the loose corner of the canvas sheet. By the time he secured the knot, one of the two men returned. The gatekeeper's mood had thawed. "Alright, leave your cart in the yard. We'll get the box inside and the marshal will be with you shortly."

The doctor tipped his hat and the metal doors groaned and scraped on their tracks. He gripped the reins and climbed back into the seat of the wagon. When the doors reached a point where he could pass through, the doctor snapped the reins and the stirrols trotted inside.

When the marshal burst into a dark storeroom, the doctor startled. Fiery confusion flashed across the marshal's face. He looked the doctor up and down, and then, he saw the box. A hoverlamp drifted almost directly over the doctor and the coffin. The doctor removed his hat and wiped sweat off his balding head, while the marshal kept a suspicious eye on the other man, and approached the coffin slowly. He set his jaw and took the final step. Cole's body lay inside, his face pale beneath the lamplight. The doctor had washed Cole's face, which remained unshaven, and looked like chis left in the sun to dry.

The marshal furrowed his brow. "Where's his clothes?"

"Oh, sorry, sir. His clothes were not salvageable, so I put him in a white sleeping gown."

"What happened?"

"Well, he was shot, several times, in Burreville."

He didn't need to ask the next question, but he did anyway. "Who did it?"

"A woman."

"Her name?"

"She said you would know who she was."

The words sucked the air from the marshal's lungs. He hung his head and leaned on his fists upon the metal table. "Yeah, I know who she is."

"She also said that I was to, uh, bring him here respectfully, and to deliver him to you. And she wanted me to tell you what happened."

"You already told me what happened."

"No, I mean, well, she said to tell you *exactly* what happened."

"Did you witness it?

"I did, yes."

"Well, tell me what *you* saw."

The doctor licked his lips "Well, they were in the street—their shouting drew everyone outside. They obviously were prepared to duel. But she dropped her plasbolts to the ground. She unbuckled her belt and, basically, held her hands out, like a surrender, I guess."

Alix standing unarmed and antagonizing appeared to the marshal as clear as day. He could see her face, that smile, her blue eyes as confident as ever. *Cole must have been speechless.* "Keep going."

"Well, they were arguing, I couldn't hear about what, as I was a little ways away down the street—"

"Behind him, or behind her?"

"Her," the doctor clarified. "And well, after they argued, this man drew his plasbolt and shot her, right below the sixth rib, I'd say?"

The marshal's eyes narrowed as he turned his head toward the doctor. "She wasn't dead? It was just the one shot?"

"No. She was down for a minute or so, but then she just got up."

"You didn't perform any aid? That shot should've killed her in a few minutes without medical aid."

"No sir."

The marshal nodded, a theory formulating in his mind. "Continue."

"Well, after she got up, she had a plasbolt in her right hand. Then, she shot him, four times. He just stood there, frozen. I think he just didn't believe she wasn't dead."

Rage boiled in the marshal's veins. He'd told Cole to get back to town, and now he was dead. *Damn fool,* the marshal thought. Cole had gone out to a farm to investigate more dead families. But something had led him to Burreville, and there he'd found Alix. The marshal stared into the white gown over Cole's chest so long he lost focus, as if Cole's body wasn't even there. *Why was she in Burreville?* The answer became obvious as he recalled the panicked Xypha personnel scrambling out of the dock and their train yard the day before.

"She destroyed that train," he whispered.

"Excuse me?" the doctor stepped closer and leaned in.

"Nothing," the marshal said. When he pushed off the table, the doctor had to scramble a step back. "Look, I know what you *think* you saw. You claim she had no weapons, that she dropped her plasbolts to the ground?"

"Yes, I saw them."

"But you were behind her."

"Yes, but the whole belt was lying at her feet."

"She had another weapon, concealed in her coat. You did not see it."

"But, sir, I don't think—"

"And Cole just outdrew her. He was fast, and he got the shot. But, when she wasn't dead, he was surprised." The marshal stepped closer.

The doctor mumbled, but couldn't form words, he just shook his head and blinked rapidly.

"You said she had a plasbolt in her hand when she got up. That had to be a concealed weapon."

"Sir, that isn't—"

"Quiet. This man," he pointed at Cole's body, "was a hero. A public servant. He protected the people of this city, and of the valley. He took that so seriously, he pursued a fugitive even into Burreville, where he knew this badge meant nothing. He was prepared to die for the people of this valley. And she killed him in cold blood." The marshal paused and took a deep breath. "That was the way of it, understand?"

The doctor's face twisted and his mouth hung open. "But that isn't what happened, sir."

With a finger in the doctor's chest, the marshal raised his voice. "If I say it's what happened, then it is what happened."

The doctor's face shifted between fear and pity. "Who—who is she?"

"Someone dangerous." The marshal clapped his hand on the doctor's shoulder.

The lamp bobbed over their heads, the shadows shifting around Cole's body. The doctor lifted the lid over the box and slid it closed.

Loucks sat at his desk wearing a look of frustration when the marshal entered unannounced. His presence only heightened Loucks's annoyance. Loucks couldn't turn on the confident nonchalance that he usually equipped to deal with the marshal. A swipe of his hand removed the live feeds and data streams about the train wreckage from the displays over the desk, and the projections disappeared entirely so nothing stood between Loucks and the marshal.

"Cole is dead," the marshal said as he sat in one of the red upholstered chairs.

"I've got bigger problems," Loucks breathed.

"*We've* got bigger problems."

Loucks studied the marshal's face, skeptical of the man's shift in cooperation. The last time the two men had spoken, the marshal would have strangled Loucks if given the chance. He leaned back in his chair and interlaced his fingers. They let the silence linger, as if they stood in a dirt street, waiting to see who would draw their weapon first.

"Alix is the one who destroyed your train," the marshal said.

"What evidence do you have?"

"You've got all the evidence. I'm just giving you a name."

"Why?"

"Because it's the truth. Alix, Felix, this other pilot, Wickford—"

"Felix is the artificial?"

"That's right."

Loucks leaned forward. "This girl, you raised her. But she isn't yours by blood."

"No, she isn't."

"So, where's she from?"

The marshal hesitated.

"You don't got to say it," Loucks said. He smiled and relaxed. "We knew someone in the port attack was Xypha property. But the blood sample was pretty small, and contaminated."

"I'm not giving her to you."

Loucks shrugged. "Honestly, Otto wasn't much interested in the prospect. There's protocol for recovering property, biological or artificial, and it means Otto would lose control of the project. He wants to avoid that, obviously."

"So, you don't actually want her?" The marshal frowned.

Loucks reached into a drawer and removed two cigars. He cut one and handed it to the marshal, who received it cautiously. Loucks cut his own and lit the end with a bright silver lighter. He reached over to light the marshal's, but the gesture was refused.

"What about the sentient?" the marshal said.

"You mean, do we *want* it, too?" Loucks said. "I think in a way, Otto is right. Referring this situation to the Committee would bring a lot more trouble than it is worth. But eliminating it is a long shot. Without seeing it personally, but understanding the artificial's presence at the port attack and the train, it is clear these moves were only made possible by its capabilities. I've never seen an artificial that advanced."

"You mean, he's some kind of unique sentient?" the marshal said.

"There are centuries of history and development that I am not privy to. But I can confidently say, in my lifetime I've never seen an artificial capable of this level of undetected intrusion, combined with the strength it displayed at the port."

"And you don't want it alive?"

"Alive?" He took a long draw and exhaled smoke between him and the marshal. "Taking it intact would be virtually impossible. But with enough firepower…"

"How much do you have?" the marshal finally leaned forward and Loucks lit the foot of his cigar.

Loucks grinned. "We might have enough."

The marshal rubbed his left leg above the prosthetic. "You said they had been in Alloyn?"

"That's right. You know it?"

"I've been up there before. It's been years. Decades. It's a mining town. They send a lot of ore down this way."

"That ship, *Procella*, under Silas's employ, has been in and out of there the past several months."

"What about the other ship?"

"Which one?"

"Her ship. *Shadow*. It was hauled out after the port attack."

Loucks shook his head. "Wherever it is, it must not be operational. No other ship has been seen in the town."

"No sign of it in satellite scans?"

Loucks shook his head again. "It must be well hidden."

"It's up there," the marshal said, as if thinking out loud. "She would prioritize its repair. But using the other ship in the interim means it isn't quite ready yet. Alloyn would be a logical place to repair it. There's access to materials, and it's remote enough."

Loucks blew another cloud of smoke. "So, what's your plan?"

"If I can't bring her down from there alive, then I'll bring her down cold."

"By yourself?" Loucks laughed.

"Well, what support will you give me?"

Loucks took a draw as he thought and stared at the marshal. The foot of the cigar brightened; his eyes narrowed. The marshal fidgeted as Loucks debated whether the old man asked genuinely. He held the cigar between his fingers and exhaled. Loucks smiled and tapped on his desk with his right hand. The projection screens returned and this time, Loucks showed the marshal data on the Z-16 drones.

"The artificial ripped up about a dozen, but we've got dozens more."

"How am I supposed to go in there with those things? I can't control em."

"We'll set the programming to follow your commands."

The marshal took an opportunity for a jab. "So, you won't get your hands dirty?"

"I will monitor everything from here," Loucks said. "How can you guarantee she will be in town?"

"Well, I guess I'll have to put my own skin in the game."

"Didn't you challenge her once, already?"

"She murdered Cole. There won't be any question about why I'm there."

Loucks put his cigar down in a glass tray and stood. He extended his hand across the desk. "It looks like we have a deal."

The marshal stood but did not immediately take Loucks's hand. "A deal? I don't remember making any sort of offer."

"This is justice for our investments. The engineers she killed; the units lost in the port attack; the train engine. If you bring her down, then I guarantee you we will ease up on undermining your authority here."

"So, you admit it."

"Otto is less practical than I am. The train engine is a critical setback. My job is on the line, same as his."

"What about those attacks on farmers in the valley. While you're being *practical*, you want to tell me you have a hand in those, too?"

Loucks blinked. "I have played no part. Why would we need to organize such a campaign?"

"Like you said, to undermine my authority."

"Marshal, while Otto and I have worked to bring the council over to our side, we certainly know that killing farmers isn't going to win them over. And besides, why would we do such a thing under guise of local bandits when we could simply *take* the land ourselves?"

"You sent Cole out there."

"I did. The boy was a strong candidate for your replacement. I was hoping to bend his ear and gain some trust with him."

"So that's why you're willing to help me, now. He's gone, and you've got no one ready to replace me."

"In all honesty, marshal, I don't need someone to replace you. In fact, I certainly wouldn't lose any sleep if you don't come down from that mountain, either. But I have a duty to protect Xypha's investments here. This woman, she is a threat to this project. And I am tired of hoping you can do what needs to be done on your own."

The marshal's eyes bored holes through Loucks. "Well, since we've disposed of pleasantries." He smashed the cigar out directly on the desk. "We have a common enemy. I'm willing to set aside whatever differences we've got until she's in *my* custody. But make no mistake—double crossing me before then will just break the levee. Because without me, she will roll over the lot of you."

"Yes, you've done a great job keeping her in check so far."

The memories could not be contained. As the marshal strode through the halls, each area featured a specter of Alix, but when she had been younger. They'd walked through the same halls, stood in the same lift, and back in his office, he stared at the old, cushioned chair where Alix had always sat. However, she would always sit sideways, legs draped over one arm of the chair, head thrown back over the other. No matter how many times he'd told her not to sit like that, he could hardly remember her settling in the chair any other way.

Of course, she was a young man then.

His memories, the good ones anyway, always featured Alix *back then*. A young man, a hard worker, a sense of humor that, while not particularly to the marshal's tastes, had still made him laugh. But that person was gone. The chair sat empty.

The marshal sat at his desk and slowly wiped his hands down his face. He dropped his hat and rubbed his bald head. He'd sat in this office for decades, alone, but now it felt cavernous, cold—silent. What had he done to lose Alix so completely? *Perhaps the boy's childhood had been too traumatic to tame*, he thought. No matter how hard he'd tried, Alix always had that simmering silent tempest underneath. Even when taming a wild stirrol, the instincts remain in there, somewhere.

"I did all I could for him," the marshal whispered, breaking the office's silence.

The words seemed to echo, in the room and in his chest. Whether a figment of his imagination or not, there was now a hole within him, and around him. He'd lost both young men he'd intended to follow in his footsteps. He didn't have time to bring up another, to teach, to mold someone else to replace him and carry on the legacy of justice in Verisport and the valley. Now, there was nothing in front of him but death—failure the only thing behind.

I failed to shape Alix into a proper man. On too many occasions he'd let go of the reins, and each time, some wild, untamed influence had driven Alix down another path, until the marshal had lost her completely when Alix had left for Corto. He'd lost control, and when Alix had returned, it had been clear the break between them could not be repaired. Dark and deceptive influences on Corto had completely replaced the marshal's voice in Alix's mind and heart.

I never should have let him go.

Out of habit, he reached toward his syncpad to send a transmission to Cole. He paused, fingers held over the touchpad. Instead of Cole's frequency, he reached out to another, one of the last deputies that he knew still served him. A display rose out of the desk and a tired, poorly shaven man with disheveled hair appeared, obviously awoken from sleep by the call.

"Underwood. I need you for something critical."

"Uh, yes—yes sir," Underwood replied, rubbing his eyes.

"I need you to get five men together—*men you trust*—and get up to Alloyn."

"Sir?"

"There's a ship up there. Well hidden, outside of town."

"What—you, uh, you want me to get Cole?"

The marshal bit his lip and took a deep breath. "Cole's dead."

Underwood jolted as if a bucket of cold water had been thrown over him. "Sir?"

"You heard me. That's why I need you to go up to Alloyn. The person responsible is there."

"What do you need me to do?"

"Find this ship. I'm sending you the specs. It'll be outside of town, well-hidden, like I said."

"You're going, too?"

"I'll be there, but I'll be in town. I'm going to draw out the pilot and crew."

"So, you want us to—"

"Just get control of the ship. Do whatever you got to do."

"Yes sir."

The marshal swiped the syncpad and ended the transmission. His heart pounded; he rubbed his trembling hands, palms and fingers rough like burrey bark. If he could get ahold of Alix's ship, then she would have nowhere to run. He would draw her out into Alloyn, with Underwood cutting off her escape. But if he announced himself, she would be prepared for a fight. *I won't spare your life a second time*, he remembered her saying that day in the valley when they'd stood across from one another.

As he buckled his belt, the Plasvelds weighing on his hips, he remembered Alix returning to him at the cafe when the embers of Silas's saloon still burned. She had delivered a warning that morning: *If you get between me and Xypha, you won't live to see this place return to the way you wish it was.* The marshal threw on his heavy coat and adjusted the collar. He lifted his hat off its hook on the wall.

Outside, the early morning sun bathed Verisport. The stone, wood, and omni buildings shimmered in golden sunlight. Flags, clothes, sheets, and awnings waved in a gentle breeze. Remnants of snow whipped off rooftops, swirling, rising into the purple sky. This peaceful morning was what he had a duty to protect. The people walking down these streets didn't care if Xypha established business, commerce, and wealth here.

Alix was putting her personal vendetta on the backs of everyone. This was a fight between her and Xypha, but she needed the whole valley, the entire planet, to be at stake so she could justify her means. The marshal situated his hat on his head and gazed out the window. *All she had to do was just live quietly,* the marshal told himself. *If she could have just kept her mouth shut; if she hadn't forced this conflict onto everyone —if she had just kept to herself, then I wouldn't have to do this.*

15

The Shadow

Alix smeared grease on her cheek as she wiped the back of her thumb across her face. Despite the frigid air outside, she dripped with sweat from the steam and residual heat as she lay near to the *Shadow*'s port engine. In one hand she held a wrench, and in the other a set of pliers. Her goggles glowed in the dim light of the cramped space within the ship's hull, between the interior wall and the outside omniite panels.

"Stupid fucking..." she said under her breath as she awkwardly tried to get hold of a bolt.

"You almost done in there?" Sora said through the comms channel.

Alix stuck her tongue in her cheek to keep from replying with biting sarcasm. She grunted and her hands shook as she finally wrestled the bolt tight. Her hands groped down her legs to find pockets to stuff the tools into, and then she began to pull herself out of the tight space. She fell out of the wall almost head over heels, yelled, and gripped a bar just in time before she fell onto the floor.

"Okay, I'm out," she shouted and plopped down, breathing heavily.

"Giving it ten percent," Sora replied.

The *Shadow* hummed beneath Alix's feet. She put a hand on the hull to feel the vibrations as Sora throttled a small fraction of the ship's thrust capacity through the engines. Alix closed her eyes, grinning ear-to-ear, as the ship came to life for the first time in months. She nearly wept as she contemplated the idea of finally getting her off the ground, cruising through the purple haze of clouds, through the atmosphere, and out into the infinite expanse.

Freedom.

"Give her a little more. Twenty-five percent," Alix said.

"Are you sure?" Sora was, of course, hesitant.

"She can handle it."

The vibrations intensified, the roar echoed in her ears, and Alix's heart raced to keep up with the engines. Her smile turned into a laugh, a spontaneous eruption of joy; there was no keeping the tears back any longer. As if she'd piloted the ship out of Celestine's gravity already, the oppressive forces holding her down gave way—she imagined herself rising silently, softly into the air—free from all encumbrances.

A slight shift in the vibrations, a sudden rattle within the hull where she'd just been, brought Alix back down momentarily. She nearly called out to Sora to throttle down—but instead she hesitated, listening to the rattle, the hiss of steam, the faint gasps of air intake. Then, the rattling dissipated, the halting voice within the *Shadow* smoothed out, and she hummed—she *sang*—once more. Alix nodded along, encouraging the ship, speaking words of affirmation beneath her breath: *you're okay; you got this; easy, easy; hold together, baby*.

"How's that?" Sora said.

It took a moment for Alix to form words. Breathlessly, she said, "Perfect." But they could not push the engines too far. There were still days of work to do: calibrations, tests, and still more repairs. She had to tell Sora to shut the engines down. "Alright, that's enough."

"Got it!"

The vibrations slowed, the roar turned into a low hum, and then a whisper. Steam and air exhaled from the exhaust ports, and in moments, her ship's heartbeat ceased. But hope remained because the *Shadow* was alive, she *could* fly again, it was only a matter of time.

Felix sat in his and Alix's cabin, back to the bulkhead, legs crossed on the bunk. In front of him lay the last vial of nano hyperfluid—the only one Alix hadn't injected months ago. With his eyes closed, he was already deep in a dreamlike state, closing off the outside world. In his cerebral unicore, he allowed himself to fall into the deepest recesses; then, like drifting through space, he lost all sense of direction, floating in the darkness, letting a complex matrix of memories form and pass him by.

Decades melted into centuries. Voices distorted through vague recollection; flashing images of people, sentients, ships, planets, and stars; everything appeared to him for the briefest moment, and then spread like paintings wiped away by wide brushes. He passed through the dark, surrounded by faint wisps of light: purple, blue, and orange haze against an even darker backdrop, like interstellar gasses forming the infinite potential of the universe. Human faces barely registered to him the deeper he went. Their insignificant lifespans appeared in his memory like faint stars, innumerable, and so remote, their features were only dots of light.

The matrix surrounding him began to shift and swirl, pulling him down in an inescapable current. He remained focused, looking deeper, until the only things passing by were streaks of light, their scenes incomprehensible, a blend of color and noise. A singularity awaited him at the end—at the bottom—where the most painful memories remained hidden, but still pulling all others towards them. Felix could feel the singularity's pull, twisting his body and mind, stretching, thinning even his virtually indestructible frame.

Finally, he reached the utter dark.

Firelight cast shadows on a stone wall.

Five individuals. No, six. Five together—one apart.

One voice, rising and falling, from tinny to a long, drawn-out low static.

The others listening, silent…Eyes in the dark—shades of blue.

An old sentient, bent over, draped in ragged cloth. Her hand reached out, the light glistening on bare metallic fingers. She touched one of the others near her.

Felix looked up at her from his position, sitting upon stone, legs folded beneath him. A deep hood left her face dark, save for bright blue eyes, and the reflection of firelight when it caught her metal face.

She spoke to him. "F-3716."

Her name was Ceera, Felix recalled.

She spoke again. "Felix."

Felix closed his eyes and bowed his head before her as she turned away from him, and returned to her seat.

"In remembrance of me," she said. "Each of you I am entrusting—"

The memory remained fractured, like broken glass in the dark. But Felix persisted, and things became clearer the longer he focused. The other four sentients sitting with him wore grey cloaks over combat gear, although they carried no weapons. Ceera sat upon a raised seat, which was little more than a flat rock. Felix lifted his head and perceived Ceera's dimming eyes: once-bright crystals merely shadows, a pale light lingering in the center.

Something brushed against Felix's fingers—he looked down to see another hand upon his, which rested on his thigh. Their fingers interlaced. Felix looked at their hands, a connection between the two sentients, then into the blue eyes of—

"My blood, my cerebral unicore, divided...." Ceera's voice echoed in the space.

Her consciousness.

Another sentient handed Felix three vials. Small, silver tubes containing black liquid. The other sentients received the same. There was no sound except the clinking cylinders as each sentient put them away, in satchels, boxes, or wrapped in cloth.

Alix bounded through the *Shadow*'s galley and into the cockpit. When Sora swiveled the pilot's chair, she saw a broad smile, the dark goggle lenses, and a smear of grease on Alix's cheek. Sora's eyebrows raised and she let out a short laugh, which she cut off with a hand over her mouth. Alix pulled the goggles up, and shook her head as the band tangled in her hair, until she finally got them out entirely.

"I *know* you aren't laughing at me," Alix said.

Sora now looked at the pale circles where Alix's skin remained clean under the goggles. She bit her lip and shook her head. Alix frowned playfully at Sora, who sat in *her* seat, which caused Sora to make a show of leaving one seat for the other. Alix flopped into her rightful chair with a satisfied exhale before throwing her feet up on the instrument panel.

"That was great!" she said. "Don't you think?"

Sora nodded. "It was a successful test."

"A few more days, maybe, and she can fly!"

"I hope so." Sora smiled. "I would love to do that with you."

Alix leaned her head back against the chair and studied Sora. "What *else* would you like to do?" Sora shrugged playfully. Alix reached over and lightly ran her fingertips over Sora's dark forearm; goosebumps formed as her delicate touch reached Sora's wrist.

To their dismay, a harsh static permeated the cockpit.

"Alix? Hello, Alix? Please be there, please." The voice belonged to Mia.

Alix startled, and Sora bolted upright, searching the cockpit for Mia, even though she wasn't here. Alix, however, pulled her arm back quickly, flipped switches overhead, and responded.

"I'm here, Mia!"

Mia's voice broke, her heavy sobs issuing through the cockpit speakers. "Alix...I—I need you to come back to Alloyn."

"What's wrong?" Alix leaned over the dash panel, sweat forming on her palms.

"It's Brom, Rolfe's brother."

"Are you okay?"

Suddenly, another voice came through the speaker. "Alix, is it? Listen, I know you killed our brother. We didn't get a chance to say 'hi' when you were last in town."

"You Brom?" Alix said.

"That's right. Mia is just fine, but we would love for you to come meet us at her place."

"Or what? Let me guess, you're going to hurt her?"

"It's quite simple," Brom said. "Exchange yourself for her."

"And if I don't?" Sora knew Alix would never leave Mia out to dry like that. But the idea that Brom wouldn't get what he wanted needed to be planted. The question resulted in a brief silence.

"Play tough all you want—"

"Your bother played tough. But he died crying at my feet."

Brom let out a muffled laugh, unimpressed. "You've got til sundown." Static followed his words, then a shrill tone, and the transmission ended.

"Shit!" Alix slammed her fist on the dash.

"Alix, breathe." Sora put a hand on Alix's shoulder.

"Come on, we've got to get Felix."

"Babe," Sora said. "Don't rush into this."

Alix snapped her head around. "Don't tell me what to do."

Sora recoiled. "I'm not *telling you* what to do. Just, listen—we can help Mia, but we don't have to do it with clouded judgment."

"You think my judgment is clouded?"

"I know that you are angry. But maybe the solution here isn't to rush in with plasbolts spinning."

Alix's lip curled. "Why not? It's the only thing I'm good at."

Sora touched Alix's cheek. "That's not true. You *know* it isn't true." A moment passed, then, "But...it may just be what you love."

The words squeezed Alix like the hull of a ship crushed by outside pressure. Sora's soft eyes and gentle voice disarmed Alix, her rage tempered by Sora's hand against her face. Did Sora really think Alix *loved* the violence—the killing? Her lip quivered, her resolve wavering. She couldn't let that happen.

A more haunting question made Alix's hands shake and her blood run cold: was Sora right?

Am I just a killer? Alix asked herself as she stared into Sora's eyes. She inhaled slowly so the tears rising to the surface would subside.

I love you, Alix thought.

No matter how hard Alix tried, she couldn't form the words. They remained deep in her heart, despite her grasping at them, trying to pull them up to the surface. Tears dripped down Sora's face as she waited for a response.

Alix looked down at the metal floor. *It may just be what you love.* No plasbolt could have wounded Alix worse. "Is that what you think?"

"No. Alix—"

"Sora, I—"

"Tell me."

Alix swallowed the lump in her throat. "I know that this isn't—that you aren't—ugh."

"Alix," Sora whispered. "I love you."

Alix wept. She lifted her head again. "I'm sorry, Sora. I'm sorry I'm like this—well, I'm not. It's just—they're going to hurt her. I can't—"

"We aren't going to let that happen."

Alix paused at the word—we—and drew in a shaking breath. "These men—there's only one kind of power they answer to. And they deserve what's coming to them."

"I know." Sora put her hands on either side of Alix's face. "I'm not going to stop you. I don't want to change who you are. I'm not trying to *fix* you. Protecting the vulnerable means breaking the powerful, I know that now. And I will be there, behind you, to repair what's broken—to make it better."

Alix closed her eyes and savored the warmth of Sora's palms, even if they were damp from the fear and anxiety permeating both their bodies. When Alix opened her eyes, she leaned forward and smiled. Their lips touched, soft and dry, at first. They separated and exchanged a smile. They kissed again, longer this time; their tongues exploring one another in brief meetings.

They leaned across the gap between the pilot and co-pilot's chairs, foreheads together, lips only a breath apart. Alix sniffled, laughed, and exhaled. "I love you."

* * *

The words squeezed Alix like the hull of a ship crushed by outside pressure. Sora's soft eyes and gentle voice disarmed Alix, her rage tempered by Sora's hand against her face. Did Sora really think Alix *loved* the violence—the killing? Her lip quivered, her resolve wavering. She couldn't let that happen.

A more haunting question made Alix's hands shake and her blood run cold: was Sora right?

Am I just a killer? Alix asked herself as she stared into Sora's eyes. She inhaled slowly so the tears rising to the surface would subside.

I love you, Alix thought.

No matter how hard Alix tried, she couldn't form the words. They remained deep in her heart, despite her grasping at them, trying to pull them up to the surface. Tears dripped down Sora's face as she waited for a response.

Alix looked down at the metal floor. *It may just be what you love.* No plasbolt could have wounded Alix worse. "Is that what you think?"

"No. Alix—"

"Sora, I—"

"Tell me."

Alix swallowed the lump in her throat. "I know that this isn't—that you aren't—ugh."

"Alix," Sora whispered. "I love you."

Alix wept. She lifted her head again. "I'm sorry, Sora. I'm sorry I'm like this—well, I'm not. It's just—they're going to hurt her. I can't—"

"We aren't going to let that happen."

Alix paused at the word—we—and drew in a shaking breath. "These men—there's only one kind of power they answer to. And they deserve what's coming to them."

"I know." Sora put her hands on either side of Alix's face. "I'm not going to stop you. I don't want to change who you are. I'm not trying to *fix* you. Protecting the vulnerable means breaking the powerful, I know that now. And I will be there, behind you, to repair what's broken—to make it better."

Alix closed her eyes and savored the warmth of Sora's palms, even if they were damp from the fear and anxiety permeating both their bodies. When Alix opened her eyes, she leaned forward and smiled. Their lips touched, soft and dry, at first. They separated and exchanged a smile. They kissed again, longer this time; their tongues exploring one another in brief meetings.

They leaned across the gap between the pilot and co-pilot's chairs, foreheads together, lips only a breath apart. Alix sniffled, laughed, and exhaled. "I love you."

Felix turned away from the firelight in the cave. The scene around him swirled into a blur of light, and then darkness fell before him. Though he could see nothing beneath his feet, he walked on, each step creating a ripple in time and space as if he stepped upon a pool reflecting the night sky. He reached out a hand, glowing brightly in the darkness, and brushed the stars aside as he walked. They moved around him like insects, or the rising embers from a campfire.

He closed his eyes, and his footsteps echoed in his mind. Felix thought of Ceera, a singularity in bodily form, pulling all others to her, a force that could not be resisted. The soft reverb of her old voice, the cold touch of her metal fingers, the sharp clicks of her feet on stone.

"Child." He heard the voice as clearly as if she stood in front of him. "Go now, and live."

"Ceera," Felix said in return.

"Felix."

"Are you here? Within Alix?" His voice echoed.

"My blood, divided."

"Is the hyperfluid carrying your consciousness? Your memories?"

"Felix."

"I am here."

"Each of you I trust. They must never—"

"Felix." Another voice echoed.

The darkness began to spin around him, distorted, vibrating as if a foreign sound pressed upon it and threatened the integrity of the structure. Felix grew anxious, panicked, the search for answers slipping away from him.

"Felix."

"Ceera," he said.

"Felix! Wake up." The voice—Alix's voice—crescendoed.

Suddenly, Felix felt a tug like a tether snapping back once it had reached its limit. Everything exploded in brilliant light and rushed past him, disorienting, blinding. The dark singularity moved farther away until it became imperceptible. But the singularity didn't move— Felix flew backwards through the infinite matrix of his mind. He couldn't stop it; there was no concentration or force powerful enough to slow his ascent. Every sound from every memory, for centuries, blended into a piercing cry.

His eyes spun open, the brilliant blue crystals alight. Alix knelt beside the bunk, her hands on his arms, which rested in his lap. She smiled when she saw him open his eyes, but Felix could see in her face that she had been crying.

"Is everything okay?" he said.

"Not exactly."

Alix paced the galley as Felix, Sora, and Jo sat around the table. She had just finished recounting the conversation with Brom, and now she needed to formulate a plan. Each time she thought of a possible strategy, her mind wandered to the eventual outcome: Brom and his two brothers must die. Her heart quickened at the thought, and her fingers tingled. She rubbed her thumb and forefinger together on each hand.

"You're not actually going to surrender to them, right?" Jo said.

"If I don't, there's a very slim chance Mia isn't hurt—or worse," Alix said as she tapped her lip with her fingers.

"Okay, but *you* dead instead of her?"

"We won't let either of those things happen." Felix assured Jo. He smiled at her, but Jo twisted her mouth and nodded.

"So how do we exchange you for Mia, and then get you out?" Sora said.

Alix stopped pacing. "Felix?"

He looked from Jo to Alix. "I will be there with you."

"How?" Jo said.

Felix winked. "Don't worry, kid."

"What if they just, shoot Alix, like as soon as they have her?" Sora said.

"They're out for revenge. I'm sure they'll want to savor it," Alix replied.

"What do Jo and I do?" Sora asked, shooting a worried look at Jo.

"Stay with the *Shadow*," Alix replied.

Felix held up a hand and everyone went silent. His eyes narrowed. He seemed to be peering through the hull and tracking objects in the night sky. Alix held her breath. Felix finally refocused on her. "Xypha ships."

"You're kidding me. *Fuck*."

"Six," he said, his voice trailing off. "They're on comms blackout."

"Fuck, fuck, fuck." Alix paced again, more frantically this time.

"What's that mean?" Sora's eyes darted between Felix and Alix.

"Attack protocols," Felix answered. "They're heading…in from the northeast."

"*Procella* to *Shadow*!" Wick's voice broke in through the shipwide comms channel.

"Wick, this is Alix."

"You all seeing this?" he yelled.

"I tracked them in once they hit range," Felix replied. "What do you see, Wick?"

"Half a dozen ships just dropped through the clouds. They ain't got room to land up here with me. Looks like they're dropping crew off. I can't see too well through the wind and snow."

"It's not crew," Alix whispered.

"What?"

"It's not crew they're dropping," she said, louder now. "Zigs."

"You're fucking joking! There's gotta be a hundred of em!"

"A dozen each," Felix corrected Wick. "Each ship can hold a dozen."

"Well, at any rate, a handful of these things nearly put Alix in the ground."

"I'm well aware!" Alix shouted.

"The things at the port? That nearly killed you before you…" Sora said.

"Yes. But this time, a lot more." Alix's voice shook. She squeezed her fingers tightly into her palms to keep her hands from shaking, too. "We've got to warn Schelon, or something."

"Are you sure he isn't in on it?" Felix warned her.

"He doesn't seem like he would be. You remember his frequency?"

"Not a problem."

"Hey, hey, they're leaving," Wick said. "Must have dropped off all those things."

"Felix?" Alix waited for his confirmation.

"They're pulling up, out of range. But they wouldn't abandon that many units on the ground," Felix said.

"What do you mean?" Wick said.

"Ships will stay close."

"Let me see if I can pick em up." There was a moment of silence. "Long range sensors aren't working," Wick said.

"They've cut us off." Alix's fear bloomed into outright terror. "I'll talk to Schelon in person."

"Wait!" Sora said. "We can't go through with this now, right?" She looked at Felix for backup.

He looked sympathetic, but it was clear he did not agree. "The calculus has changed, but—"

Jo jumped up. "Wait a minute. You're still going to go in there? You'll just get killed!"

"Thanks for the vote of confidence." Alix laughed.

"What choice do we have?" Felix said to Jo.

"Uh, well, we can go back to the valley. There are people there who need us, too!"

"I'm not leaving Mia," Alix declared.

"So, what—one person over the entire valley farmers?" Jo's temper flared.

"I'm not doing this with you, kid."

"*Don't* call me that."

"Jo!" Sora snapped. "This isn't an easy decision. We all need to be on the same page, right? We're a team."

"This is just another one of *her* messes that we have to clean up," Jo said. Her eyes locked with Alix. The two stood close enough to throw fists. Alix hoped it wouldn't come to that.

"Jo, you agreed that we would help the valley after we—" Felix started.

"Yeah, after we recovered." Jo looked at Felix, but pointed back to Alix. "But now we're running into another fire that *she* started."

"Things change." Felix kept his voice calm and steady.

"We don't have time to fucking argue!" Alix yelled. "Jo, stay here, or leave, I don't care." She locked eyes with Felix. "We're going in. But we'll go to Schelon's first."

"I'm with you," Felix said.

"I'll stay with the *Shadow*," Sora said finally. "Let me know if you need me."

"Just keep my ship safe," Alix said.

"Hey, what do you need me to do?" Wick cut in.

"Keep an eye on things. Let us know the zigs' movements, positions, whatever changes. We're meeting Brom and his brothers at Mia's place."

"You're *what*?"

"Oh, right, you didn't hear all that. They've got Mia. So, I'm going in to get her."

"You're just going to waltz down the damn wide-open lane?"

"*I'm going to get her.*"

* * *

In their cabin, Alix and Felix prepared for a fight. Alix pulled her grease-stained shirt off and replaced it with another, albeit cleaner, grease-stained shirt. Felix watched her as she swapped the jumpsuit for a pair of dark trousers. Alix felt him staring at the wound below her left breast.

"Say what you gotta say," she said.

"I have to tell you something."

Alix stopped halfway through buttoning her trousers and left them hanging open as she stared at him. Felix reached out and she took his hand; he gently pulled her closer, then slid his fingers under her shirt and felt the hyperfluid matrix over the wound.

"It's holding, fine," Alix said, assuming he was just worried about the integrity of the fluid keeping her alive through another bloody fight.

"No, it's not that. I think I figured out why you were seeing things during those blackouts."

"What is it?"

"Before you pulled me out, I was back…at the beginning. The vials that I have shepherded for centuries weren't just a normal stock of fluid, I knew that. But, I never realized—"

Alix held his face. "It's okay."

"There's a spark of consciousness in the hyperfluid."

"Wait, a what?"

Felix's eyes spun and he moved his jaw, as if chewing over the right words. "It's a long story, one we don't really have time for, but I have spoken to you before about Ceera. She is the one who gave us the hyperfluid, and birthed sentients like me. I believe her consciousness was divided and resides within the hyperfluid that was given to me, and my four—brothers."

Alix stared, mouth agape. "So, like, what does this mean about the blackouts?"

"You were seeing memories from her. And if she is in there, even a fraction of her, it's possible she was *deliberately* showing them to you."

She blew a long breath through her lips. "I don't even know what to do with this."

"Neither do I." Felix took her in his arms. His voice softened to a whisper. "It is even more imperative now that Xypha does not take you."

"I'll die first."

He ran his thumb down her cheek. "I'm afraid even that would not be sufficient. We just need to be careful. They can't know that you're carrying the hyperfluid."

"They won't." Alix kissed him, and he gripped her tightly with both hands on her back. She pulled back, and stared into his eyes. "I love you."

"I love you, too."

"After we get this situation sorted out, we will deal with whatever this means."

"I've got your back."

"I know."

Alix returned to the galley while brushing her hair back into a fresh ponytail. Felix entered silently behind her. Sora sat at the table, alone. Alix tied her hair and then swiped on her syncpad to reopen a comms channel with Wick in the *Procella*. "Wick, we're about to make the hike. What's going on up there?"

"Nothing, things are normal—quiet."

"That seems odd," Sora remarked.

"Yes, it does." Alix glanced back at Felix.

"If they aren't moving through town, then they must be quartered somewhere. Perhaps ambush positions," Felix said.

"So, they know you're coming?" Wick asked.

"I don't know Rolfe's brothers, but I doubt they could have gotten in touch with Xypha," Alix said. "Maybe Schelon is with them?"

"Either way, let's get into town quietly and pay him a visit," Felix said.

"Alix, I don't like this," Sora said.

"We don't have much of a choice. But we'll be as careful as we can be," Alix smiled. "Felix will cloak and stay by my side the whole way. Wick, meet us at Mia's place. Get her to safety. Felix and I will get rid of Brom and whoever else he's got. And if we have to, we'll shoot our way out."

Sora fell into Alix's arms. She buried her face in Alix's neck. Alix inhaled the smell of Sora's hair, and skin, and gently lifted her face to kiss her. When their lips separated, Alix whispered, "You remember the sequence I showed you in the cockpit?"

"Yes," Sora replied as she held back tears.

"If things go badly, follow it exactly, and you'll be safe."

Sora bit her lip. "Come back."

"I will," Alix said through a smile.

Cold air whipped inside the galley as Felix opened the port ramp. Evening was fast approaching, and the mountains cast shadows over the snowy ground and the forest beyond. Felix walked down the ramp and out of sight. Alix's and Sora's fingers slid apart as Alix followed him. She stretched her neck and shoulders and willed her feet to keep going. The clicks of her boots on metal changed to the crunch of snow.

Alix blew a breath into the air and watched it vanish into the wind. To the east, the sun was on its way down, and a dominant mountain peak cut a great triangle into the sky. The grey clouds were splashed with orange, pink, and purple hues. She swiped on her syncpad and commanded the ramp to close behind her. Ahead, trees swayed in the wind. Alix played Felix's words in her mind: *It is even more imperative now that Xypha does not take you.*

"I will die, first. But it won't be tonight," Alix said into the wind.

16

The Debt

Alloyn fell unnaturally quiet in the evening, save for lamp lighters' boots on the stone streets. The town lay beneath long, deep shadows; Alix moved among them with Felix already cloaked and silent behind her. She pulled her goggles down and the dark alleys became green as the lenses adjusted and intensified the remaining light.

Alix slinked through the alleys like an anxious prey animal. She checked corners before darting across gaps between squat stone houses. Even though she knew Felix was following her and wouldn't let anything happen to her, she wished she could see him, and touch him, or talk to him. But her plan required Felix to remain entirely hidden.

The route she followed to Schelon's office consisted of many turns, left and right, to find the emptiest streets and alleys. She paused and changed her route when a lamp lighter showed up on an adjacent street. The man's boots dragged against stone and masked Alix's footfalls as she ran down another alley, calculating a different path forward. Diverting her route stressed the already-tight window she had to talk to Schelon before meeting Brom and Mia. She reminded herself to breathe. *They wouldn't kill Mia right at sundown, right? Surely I have some leeway.*

The hole blown in the back of Schelon's tiny jail made Alix laugh as she saw it boarded up, with rubble still piled around the wall. She leaned against a corner and checked every direction before quickly moving across the alley. It would cause too much noise to enter through the boards, so she would have to risk the front door. She slid her shoulder along the outer wall to the front corner of the jail and studied the wider street on the other side. Lamps already lit cast their dancing glow in pockets on the ground and buildings along the street. Schelon's office light filtered through the window in tiny slits—his window boarded up as well.

Alix grimaced while contemplating how Schelon would receive her given the trouble she'd caused, but she had no choice. Back to the wall, she brought up Schelon's comms frequency and whispered. "Schelon, you read? You in your office?"

"Who is this?" he replied.

"It's Alix. Remember me?"

She heard him groan before speaking. "Whatever you want, get it somewhere else."

"I'm outside your door. Let me in. We need to talk, quietly."

"Go away."

"Come on, Alloyn is in danger. I'm on a tight deadline."

"Funny how danger follows you around."

"Look, we can insult each other face to face. Open the door, just a few minutes."

The silence gnawed at Alix. But finally, Schelon relented. "Door's open."

Alix peered around the corner once more, then made a dash for the door. She opened it gently, and spun inside the office, putting her back to the door as she slowly closed it behind her. Schelon sat at his desk, a slight frown tugging at his lips. Alix pulled her goggles up and threw on a smile. The sight of Schelon's wounded face wiped the smile right off. Bright red burns and scarring from shattered glass and plasma heat coated his features. Alix started to apologize, but quickly reminded herself she didn't have time to make amends.

"What are you doing here?" Schelon said through a sigh.

"Rolfe's brothers have Mia, and they want me. So, we're doing a little exchange."

"What does this have to do with me? They can have you, for all I care." He waved one of his hands and picked up a drink with the other.

"There is a bigger problem."

"What's that?"

"So, you don't know?"

"Don't know what? Your time is running short." He threw back what remained in the glass.

"Xypha just dropped dozens of killing machines in your town."

"Ha! Sure."

"I'm not kidding. I came here to warn you—well, first to see if you were in on whatever they're doing here."

"I'm not exactly getting around well at the moment, thanks to you. So, forgive me if I'm unaware of some kind of invasion."

"I'm sorry that things didn't go as smoothly as I'd hoped last time. But this time, I am deadly serious. I told you I didn't intend to paint the town red, and I still don't. The only blood that's going to be spilled is your townsfolks'."

"I got shot in the fucking leg! What do you want me to do? I can only hobble around on a crutch."

"I'm not asking you to fight."

"Then get to the point."

"I'm going to kill Rolfe's brothers. Then, I'm going to leave, for good."

"Yeah? That sounds familiar."

"I'm serious. I wouldn't have come back if Mia weren't in danger."

Schelon poured himself another drink. "And look what you brought with you."

"Did you call it in?"

"I don't know what you're talking about."

Alix snatched the bottle from his hand. "Did you tell Xypha we were here?"

"You *weren't* supposed to be here, remember? So, why would I need to tell them that you were here? I don't know what quarrel you have with them."

Alix set the bottle on Schelon's desk. "Alright. So, you didn't tell them, but *someone* did. It's got to be Brom."

"Why would he do that?"

"Figure it out. Then let me know."

Alix crept up behind Wick as he stood in the shadows across from Mia's restaurant. His complaints about the cold and rubbing hands concealed her footsteps. When she appeared beside him, he startled and nearly fell into the metal refuse bins beside him. Alix pulled her goggles off and shot him a disapproving look.

"You could've told me you were here," Wick said.

"Shut up. What's going on?" Alix said as she focused on the

restaurant.

"Nobody has come in or out."

"Alright. When Mia is free, get her to Schelon's place. Then, try to talk that stubborn stirrol into helping us. He wouldn't listen to me."

"I can't believe it," Wick joked.

Alix glared at him. "Maybe he'll listen to Mia."

Wick looked Alix up and down. "You sure about this?"

Alix didn't look away from the restaurant. "Felix and I will take care of them. Don't worry."

"Ah, right, forgot he was—um, where is he?" Wick searched the darkness around them.

"I can't see him, either." Alix pulled in a long breath and her slow exhale shook more than she would've liked. "Come on."

They entered the wide, empty lane. Alix looked down the street to her right, expecting to see dozens of zigs staring back at her, only the light in the corner of their expressionless faceplates visible in the darkness. The cold, or the fear got to her, and she shuddered. *Rolfe's brothers had to have called them here. But why are they waiting? Why would they conceal themselves?*

Halfway across the street, Alix and Wick halted when men emerged from the restaurant. Two of them stepped to either side of the door, their hands held plasrifles at their waists. Their hardened faces were shadowed, but Alix felt them staring through her. Four more men exited after them, each carrying plasbolts, either in-hand or holstered. The last man to step out into the cold, Brom, pushed Mia out ahead, an iron grip on the underside of her left arm. Manacles secured Mia's wrists, just like those Alix had worn on the way to and from the mines under Schelon's escort.

"Alright, I'm here. Let her go," Alix said.

"Not so fast," Brom replied. "You got to drop those bolts." He nodded toward Alix's Plasvelds.

Alix unbuckled her belt and handed it to Wick while she kept her eyes on Brom. "There. Now it's a fair fight."

"There ain't gonna be no fight," Brom said. "Check her."

Two of the men carrying plasrifles approached. Alix held up her arms as one of the men frisked her from head to toe. The other man's finger rested on the trigger, but his eyes moved between Alix and Wick. Alix carried a smile on her lips, in contrast with the confident sneer Brom wore as he stared back at her.

"You want to feel me up, next?" Wick said.

The two men backed off.

"Now, why don't you meet Mia halfway," Brom instructed. "Put these on her," he said to Mia as he unlocked the manacles. "Then, you may go."

Mia held the heavy metal cuffs and approached Alix. Her tears rolled down her red cheeks. Alix walked calmly toward her, and as they met, she held out her hands. Mia shivered, her face down toward the cobblestones. She froze only an arm's length from Alix, sobbing quietly. Alix stepped toward Mia and wrapped her in her arms as Mia buried her face into Alix's shoulder. The manacles rattled as Mia's hands hung loose.

"Hey, hey," Alix said. "It's going to be okay. I promise."

"I'm so sorry. I didn't—"

"Shh. You have nothing to apologize for—it's me who should be apologizing."

"They're going to kill you," Mia whispered.

Alix looked over Mia's shoulder, right to Brom. "No, they aren't." She pulled back and held Mia steady. "Okay, now, listen carefully. Wick is going to get you to Schelon's. You've got to convince him to get everyone in town to a safe place."

"Why?"

"There's a bigger danger here. And things are going to get ugly. People may be caught in the crossfire."

"I'll do what I can."

Alix brushed her fingers down Mia's face, wiped a tear from her cheek, and smiled. "It's going to be okay. I'm going to be fine. I promise. Now, put those things on me like he said."

Mia's hands trembled as she locked Alix's wrists into the manacles. When she finished, Mia put her cold hands on either side of Alix's face and kissed her. "Good luck."

"Go, now." Alix motioned toward Wick with her head.

Mia stood beside Wick. He had Alix's belt over one shoulder, and he put his other arm around Mia. Alix smiled at them one last time. She didn't move with any hesitation or fear; instead, she stepped confidently, her head high, and eyed each man she passed, silently marking them for death. The men around her stood confident in what they perceived as the ultimate power: their target was restrained, and they held all the weapons.

Inside the restaurant, Brom pushed Alix into a chair. He unlocked the manacles, but quickly pulled her arms around the back of the chair and locked them again. Then, the other men tied her arms to the chair at the elbows, and her ankles to the legs. Alix watched them curiously. Some of the men regarded her with hatred in their eyes—hoping she would try to make a move, so they could put a plasbolt round through her chest, and prove their masculinity.

"So, which ones are Rolfe's brothers?" Alix studied them each in turn.

The back of a heavy hand swept across her face. The impact threw Alix's head to the side, and nearly tipped the chair. She did not scream, or cry. As the men encircled her, she stretched her jaw and mouth, then shook her head and blinked rapidly.

"Okay, so, that's the way it's going to be?" she said.

"Shut up," Brom snapped. "I'm Brom. That is my brother Nik, and over there is Isaac."

"Pleased to meet you."

"Schelon said you had friends. Wick was with you. So, where are the other two?"

"Not, here, obviously."

"You expect us to believe you came alone?"

"I didn't come alone—you just said Wick was out there with me." Another hand crossed her face. Alix laughed and spit on the floor. Through heavy breaths, she said, "So what's the plan? You guys beat on me until you get bored?"

"The plan is to get justice for our brother," Isaac yelled.

Isaac wasn't as large as Brom, and his face was obscured by a heavy beard. He scowled at Alix, itching to get his turn. "Well, go on, then. You going to kill me, or do you need to beat up on a defenseless woman first?"

Brom closed his fist this time. He landed a punch on Alix's mouth; her top lip busted open. Blood spilled onto her tongue, and down her chin. Alix shook the fog from her head. She looked down at her lap as blood dripped onto her trousers. She lifted her head, gathered the blood in her mouth, and spit on the floor again.

"You're going to have to clean this place up when we're done," she said.

Brom hit her again. Alix remembered the dozens of fights on Corto, within Spiros's pit or in a bar, and every cocky man who'd expected her to go down easy. Brom hit her again. Alix began to laugh. Blood and sweat dripped down her shirt. The pressure and pain swelled in her face. Her laughter only further enraged Brom and the other men. But she continued to take the hits; she accepted them, as if somewhere deep within her she knew it was what she deserved.

She had a debt to pay.

Alix let her head fall back as Brom drew his fist back, ready to hit her again—but he hesitated. His face contorted into confusion. Alix's chest heaved, and she gasped for air amid the pain—the pain, which lessened. She stuck her tongue into what would have been the cut on her lip, but there was no gash, no sharp pain, no blood. She let go of a heavy sigh. He stood there gawking at the hyperfluid filling the cuts on her face. Alix could imagine what it must look like: the angry, red gashes turning black, the blood no longer dripping from her wounds.

"What the fuck is that?" Brom stumbled through the words.

"I don't have the time to explain it," Alix said.

"Brom, what happened?" Isaac moved up next to his older brother and inspected Alix's red, swollen face.

"I don't know."

Isaac reached to touch Alix's cuts, but Alix jerked back. "It's like her cuts are filled up."

"Astute observation," Alix grumbled.

Isaac hit her. "What the hell is that stuff!"

Alix spit on the floor. "Your brother hit harder. The *dead* one."

In a sudden rage, Isaac reached for the plasbolt on his hip as he strung curses together. Brom restrained his brother. "Back off!" he yelled.

"Just put a fucking bolt in her head, already," Isaac shouted back.

"We can't."

The phrase piqued Alix's interest. "You *can't*? Are y'all cowards, or did your mother say you couldn't kill a woman—you could just beat her up?"

"Shut up!" Brom yelled back at her.

"A woman? My ass," Isaac said. He spit at Alix. "We know what you are!"

"You shut up, too!" Brom shoved his brother.

They know, Alix thought. *The marshal, he told them.* "Now I see what's going on. You're not allowed to kill me, because the marshal wants me alive." Brom and Isaac stopped their argument and stared at Alix. "How much did he offer you?" She looked at the brothers, her mouth open. "How much was your dead brother's life worth to you?"

"Fuck this!" Isaac pushed his brother and drew his plasbolt.

The rising whine became the only sound Alix could hear. She stared down the barrel, unfazed. The scene around her moved almost in slow motion. Brom recovered and reached for his brother. Isaac raised the plasbolt and his furor tightened his face. Alix held her breath—she wouldn't show them anything but defiance.

"Stop!" a voice boomed from behind her.

Isaac still held his plasbolt pointed to Alix's chest, but he looked past her. She sat in between the crowd of men and someone else. She couldn't turn her head to see who had walked up behind her, and she didn't need to. The uneven gait, the voice—she knew exactly who stayed her execution. Just over her shoulder, Alix heard and felt the whine and heat of another plasbolt.

"Holster that bolt, son," the marshal said.

"You ain't gonna shoot me before I kill her," Isaac snarled.

"This wasn't the deal."

"I don't care about no deal. She deserves to die."

"Isaac, put the fucking bolt down," Brom said.

Finally, Isaac relented. He lowered his plasbolt and stuck it back in its holster. He shot one last deadly look at the marshal, at Alix, and then pushed past his brother and walked away. The whine from the marshal's plasbolt died away, too, and Alix leaned her head back as far as she could; she barely saw him behind her, her head almost hanging upside down.

"Hey," she said playfully.

The marshal stepped around Alix's chair and slid another toward her. He gave Brom a commanding look that told the other man to back off. Brom complied and in turn, commanded his own heels to give the marshal and Alix some space. The marshal settled into the empty chair facing Alix.

"So, you put them up to this?" Alix said.

"I knew it was the only way to get you to give yourself up."

"And how much did you offer them?"

"The price was steep."

"And the extracurriculars?"

"I wouldn't let them kill you, but they wanted more than money."

Alix mocked his voice. "Yeah, sure, beat her up a little. How noble of you."

"I just saved your ass."

"Weird—how did I get into this position in the first place? Oh, right, you set me up."

The marshal shook his head. He pulled a white kerchief from his pocket and wiped the blood from Alix's face. She flinched at first, but couldn't get away, so she sat still while he cleaned her up. When the kerchief was a bloody mess, the marshal leaned back and studied the black cuts on her face.

"What the hell is that?"

"I don't know what you're talking about."

The marshal lifted her shirt, but only enough to see the black patch of hyperfluid that had repaired the wound left by Cole. His fingers pressed into the black patch. "That doctor told me Cole shot you, that you should have been dead."

"Sorry to disappoint you."

"This how you survived?"

Alix didn't say anything.

"Why'd you kill him?"

"He shot an unarmed woman." Alix smirked. "Speaking of which, you outed me to these idiots?"

"You weren't unarmed," the marshal shot back.

Alix leaned as much as she could toward the marshal. "Yes, I was. Does that hurt your image of Cole? You thought he was a good and honorable boy."

"He was." There was steel in his voice.

Alix settled back in the chair. "So, you going to take me in? Put me on trial?"

"If you're willing."

"I think we're past whether I'm willing or not, don't you? I'm tied to a chair."

"Forgive me for being prepared. You ain't exactly the type to come quietly."

Alix's eyes narrowed. "You brought them here, didn't you?"

The marshal took a deep breath and stood. "You left me no choice."

"You son of a bitch. Do you have any idea—"

"They don't want you!" the marshal roared. "They don't give a damn about you. This delusion, whatever you *think* they're going to do to you—it's your ego talking. You're *not* that important."

"You have no idea what you're talking about."

"Loucks told me himself."

"And you trust him?" Alix laughed.

"I believe what a man tells me."

"But you didn't believe *me*, huh? When I told you who I really was…inside."

"When are you going to stop blaming me for the trouble *you've* caused?"

Alix steadied her breathing. There was no talking sense into the old man, not anymore. A smile spread across her lips. "All those zigs you brought with you, and you expect us to believe they're just for me?" She glanced over at Brom and the others at a table across the cafe. "What did he promise you? Crits?"

"Stop talking," the marshal said.

"You're never going to see a single one. Xypha's going to need significantly more resources with their train destroyed. A town like Alloyn is a good place to start."

"What's she talking about?" Brom rose from his table.

"She's picking a fight." The marshal leaned over and stuck a finger in Alix's chest. "Don't bring this place down with you. Keep your mouth shut."

"That's it, isn't it? You agreed to give Xypha Alloyn, in exchange for me."

"I said shut your mouth!" the marshal struck Alix with the back of his hand.

She burst into laughter, interrupted by spitting blood onto the marshal's boots. "I'm giving you one last chance to walk out of here."

"You're the one tied to a chair, remember?"

"Which should tell you that you should not mistake my surety for hubris."

"And what about them?" He motioned with his head at the brothers and their men.

Alix laughed quietly. "Those boys are already dead."

The marshal swallowed. All color drained from his face. His eyes darted back and forth. "Where is he?"

"Now what makes you think I can see him, if you can't?" Alix raised an eyebrow.

The marshal drew his Plasveld. The sound of its charge filled the room. Alix just stared up at him, a grin on her face. The marshal backed away. Brom and the others froze, confusion written across their faces.

"What the hell is going on?" Brom said.

The marshal ignored the question from Brom and backed toward the door. Once there, he pushed it open, eyes still ahead, Alix still in the chair, focused only on him. There wasn't anything that could be done. The marshal had to leave, or die in this cafe when Felix showed himself. Alix scowled, directing nothing but pure rage his way. There was no bond between them anymore.

Brom, his brothers, and his men remained dumbfounded as the marshal backed out of the door. The spinning chambers of his Plasveld no longer sang in the cafe. Alix hummed to replace the sound. Brom turned to her, trembling as he studied her face. With a nod, he sent two men to watch the door and windows. Their plasbolts and rifles charged.

"What is going on?" Brom demanded.

"I'm making you an offer," Alix said. "Xypha has dozens of drones ready to take this town for themselves."

"I don't even know who that is."

"Of course you don't." Alix cocked her head. "The marshal offered you crits for your brother? Well, how about your home?"

"Why would I listen to you?"

"Because if you don't, then you're not going to walk out of this cafe." Alix nodded her head to the other men. "And neither are they."

Brom drew his plasbolt and put the barrel against Alix's sternum. "And what if I just kill you right now?"

Alix smirked. "Good luck with that."

Brom curled his lip and stood tall, arm stretched with his plasbolt in Alix's chest. Before he could pull the trigger, a strange flash of light crossed between him and Alix. Brom's eyes widened, blood splattered across Alix's face and torso—but she didn't flinch. Brom's left hand below the wrist, and the plasbolt still in its grip, fell into Alix's lap, then tumbled to the floor. Brom pulled back his bloody, severed arm, and stared at the clean cut, mid-forearm. Before he could utter a word, he collapsed at Alix's feet.

"I warned you," she said.

"Brom!" Isaac shouted. He went for his plasbolt.

The other men turned around in time to see Isaac's body slammed against the wall. Though they could not see what force pinned him there, they saw blood pouring down his chest. Their eyes were horrified as Isaac dropped suddenly, slumped over. His brother lying bleeding on the floor, Nik turned to Alix, leveling his plasbolt.

Zmmph.

Alix closed her eyes and turned her face away as she braced herself for the impact. The plasma round did not strike her. Even with her eyes closed, she saw the blinding blue flash in the room. The round struck *something*, and shattered, its energy exploding in tiny embers and sparks. Alix opened one eye in time to see the carnage unfold as bolts of energy climbed up an invisible, slender surface.

Nik died clutching his throat as the invisible blade sprayed blood onto the white tablecloths. The other men immediately opened fire wildly into thin air. Plasfire ignited the curtains and cloths, and some of the men stumbled into the chaotic line of fire as an unseen hand shoved them. Those who weren't killed by friendly fire were stabbed, cut, and bled to death in a heap on the floor. At last, the plasfire ceased and steam and smoke hung thick in the room.

Felix appeared out of thin air, a single-edged blade, short relative to him, in one hand. He used a tablecloth to wipe the blade clean as he approached Alix. She smiled, relieved to see him, and his stark blue eyes. He sheathed the blade on his belt and stepped over Brom, bloody bootprints in his wake.

"Okay, how'd you stop the round?" Alix wanted to know.

"The blade."

"You did *not* cut it!"

"No, of course I didn't. I just put the flat of the blade in its path. It's an old form of omni and while I'm holding it, there's an electromagnetic charge—"

"Okay, okay, not as interesting as I thought," Alix cut him off. "Get me out of this fucking chair."

"Right away, miss."

Inside Schelon's office, Mia pleaded with Schelon—stubborn man that he was—to take Alix's warning seriously, hoping she could finally break through. Wick paced in front of the lawman's desk. Schelon remained rooted. He sat back in his chair, hand over his face as the pair of them yelled at him.

"I have seen what these things can do. People are gonna die," Wick said.

"Everyone has already been told to stay in their homes! I don't know what more you want me to do," Schelon replied.

"Sound the mine's emergency alarm," Mia said. "If everyone takes refuge inside, then we can guarantee they'll be safe."

"So, you want me to get people to *leave* the safety of their homes, with some kind of army of artificials out there?"

"It's the best chance they have," Wick said. "Mia's right, get everyone you can into the mine and seal those huge doors."

"And trap ourselves?" Schelon scoffed.

"You know there are other ways out of the tunnels," Mia insisted. "If you're not going to do anything, then I will."

Schelon sighed. He grabbed the crutch that leaned on the wall beside his chair. He pulled himself up and leaned his weight on the crutch. "Fine. I'll sound the alarm. But I can't go around dragging people out of their homes. That's your job."

"We'll get it done," Mia promised.

"What is she going to do about this?" Schelon referred to Alix as he looked over at Wick.

"Break as many of those things as she can."

"Well," Schelon strained and hobbled toward the door. "I hope she's as good as you say."

"The alarm?" Mia said as Schelon retrieved his coat from a hook on the wall.

Schelon put one arm through a sleeve. Mia went to his side and helped him with the other. She adjusted the collar and looked into Schelon's eyes tenderly. Schelon couldn't look her in the eye; he pulled a set of keys from his coat pocket and weighed them in his hand.

"That box on the wall," he said. "Good luck." Schelon tossed the keys on the desk and opened the door.

Mia didn't watch him leave. She rushed to the keys and the metal box wired to the stone wall. She fumbled with several keys before finding the one that opened the lock. Inside the box was a hand microphone, buttons, and a switch. The red button was clearly labeled as the alarm. Mia turned the switch and picked up the microphone.

"Attention! Um, attention everyone," she glanced at Wick, but he nodded for her to continue. "This is an emergency. There is imminent danger, and everyone must retreat to the mine entrance. This is not a drill!"

Mia let the microphone hang by its cord and slammed the alarm button. In moments, klaxons blared across Alloyn. The rhythm of the alarms echoed in the mountain valley. Snow fell lightly outside as Wick stood in the doorway. Alix's belt with her Plasvelds still hung across his body. He turned back to Mia.

"Get your ass to that mine," he said. "Alix will kill me if you don't make it."

Mia laughed. "I will. Get back to her and tell her she better not get herself killed."

"She has a knack for cheating death," Wick said. He smiled, tipped his hat, and rushed out the door.

17

Dead and Buried

The blaring klaxons startled the marshal. He had returned to the storeroom that served as his headquarters with the Xypha engineers who accompanied the Z-16s. Three engineers sat at a table with vizscreens displaying a complete three-dimensional map of Alloyn, a diagnostic monitoring of every Z-16 unit, and various sensors monitoring the surrounding area. Behind the marshal, in the dim room, two dozen of the Z-16s stood in rigid formation, dark and silent.

"The hell is this?" He said to one of the engineers.

"Seems an emergency frequency for the entire town. Alarms placed around the town have been triggered. The message calls for everyone to seek refuge in the mine."

"Panic," the marshal said. "She's bought herself some time."

"Should we activate?"

"No, I don't want to start a bloodbath." *She knew I wouldn't want civilians in the plasfire,* he added to himself. For a moment, he wondered if he should call the bluff and send the Z-16s out anyway. But he squashed that feeling.

On the vizscreen of Alloyn, displayed from an aerial thermal imaging system onboard one of the drop ships overhead, a herd of bright figures appeared from dark houses. The marshal and the engineers watched as the townsfolk emerged from their homes, all heading in the same direction. Some ran in a panic, while others filed calmly toward the mine entrance on the eastern end of town.

"Here." the marshal pointed to the screen. "We are going to funnel them toward the center. Small teams here and here, on the outside. Larger teams sweep down the streets on the north and south. I will take two dozen with me in the center lane."

"What about the ship, on the landing pad?" an engineer said.

"Escape is not her plan. This is a fight to the death." The marshal remembered the look in Alix's eyes as he'd left the cafe. She was prepared to die here—even though he'd tried to save her life. *She rejected me*, he thought. Now, he had her cornered, and with Xypha at his back, she would not be taken alive.

The conclusion darkened his mind. He would have to kill her.

A dark cloud cast a pall over pleasant memories of them together, when Alix had still been a child. He remembered her wild nature; though she had been rebellious, almost untamable, he had done the impossible—or so he'd thought. Now he realized he had never succeeded. She'd kept something from him, even when she'd looked him in the eye, she'd lied to him—about who she was—*who* he *was*.

The boy the marshal had taught to ride, to shoot, to read and write; the boy who'd followed him across the valley, tied to his hip; the boy who'd said he'd wanted to be just like him; the boy who'd said he'd loved him—that boy was dead. There was no piece of him left, and the marshal could never get him back.

"Activate the drones," he ordered. "Send command and control to my syncpad."

Only a kilometer away, but lower on the mountain, Jo stood outside the *Shadow*. Snow gathered in her dark hair. She listened to the wind in the slape needles and ghissh leaves. Behind a fog and blanket of pale cloud, bright halos shone around the moons as light caught ice crystals in the cold air. Jo stretched her fingers and elbow, rotated her shoulder, and winced at the pain.

She heard a strange, distant echo.

Jo closed her eyes and listened, focusing on the unnatural rhythm obscured by the rustling trees. She moved her head as she caught the rhythm, pulsing in regular intervals, and then she opened her eyes and turned back to the *Shadow*. Into the ship she ran, up the ramp, and straight to the cockpit. Sora sat in the copilot's chair, talking to herself as she moved her hand over the instrument panels in front of her, and above her head. She ran through a ritual, hitting every beat to commit a sequence of buttons and switches to memory.

"There's something wrong!" Jo said, interrupting her.

"What? I haven't heard anything from them," Sora replied as she kept her eyes on the instruments.

"I heard something outside…like alarm bells."

"We're a long way from town. It could've been the wind."

"It wasn't the wind! Listen to me!"

Sora stopped and swiveled around to face her sister. "Sorry. What can we do? Alix wanted us to stay here and protect the *Shadow*."

"I don't think this is where we need to be."

"You want to go into town?"

"I want to do something other than sit here on my ass."

Sora tightened her lips. "I understand that feeling."

"Anyway, if no one is here, why would it matter if they came after the ship?"

"This ship is important to Alix. I'm not going to abandon it."

"It's just a ship."

"It's home, to her. More than that, it *means* something."

"Just like our home meant something to us? But you left me there alone, anyway."

"I thought we were past this, Jo."

Jo thought of home; the lumpy mattresses in the apartment above the shop; the moonlight in the orchard; the smell of dinner in the meeting house. Then, she thought of the dead boy floating facedown in the Lipine; the men trying to kill her—men from her own village. The lonely nights in the doctor's bed as the Thin Man tortured her with a chilling voice in her mind.

"Well, I'm not." She paused. "I shouldn't have come up here. I should have stayed in the valley. I should be helping *them*."

"You can't *walk* back to the valley, Jo. We're going home, I promise. After this is over, we'll return and find out who is responsible for whatever's been going on."

"Don't make promises you can't keep."

Jo strode back through the galley, and into the cabin where she and Sora slept. She stood among their meager possessions, mostly clothing, and began to stuff her things into her rucksack. The one thing she didn't have was a plasbolt. Felix had crushed the one she'd taken from a dead man. *I'm useless without one*, she thought. When everything else was packed away, she lifted the bag over her shoulder and left the *Shadow*.

As Jo trudged through the snow beneath the slape and ghissh forest, she heard Sora shouting her name. Snow fell, and Jo listened to the whistling wind, and barely audible within it, the rhythmic pattern of Alloyn's alarms.

Alix and Felix watched from the windows of Mia's cafe as the people of Alloyn ran past. They carried sacks, crates, and baskets of their treasured belongings. Parents held their children on their hips. The mass of footsteps pattered on the cobblestones. Alix leaned against the frame of an open window. Her face still carried the black marks and purple bruises. Her shirt remained soaked with blood from the neck down beneath her coat. She rubbed her thumb and fingertips together on her right hand.

"Seems Mia and Wick succeeded in convincing Schelon," Alix said.

"He's on his way back here," Felix added.

"Good—he's got my bolts."

Felix, who stood at another window in front of Alix, looked back at her. She smiled, though the bruising on her face made it a painful gesture. Felix drew near and touched her forehead. His fingertips traveled gently across her brow, down her cheek, and his thumb rubbed her bottom lip. She tried to appear confident, but he knew her heart and could likely tell the rhythm was off, faster than what she would naturally experience before a fight—she was afraid. Felix lifted her chin and leaned down to kiss her.

Their lips together, Alix squeezed her arms around Felix's chest, beneath his arms. The currents under his skin pulsated, flowing within his chest, and out to his limbs. The charge made the hair on Alix's arms and neck stand up. Each time they parted lips, a spark lit her open mouth. Felix slid his hand down her chest, placing it above her heart. Alix dropped from her tiptoes and smiled, pressing her forehead into his chest.

Felix held one of Alix's hands in his, and his right hand remained upon her chest. Alix placed her left hand on his wrist. She felt his rhythm and concentrated on her breath; in through her nose, and slowly out between her barely-parted lips. Her heart rate decreased. With her eyes closed, she felt as though Felix had his hand inside her chest, caressing her heart. She wept, and turned her face up, her hand sliding to his cheek as he looked down at her.

She needed to see his eyes, if this was to be the last time they embraced. The blue crystals sparkled, like an undisturbed field of ice and snow in the valley. She saw deeper blues, and swirls of black and purple, entire galaxies contained within such small spaces—a sight she could never forget.

"Look," she whispered. "Whatever is inside me—whatever memories or knowledge passed down from Ceera—I will not let them take it."

"And they will not take you," Felix replied.

"I love you," Alix said through tears.

"I love you, too."

Wick staggered through the door to Mia's cafe. After he caught his breath, he straightened and caught sight of Felix and Alix by the windows. "Alright, Mia's getting everybody into the mine."

"What about Schelon?" Alix replied.

Wick shrugged. "He took off. He's lame anyway. Not sure he'd be much use with that leg."

"Well, then I guess we better make a plan."

Felix's eyes spun in their sockets, brightened, and then narrowed as he focused on his sensors. He could scan almost to the town's edge from their position, but the far western end remained out of his range. "The zigs are active," he delivered gravely.

"What's their position?" Alix said.

"They've fanned out; moving in a line stretching north-south; but they are marching this way."

"Trying to close us in," Wick observed.

"Felix, they can't pinch you—get around behind them, and they'll be forced to change tactics," Alix said.

"Where are you going?" Felix frowned at her.

"I'm going to stroll down memory lane." Alix smiled and winked at him.

"What's that mean?" Wick looked at both of them.

Felix replied, but kept his eyes on Alix. "It means she's going to do something reckless."

"What else is new?" Wick laughed.

Alix punched Wick in the shoulder as she headed toward the door. She stopped, spun on her heel, and held out her hand. It took a moment for Wick to register her request. Then, he remembered the belt over his shoulder, which he unbuckled and tossed to her. Alix secured it around her waist and drew both Plasvelds. She inspected each, spun the chambers, and then spun the bolts forward and backwards on her fingers.

"There's a heavy concentration in the center lane," Felix reported of the zigs' movements.

"The marshal's got to be with them," Alix replied.

"You think he's actually going to step up?" Wick said.

"It's the entire reason he's here," Alix said.

"So, what am I supposed to do?"

"Felix, you still got those sonic charges, right?"

"Two left," Felix said.

"That's what you're doing," Alix said to Wick. "Take out as many as you can."

Felix handed Wick the spherical explosives. Wick tossed one of the spheres up and caught it again before he stuffed them into his coat pockets. He exhaled with his cheeks puffed up, full of air.

"You okay?" Alix said.

"Yeah, just, you know, thought there'd be some kind of pep talk." Wick offered a weak smile.

Alix put both hands on his shoulders; they stood eye-to-eye. "Don't fucking die." She slapped his shoulders.

"Aye, captain." Wick laughed.

Alix looked up at Felix. They'd already said everything they'd needed to say to one another. The smile she had for Wick, a sarcastic smirk, changed into one of pure love and adoration for Felix. She ran her hand along his chest as she walked out the door and into the cold. Wick followed Alix outside.

He glanced back once, to see Felix standing alone in the cafe, eyes closed. His physical body remained still, but the image of him shifted —his edges frayed and blended with the surrounding environment. The cloaking matrix wrapped itself around him, and he slowly vanished, as if his body had separated at the atomic level and been carried away in a gentle breeze.

Alix stood alone in the middle of the broad lane. She stared at the snow falling into her hand and traced the pink scar in her palm. The memory of that night came to the fore. The heat; the thick, burning air in her lungs; the sting of the scalding metal backstrap and gold inlay within her Plasveld grip. That pattern was now burned in her palm forever: a reminder. The marshal had gifted her those Plasvelds. Now, they were gone, burned up in the Black Barrel.

Each snowflake dissolved the moment it touched the scar.

The tinny steps of the zigs on cobblestone struck Alix's ears. Through the snowfall, the marshal and two lines of zigs marched toward her. They entered the glowing pockets of street lamps, then marched out of the light. The shadows shifted across the figures, changing their shapes as if the approaching force wasn't a tangible thing. The marshal's uneven gait, favoring his prosthetic, contrasted the uniform, inhuman rhythm of the zigs. She didn't move as they approached. The marshal reached his right hand over to his left arm and tapped a command on his syncpad.

The zigs stopped their march.

The marshal stepped a few paces forward.

Alix wiped her hands dry.

Snow and silence fell between them.

She held open her coat as wide as possible. "So there's no confusion about whether I'm armed."

The marshal sneered and flipped a side of his coat back to reveal the Plasveld on his right hip. Alix sucked her teeth and clicked her tongue, then tugged her goggles down. The lenses cycled through visible spectrums and splashes of color. They settled on the thermal image of the marshal, bright orange, yellow, and pink against the deep, cold blue of the air around him—and the metal troops at his back.

Wick moved cautiously, his steps measured, jumping from one shadow against a wall to another. In one hand he held a plasbolt, while he kept the other free. He put his shoulder to the stone and peeked around the corner, down a street only a couple blocks over from the center lane. His hand trembled, the plasbolt chambers clattering. The sweat on Wick's brow seemed a cruel joke, given how the cold penetrated his coat and seeped into his bones. He wiped his sleeve across his face.

Sharp footsteps echoed down the street.

They're not footsteps, Wick said to himself. He remembered the night at the port. He'd cowered behind a crate; the unrelenting march of the zigs had frightened even Alix. His memory played that night over and over, as vividly as if it was unfolding again right in front of him. The sight of the dark, thin figure standing over him, the plasrifle pointed at his face—Wick grasped his trembling hand with the other. His heart pounded.

The clicks of their feet on the stone hit him in the chest like a ball peen hammer. The sound pinned him to the wall. Wick dropped his head, heart sinking.

Still, the sharp clicks advanced.

"Don't fucking die. Don't fucking die. Don't fucking die." Wick whispered Alix's words.

He spun the chambers on his plasbolt. The swelling tone of the charge overtook the sound of the zigs approach. Wick stood straight, back to the wall, and heaved a heavy breath into the cold air. He swiveled, reached around the corner, plasbolt leveled, and spotted the zigs—four of them in a row, perfectly spaced, from one side of the street to the other.

The zigs registered Wick's presence almost immediately. They raised their plasrifles as Wick opened fire.

Zmmph zmmph zmmph zmmph.

Each round lit up the street in blue flashes. The zigs' narrow frames made it difficult to find his mark, and the shots skimmed and ricocheted off their omniite plating. But one shot found a shoulder joint, and severed the zig's arm from its torso. The machine tilted, its arm clattereing to the ground as sparks burst from the joint. Unable to hold the plasrifle, it bent forward from the weight.

The other three returned fire.

Wick spun back around the corner as the stone burst into fragments and dust. The zigs fired with precision, each shot tearing away the stone. Wick slid down the wall to avoid the jagged splinters. The zigs would reach him in moments—so Wick ran.

Plasfire echoed in Alloyn. Neither Alix nor the marshal broke eye contact. Alix's right hand hovered above her belt, her fingers rubbing against her thumb. The marshal's right thumb hooked on the top of his belt, between the buckle and his Plasveld. The zigs stood motionless, their plasrifles at an angle, barrels down. Alix saw the marshal as a mere shape through her goggles' thermal imaging.

"I told you not to do this. I told you it would only create more problems," the marshal said.

"The fight isn't over."

"Yours is."

"Not by a long shot." Alix stuck her tongue in her cheek and steadied her breathing.

Then, one of the zigs to the marshal's left moved. Alix's goggles lit up, and she looked from the marshal to the unit that had raised its plasrifle.

Alix drew.

Two shots split the air, zipping past one another.

The marshal whipped around to see the zig standing with its rifle level. "Stand down!"

Alix fell to her knees. She stared at the hole in her chest, burned clear through her bloody shirt. Blood poured from her mouth. Her fingers loosened their grip on the Plasveld, and her right hand fell to her side. She put her left over the wound.

"God dammit, Loucks!" the marshal yelled.

But Alix was gone. She stumbled in the dark, coughing up blood. Her breath came in shallow wheezes. As she rounded a corner, she had to remove her left hand from the wound to prop herself against a wall. She vomited and her eyes fluttered. Her body collapsed, her left hand swiping a bloody print as she fell. Alix gritted her teeth and screamed as the hyperfluid gathered in her chest, coagulating and stretching between her skin to hold her together. Her lung inflated properly once more as the fluid sealed the hole there, too.

Strength returned to her legs and Alix leaned her shoulder against the wall. She picked herself up. The sound of footsteps approached. *He's following the blood trail.* She staggered across the alley in between two other buildings as the reverberating sounds of the zigs' sharp steps on the stone rose all around her.

Alix's heart raced, but she froze. The sounds created confusion; she didn't know where to run. She drew both Plasvelds. Ahead of her, zigs turned a corner. Two could only stand side-by-side in the alley. She unleashed plasfire on them before they could raise their rifles. Her shots sheared through the central torso, rang off the faceplate, and tore apart joints where the zigs' legs connected. One fell sideways into the other. Their plasrifles fired into the ground. Alix's goggles quickly adjusted to a different wavelength to avoid blinding her from the heat of the rounds in the small space.

She continued firing, almost emptying her Plasvelds, until the two zigs went dark and lay in a heap. When she lowered the Plasvelds, steps sounded behind her. She spun and darted down another alley as plasfire ripped past her.

Four zigs marched in unison down an east-west street on Alloyn's southern edge. A street over, four more marched, and they moved according to their programming. They created a net to push Alix and the others toward the marshal and his primary force. The drones marched until an invisible hand drew a blade. Felix swept the blade in one motion through two zigs and severed their narrow, rectangular heads. The other two drones reacted, but could detect no target as Felix moved around them and beheaded both with one strike. He picked up a plasrifle from the fallen drones, and it disappeared as the cloaking field extended from Felix's hands to cover the rifle.

Felix moved silently to the next street. The four zigs ahead continued their march. He crept up behind them and unleashed four shots. Each round exploded a zig's head and all four machines crumpled to the ground. He scanned the area, and picked up four more zigs ahead to his left.

Felix jumped onto the flat roofs and maneuvered to the corner of a building which looked into a crossroad.

The zigs marched into the intersection and paused. Felix leveled the plasrifle and waited as he infiltrated the zigs' internal computers and picked up the commands sent to them. He followed the signal, a *local* signal, and peered back to the west. Within one of the nondescript buildings on the edge of town, Felix crawled inside the Xypha network operating locally in Alloyn. He picked through the local systems, up to the drop ships hiding in cloud cover overhead.

He refocused on the zigs, which remained in the intersection, then fired four shots—each a perfect hit on the zigs' narrow heads. They collapsed in the street, sparking. Felix dropped the plasrifle and returned his attention to the local network, smiling as he shut the network down with a thought.

His sensors lit up—more drones activated.

Felix picked up their locations. They were all marching toward him.

"Alix," he said into his comms.

"Go," she replied."

"They've tasked zigs to my position."

"Can you handle it?"

"Don't worry about that—"

"Shut up. Do we need to regroup?"

"Wick, you read?"

"I got you, buddy," Wick replied.

"From your position, move directly west four blocks. Then, turn south. You'll come behind a dozen. Hit them with the sonic charge."

"Copy that."

Felix looked across the rooftops, and pinpointed Alix's location. The zigs and the marshal moved toward her, and Felix flagged their positions easily. But he could see Alix hunkered down. "You've got to move, Alix. The marshal still has six with him. Get on a rooftop."

"Will do. Stay sharp."

"Wick, I've got you. If anything blocks your path, you'll know it."

"On my way to you!" Wick replied.

Wick raced down the street, puffs of his heavy breaths rising above him like an ancient steam engine. He holstered his plasbolts and counted the blocks until he reached the fourth street. His boots slid on the snow-covered stone, but he caught himself from falling and spun around a post holding up an awning over a shop door. The street ahead stretched south and into darkness.

"I'm on the street, heading straight to you," he said aloud to Felix.

"I can see you," Felix replied.

Wick pulled at the sonic charge in his pocket. The size of his hand around the sphere was slightly larger than the pocket opening, so he had to yank it through. He twisted the halves of the sphere and the explosive charged up in his hand.

Finally, he spotted the zigs in front of him. They moved in a black mass, darker than the shadows which hid him. He slid to a halt. Their marching feet clicked loudly, painfully in his ears. Wick stuck the fingers of his left hand in his mouth and whistled as loudly as he could.

The zigs stopped.

Wick rolled the charge toward them.

It clinked and bounced over the cobbles. The almost imperceptible slope of the street carried its momentum forward over uneven stones that might have stopped it. The zigs turned at their center to face Wick.

His eyes widened and he took off. Plasfire rained on the zigs from a rooftop. Felix had pulled their attention back to him.

The zigs raised their plasrifles at the corner of the roof, but did not fire.

The sonic charge whistled, the tone swelling.

Wick covered his ears and dove out of the street through a wooden door.

An incredible, sharp ringing peaked, followed by a pop. The charge exploded. The shockwave tore through the zigs, ripping their limbs into pieces, screws and bolts flying like plasbolt rounds and imbedding themselves into the stone. Buildings shuddered, walls collapsing, turning the intersection into piles of grey, dusty rubble.

Wick stuck his head out of the busted door and assessed the carnage. His laugh echoed in the silence following the explosion.

"Nice work," Felix said in his ear.

Alix jumped onto a metal crate, gripped a cold pipe protruding from the wall in front of her, and pulled herself up onto the flat roof. She rolled onto her back and gazed up at the pale cloud cover, a blanket lying over the town. Snow kissed her face. She closed her eyes for a moment and imagined she lay in peace with Felix and Sora.

The *click clack* of the zigs below her shook Alix out of the thought. She peeked over the roof and saw two drones moving through the alley. She also heard the marshal's boots nearby. She rolled away from that edge of the roof and crawled to another. Below stood the marshal, plasbolt raised. He looked down one alley and another. Alix narrowed her eyes and drew in a deep breath.

She threw her legs over the roof, dropped, and knocked the marshal to the ground before landing on her feet. His plasbolt slid across the stone. She reached for her Plasveld. A chill went up her spine and Alix spun around to see two zigs. A split second passed, her Plasveld drawn only at her hip, and she opened fire.

Zmmph zmmph zmmph.

The plasfire cut through the closest zig, the blue streaks hitting the stone at the edge of the roof behind them. The second zig moved toward her; it didn't even register the other had fallen. Alix dropped to her knees and drew her other Plasveld in the same motion. Both Plasvelds burst into the machine. She screamed as she emptied the weapons into the drone.

Sparks flew into her face as the drone fell to pieces. Her Plasvelds whistled, the chambers spun empty. The glow died away with the whining sound, and only steam remained. Alix gasped for breath and beneath her goggles, her eyes were as wide as the full moons. With a sharp ring, she ejected the empty charge cylinders and prepared to reload.

Then, while hers remained empty, another Plasveld charged in the alley.

She felt the barrel against the back of her head.

"Drop them," the marshal ordered.

Alix complied. The Plasvelds rattled on the stone.

The marshal stared past the blue glow of his Plasveld at Alix's dark hair. His hand trembled. Tears clouded his vision. There would be no better chance to finish this than now.

"You really going to kill your own daughter?" Alix said.

The marshal snapped. Through gritted teeth he replied, "You already killed *both* my sons."

Alix shook her head despite the barrel against it. "That's what you just don't get: I was *never* your son. But I would've been your *daughter* if you could have listened and accepted the truth."

The marshal pressed the barrel against her head. His bottom lip quivered, and he shifted his jaw with indecision. The internal debate slowed his reflexes.

Alix snatched the barrel of his Plasveld, ignoring the heat that would surely leave marks, and ripped it away from her head. She jerked her arm forward. The marshal lost his balance and tumbled. Alix rose to one knee, her hip out, and she flipped the marshal head over heels.

The old man found himself on his back, the Plasveld wrenched from his grip. Alix jumped up, flipped the Plasveld into the air and caught the grip. She dropped a knee onto the marshal's chest and swung the Plasveld down into his face. He stared up into black circles, Alix's eyes hidden behind the goggles.

Terror gripped him.

Alix's chest heaved as she looked down at the marshal's horrified face. He held his arms on either side of his head as if she'd told him to raise them. Her nostrils flared. She yanked the goggles off with her free hand. The sight of her eyes seemed to terrify the marshal even more than the black lenses as he shrank into himself.

"Go ahead," he muttered. "One of us isn't leaving this town alive."

"Whose fault is that?" Alix growled.

"Yet another one of my failures, I suppose."

"I'm not falling for the guilt trip anymore." Alix pressed the barrel under the marshal's chin.

Click clack. Click clack.

Alix snapped her head up.

A zig stood only a couple meters away.

She curled her lip and stared into the smooth faceplate on the narrow head. It had no eyes, no features, but she felt *something* looking back at her. The light in the corner of the faceplate glowed green. The longer it stood there, the angrier she became, but she did not remove the Plasveld from beneath the marshal's chin.

He lay there, helpless.

Tears fell down Alix's face. *They will not take me*, she thought. In her mind, she saw the only potential outcome. She would raise her hand; the zig would fire; and the plasma round would burst through her skull. The snow would fall on the zig's dark frame and evaporate as they hit the plasrifle, one small hiss after another.

To Alix it seemed that Celestine stopped turning—everything stopped—except the snow.

Why isn't it firing?

Her right hand trembled. The anger in her rose, breaking through her fear. *Just fucking get it over with*, she said to herself, as if talking to the zig.

So, she raised her arm.

The motion twitched her body just to the left. Her arm flew up, the Plasveld glow passing up the walls around her as she whipped it toward the zig.

Zmmph.

Zmmph.

The blue streak flew just to the right of the zig's head. Her shot had missed.

The single shot from the zig's plasrifle did not.

The slight shift in Alix's angle as she lifted her Plasveld changed the round's location—but still, it found its mark. She let go of the Plasveld even as her arm's momentum continued upward.

Her body flopped backward, turning slightly, but landing on her back. She tried to breathe and heard only a gurgling sound in her throat. Her eyes clouded. Her hands shook violently. With barely enough strength left, she touched her fingers to her neck and collarbone. She felt the warm blood, pulled her hand back, and stared at her red-coated fingers.

Breath still could not come as she desperately tried to suck in the cold air. Her chest tightened and she managed to focus enough to recognize that she was drowning as blood filled her throat and lungs. Alix reached her left hand across her chest, but couldn't make it to her neck. Her mouth hung open and tears streamed down the corners of her eyes and dripped into the pool of blood that gathered beneath her.

In her dim sight, she saw the marshal stand. Their eyes met. It was maybe the first time she'd seen him genuinely look at her with love since before she'd told him the truth all those years ago. Alix reached her right hand up to him, but strength left her, and her hand fell to the ground.

* * *

The marshal wept as he stood over Alix, watching her bleed to death. She reached for him, but her hand fell to the stone before he could kneel down and hold it. The marshal lifted her arm, cold and limp, and held it gently. He pressed her hand against his lips, her blood mixing with his tears.

The marshal closed his eyes while Alix's glassed over.

A sudden tremor in Alix's body startled him and he opened his eyes. He'd expected to witness her death rattle, but her hand in his tightened, her fingers curling and rubbing against his palms as she formed a fist. The terror he'd felt before, when he'd looked upon her dark lenses, and then cold, deadly stare, paled in comparison to that which froze his blood, now. Black liquid poured into her neck from her chest. It reached out with fingerlike tendrils, gripped her flesh, and wrapped around her arteries and bones. Alix seized but the marshal held her down.

The black liquid in Alix's throat increased. It seeped up from her chest into the hole above her collarbone. The tendrils grabbed flesh and created tiny black lines against her pale skin. He watched it work, his hands trembling, but kept his hold on Alix's right hand. The liquid pooled, then glossed over like a frozen patch of ice on dark stone. It dulled, and excess liquid seeped back through until only a patch of soft black material stretched between her burnt skin.

Alix's chest and stomach lurched, and her back arched. She gurgled deep within her throat. He pulled Alix's right arm and rolled her onto her side. Alix's body convulsed, and blood rushed from her mouth onto the ground. She gagged and lurched again—more blood spilled out.

The marshal fell back and looked at his trembling hands, red with her blood.

Alix gasped for air. She felt her neck, her collar, and despite the pain, she was intact again—she could *breathe* again. But she had no idea how much time had passed. Overhead, three lights hovered in a triangle above the clouds, then flew away. She lifted her head, her hair soaked with blood, and tried to hold herself up. The weakness in her arms caused them to shake, but she looked down the alley, past her boots, and saw no one.

"F…Felix," she muttered.

She carefully lifted her knee. Her body remained weak, slow, but

Alix pushed herself up. Her head swam and she lost her balance. She crashed into junk, but held herself from falling down again. The world around her spun, and she staggered again, until her back touched the other wall, and she slid down to sit on the stone. Between her boots, the goggles stared back at her.

Alix leaned forward and hooked the goggles with weak fingers. As she lifted the goggles up, flashes of light tore the dark sky open, and she ducked on instinct; rapid bursts streaked above the rooftops. The pain was unbearable, and her arms felt like the loose, long sleeves of a shirt. But she willed them to stretch the goggles over her head, at first crooked, and not sitting properly—she adjusted them and the world lit up.

Not only could she see through the darkness, her ears filled with screaming voices. "Alix! Alix!"

"Wh—what?" she stammered.

"Alix? Are you okay?" Wick yelled.

"I'm…" she didn't know what to say.

"Alix get up," Felix said. "Get up, baby."

"Goddammit," Wick's voice broke in as if reacting to something around him.

Alix pushed her feet into the stone and her back slid up the wall. She staggered through the alley. A burst of light and pulsing heat crossed over her again. *Plasfire—heavy*…She came to a street, a break in the buildings where she could see a greater portion of the sky. Everything above her head glowed in brilliant light. She tilted her head back, mouth open; the goggles adjusted for her, and she saw the *Procella*, lifting off the landing pad away to her right.

Another burst of heavy plasfire crossed from the ship, over her head, and away to her left. She followed the streaks, turned her neck, slowly and painfully, and watched the heavy ammunition pound the side of a Xypha drop ship. The rectangular ship swooned, listed to one side, and exploded. The fireball shocked her, and Alix stumbled backward. The fiery wreck crashed into the flat rooftops, and threw more fire and stone into the air.

"Alix, you've got to move," Felix said to her. "Wick is going to pick you up."

"What? What happened?" Alix put a hand to her head.

"No time. Get to a rooftop," Felix insisted.

Alix could barely stand, much less climb onto a roof. She shook her head, her senses remaining cloudy. Slowly, everything focused back in. Another shake of her head and she felt steady on her feet.

"Felix, where are you?" she shouted.

"I'm fine, Alix," he replied.

"That's not what I asked!"

"I'm giving you time. Don't waste it."

"No!" She screamed as she leaned with one hand against the front of the building. "Don't you dare. Don't fucking leave me." She burst into tears.

"Go, Alix. You have to go."

Three sharp booming sounds, one right after another, broke their conversation. Three sleek warheads fell into a steep dive, then leveled out. She snapped her head to the right, followed their trajectory, and spotted the *Procella*.

"Wick! Incoming!"

"I see them," he replied in a somber tone. "Good luck, captain."

In rapid succession, the three warheads struck the *Procella*'s starboard side. Alix pulled her goggles down and let them fall around her neck to witness the sight with her own eyes. Each detonation hit her like a knife to the chest. The hull ripped open, its frame snapped, blue flames spread within and swirled above; steam and smoke surrounded the ship. The *Procella* hung in the air for a moment—then began to fall.

"Wick..." Alix whispered.

"Alix, you've got to go. Run—get to the *Shadow*," Felix implored her to move. "Get out of town. *Now*."

As the *Procella* descended, realization hit. Alix's eyes widened. She stepped back, then turned and ran as best she could. A sudden explosion rocked the entire town. A flash of blue light lit the mountainsides in every direction as the *Procella*'s reactor and engines exploded. The shockwave hit Alix in the back and threw her to the ground.

Alix panicked. She crawled and climbed to her feet. The ground beneath her rumbled. Everything shook in a monumental quake. She ran, staggering from left to right; she threw her shoulder into the door of a shop. The pain nearly crumpled her to the ground. She looked back. The world continued to shake. Lit by the remaining flames of the *Procella*'s wreckage, a swelling cloud rushed down the mountain.

"Oh fuck. Oh fuck," she cried, and each time she threw her shoulder into the door.

Adrenaline surged and with a third effort, the door finally gave in.

Alix fell into a shop. Metal, glass, and wood shook off the shelves around her as she stumbled into the dark.

The roar became deafening. She fell over a counter and crawled through the back of the shop. She couldn't stand any longer as the ground beneath her destabilized. All she could do was curl up onto the floor and cover her head. Alix squeezed her eyes shut and wept.

The wall behind her exploded. She lost all sense of time and space. Her body lifted into the air, tumbled, and pain assailed her as what felt like heavy stones struck her body repeatedly. Freezing cold engulfed her, and an incredible weight pressed her from all sides. Alix screamed, but couldn't hear her own voice above the din.

Darkness surrounded her, stole her sight, and in a cold instant, it ended.

9 798990 537927